DAVID RAYMOND

For Sherlock

1

I breathe her in deeply, and the most primal part of my brain pumps to life. It's not just her. This house is full of scents which overwhelm me: bleach, cheap pinot noir, and a singular rusty aroma. Blood. Jackpot! Another Miami murder scene home listed for sale by the enigmatic Shadow Holmes. Never heard of her, you say? Fortunately, I know every minute detail of her adventures. I'm her confidant, partner, raconteur, and we share a bed. Watson's the name.

To the uninitiated, Shadow Holmes appears the odd duck. Don't get me wrong, mate, her face looks nice enough on a real estate sign, however I'd wager the average bloke couldn't pick her out of a book of mug shots, unless you were fortunate enough to gaze upon Shadow's eyes, which are watery grey, simultaneously ever-present and far-away, and possess the ability to make one feel naked; and not in the good way. As to her form, her body is Rubenesque perfection. Not that you'd know it, because she dresses like a nun on a night out. When she speaks though … when Shadow Holmes utters a single word, people hang on each syllable as if attending the book reading of an acclaimed novelist who holds the key to world peace, eternal life, global warming, delicious vegan cupcakes, and hour-long orgasms. Each of Shadow's words is chosen with care. They must be. People have profound expectations of the great-granddaughter of Mycroft Holmes, Sherlock's older, smarter brother.

Shadow inherited a great many traits from her great-grandfather Mycroft: an unrivaled analytic mind, a fondness for tasty food, and the laziness of a lion. Fun fact, mate. Lions sleep 18 hours a day. Shadow used to sleep late into the morning and top it off with an afternoon catnap. Thus, the schedule of a Realtor suited her. Additionally, with a mind like hers, she could do the job in but an hour a day. Once her life lacked rigor, until with my help, she found her true calling—solving murders. Mind you, not just any murders. Those which take place in the sanctity of one's own home. Afterward, naturally, we sell the domiciles. Don't get judgy, dear reader. It's not as mercenary as it sounds. We are well compensated, however we only list homes with unsolved murders, and subsequently solve them. Being Florida, selling these homes, is a growing market. Turns out some twats *want* to buy houses where people were murdered. Once they're settled in, some buyers go so far as to host murder mystery reenactment parties, with dinner guests trying to figure out who was offed and who did the offing. In fairness, some of the crimes we solve do lend themselves to such theatre. For example, last year we sold a home where a man had been killed by a falling coconut which broke through a screen porch, landing upon the victim's head. Shadow and I discovered the widow had murdered her husband and framed the coconut.

A decade ago, Shadow was far from the cool, composed, occasionally brooding, celebrity crime-fighting Realtor she is today. I came into her life right after the tragedy that forever transformed her existence, and mine. Finding your parents murdered in your childhood home would unhinge anyone, however, knowing you could have prevented it would have sent a weaker human over the bloody edge.

After the murders, Shadow tortured herself with *if onlys*. If only she hadn't missed a lifetime of clues. If only she'd deduced it earlier. If only she hadn't let her guard down. If only she hadn't gone on that date. About that. Trust me, Shadow Holmes could easily be voted lady least likely to swipe right on Tinder. When she wasn't working, Shadow was typically sitting quietly at home reading. This girl reads all the greats— Kafka, Hemingway, Twain, Heinlein, Raymond, Doyle, Sagan. Books and scientific research about everything from string theory to string cheese. They publish it, she reads it, and recalls every word. Her appetite for knowledge is voracious. Her appetite for human intimacy—not so bloody much. Knowing her as I do now, I found it difficult at the time to comprehend why she went on that date. The woman who asked her out was intelligent, well-read, charming, and although at 4'8' considered a dwarf in medical terms, she was built like Beyoncé. Indeed, that Beyoncé part, likely explains the date, right, mate? Hang on. The scent of blood aggravates my bladder. I'll just duck outside behind this mango tree, and ahhh. Much better. Don't want to muck up any evidence. (You'll never catch a proper CSI using the loo at a crime scene, will you?)

Shadow was thirty-three when it transpired. She had three previous relationships. One with a man, two with women. They met at a real estate symposium on Miami Beach. During two days of otherwise mind-numbing seminars on topics such as the best shade of grey to paint a home for a quick sale in the trendy South Florida marketplace, Shadow, who at that time nearly held doctoral degrees in astrophysics and mathematics, found Mary Janetori's presentation on the predictive analytics of real estate sales data stimulating. Mary asked her out for lunch the next day. Shadow's first instinct was to decline the offer, however she found herself indescribably aroused.

Whilst it was a short drive from Shadow's home in Biscayne Park to Jimbo's on Virginia Key, Mary had a better idea—taking her jet boat, because you'd have to be an absolute wanker not to love a boat that does 200 kilometers per hour. A loosely assembled collection of wood shacks, old trailers, and older drunks, Jimbo's was a ramshackle open-air waterfront bar/fish-shack/bait shop, with ice-cold beer, and even cooler patrons. Models, bikers, rappers, businessman, and fisherman, all hoisted a few back in Jimbo's heyday. Shadow had never been and was excited. A rare emotion for Shadow Holmes. Indeed, before our adventures commenced, Shadow's emotions were as guarded as a flock of sheep on a border collie farm, however as soon as the boat sped from the dock, she felt liberated.

They arrived at Jimbo's in 12 minutes flat. Mary skillfully squeezed into the last spot of dockage along the mangroves. They ordered beer, fish dip, and a sleeve of saltines, and wandered about, sipping beer, and taking in the gritty ambience until they located a suitable spot at one of the creaky wooden tables fashioned from a repurposed door. Mary stretched across the table, her fabulous form fighting the containment of her polka dot bikini top and shot Shadow a disarmingly sinful smile. Her lips were upon Shadow's before she was fully seated. It was a sensual kiss, with a delicate tongue twirl, which caused Shadow to tremble. She had never experienced such titillation and being a Holmes, needed to understand why. Shadow opened her eyes, studying all around her, especially Mary's face. A face reveals a great deal to the astute observer.

To Shadow's surprise, Mary was staring back. Until that moment Mary's eyes had been hidden by sunglasses. Shadow recognized something peculiar and familiar in Mary's face that she failed to observe before. There was a glint of scarlet in Mary's eyes, and her forehead was the least bit pronounced. Shadow pulled away. Mary's smile turned sinister. Her head sluggishly oscillated side to side in a cobra-like fashion, whilst she emitted a most curious, "Ttssssss!"

Shadow's blood ran cold. She fled, shedding her flipflops, running barefoot on the dirt, smacking herself in the forehead over and over and over again for being such a lust-struck blithering idiot; blind to the obvious. She ducked into the woods, frantically calling her parents on her cell phone. Nobody answered. Her heart plummeted to her gut. She rushed to the dock covered in a mist of cold, grimy sweat. Naturally, her date along with the jet boat, were nowhere in sight.

Halfway into the cab ride to her parent's home, the poison Jane secreted into Shadow's beer began to take effect. Her chest tightened. Her heart skipped a beat, then another. She phoned their house again and again. Her calf muscles twitched. Her breathing became labored. Saliva filled her mouth. She had to make it home. If the directive her father issued long ago wasn't a fairy tale, Shadow knew she was their only hope.

When the cab finally arrived, she struggled for each breath. She battled her legs through the front door into the living room. It was there she discovered her parent's bodies slumped on the couch; drool stains pooled on the flowered pillows beneath their lifeless heads.

Grief struck like a thunderbolt. Shadow's chest tightened. She could barely breathe, let alone stand. The room spun round and round. Her hand twitched along the top of the couch, deciding if its job was to steady her or guide her down to die next to her parents. The idea of succumbing to death became more appealing with each gasp for air, yet the thought of the Holmes clan being wiped out by a Moriarty roused the last of Shadow's strength. "NEVER," Shadow shouted, determined to follow her father's command with her dying breath.

She stumbled to the backyard, seized a shovel, and fought her way to the ancient oak tree standing sentinel between her parents' house and her modest guest cottage. She only had to walk thirteen paces. Shadow steeled herself against the mighty tree, wheezed, aimed southeast, and counted her steps aloud. She made it to eleven, fell, and crawled back to start anew. Focusing her immense brain power on her goal, Shadow gulped a shallow breath, lurched thirteen paces, and thrust the shovel into the ground.

She dug until she heard a ping. Her addled brain barely directing her limbs, she threw the shovel aside and burrowed with bare hands. She retrieved a cylinder from the moist ground, broke the seal with her dirt filled fingernails, removed the yellowed envelope and opened it, revealing a bit of old parchment. She wrestled her phone from her swimsuit top and dialed the number, which even in her diminished state, she recognized as having been written in Great-Grandfather Mycroft's hand. A young woman answered. Shadow managed to get off four words before collapsing on the damp bed of oak leaves, "The game is afoot."

2

Dr. Tuesday Hudson phoned Scotland Yard, "The game is afoot, Lestrade!"

"None of that until after rehab, Hudson," snapped Inspector Lestrade.

"Listen to me, Lestrade—"

"You didn't go! Bad form, Hud—"

"SHUT UP, LESTRADE. It's a matter of life or death. Name and number of the Albanian compound pharmacist from the Dawkin's case?"

"You don't recall his name? You slept with him—twice. How high are you? Rehab, Hudson, before I'm compelled to lock you up," Lestrade huffed.

"Listen carefully, you ninny. If what I feared has occurred, the antidote must be administered precisely. If done improperly, the cure will be worse than the poison. Name and number, Lestrade! Do you hear me? NOW, Lestrade. NOW."

"Now! Now!! Now, who do you think you are, ordering a chief inspector around like this?!!"

"Lestrade, please."

"Did the great Dr. Tuesday Hudson just say please?"

"Lestrade!"

"And rehab?"

"On my way."

"Liar. I just texted you the contact," Lestrade replied.

"Lestrade …"

"What now, Hudson?"

"Thank you."

Shadow awoke two days later to find a tall, lean woman, perched over a clipboard beside her hospital bed. An abundance of strawberry-blonde curly hair softened a pale angular face and hung below her schoolgirl skirt like a long jacket. A magnifying glass tattoo adorned the back of each thigh. Between a set of familiar, piercing grey eyes and lips which seemed permanently fixed into a naughty smirk, stood a thin, lightly freckled, falcon-like nose. Overall, she had the appearance of a bird of prey on the hunt—at Coachella. Realizing Shadow was awake, the woman grinned broadly and was greeted by a groggy gaze.

"Holmesian ears, cheekbones, eye coloration. Given the incalculably low probability of my insanely loyal father knocking up your mother, it's obvious Great-Granduncle Sherlock spawned," Shadow yawned.

"Sherlock was my grandfather. Fatherhood came to him late of age. Hello, Cousin. Tuesday Hudson," Tuesday said, stepping lithely to the side of the bed to shake hands. "Sorry about your parents."

"You answered the phone, 'Hudson'. So, Sherlock and his landlady?"

"Eww and no!" replied Tuesday.

"The poison. Snake venom synthesized for oral administration," Shadow stated, whilst giving Tuesday a firm handshake.

"Yes, A highly unusual strain of cobra venom. I confirmed it in your blood work, as well as your parents'," Tuesday said.

"Their bodies?"

"With a discreet friend at the medical examiner's office until you make arrangements," Tuesday replied.

"You developed an antidote."

"Yes. Using tetrodoxin derived from pufferfish," Tuesday replied.

"I thought tetrodoxin only delayed the effects of other poisons. What made you think it would work?"

"For a Realtor, you know a great deal about toxins, as did Sherlock. He wrote an unpublished paper postulating the addition of bee pollen to the antidote for viper bites. I only recently developed it. After Moriarty murdered a colleague, I thought it might have future applications."

"The number I called triggered a video feed, you assessed my condition and treated it, which makes you a physician," Shadow said.

"I am indeed a physician, however I only practice medicine when called upon. You know, Hippocratic Oath, and all that muck."

"You could have saved my parents!" Shadow said, bolting up.

"I didn't know you were poisoned until you rang and by then it was too late for them. The antidote hadn't even been tested on rats. You're fortunate it worked."

"Fortunate!! I'm an IDIOT!! And my parents are dead because of it! Jane Moriarty masquerading as Mary Janetori."

"Quite! Barely disguising her name by rearranging the letters. Moriarty didn't even think you clever as a Wordle player, my dear cousin," Tuesday said.

"A Moriarty in front of my eyes and I was blind to her," exclaimed Shadow, bolting up in bed, holding her head in her hands.

"Not exactly blind, Cousin. I've heard she can crack walnuts with those thighs of hers," Tuesday smirked.

"Ughhh! I can't believe I kissed her," Shadow groaned.

"Permit me to ease your guilt. I witnessed Moriarty's seductions on many occasions and developed a theory. I recently obtained and tested a sample of her hair, which proved my notion correct. Moriarty's body emits 1,681 times the amount of pheromones as the average woman. I'd wager she had you slimy as a snail," Tuesday joshed.

"That explains why I was so freaking horny, and don't you dare joke about that maniac."

"There, there. You're awfully stuffy for a Yank. Are you well enough to get out of here? I hate hospitals," Tuesday grinned.

"A doctor who hates hospitals?"

"All my patients are dead," Tuesday responded.

3

"The poison and/or your antidote must have dulled my deductions. You're a coroner, a side hustle to cover up your real job—a consulting detective," Shadow remarked.

"Correct, however, being a medical examiner augments my work. The dead are often more articulate than the living. There's no better way to understand a murder than observing what a dead body reveals," replied Tuesday.

"How morbid."

Hands behind her back, Tuesday paced the room, studied Shadow, and commenced her observations. "Despite your obvious level of intelligence, my dear cousin, in lieu of a challenging career in one of your chosen fields of study, you squander your time reading to excess, gourmand pursuits, and the moderate consumption of wine. Moreover, for the past year following the termination of an intimate relationship which provided the singular spark to your bland existence, beyond your limited interactions with clients engaged in real estate transactions and your parents, you live the life of a hermit. How ever do you tolerate being a Realtor?"

About that, mate, even though she was dissing Realtors, Tuesday was endowed with, amongst other things, a certain charm; a characteristic Sherlock Holmes was known for. Shadow's DNA was dipped from Mycroft's gene pool; thus, she was more of a charm school dropout whose gruff demeanor rendered her oddly beguiling—like a French bulldog.

"Same way you get off on sniffing corpses," Shadow sniped.

"Let's get you out of here, my rude relative, before Moriarty turns you into one. She has operatives everywhere and I don't want us to be the last of our lot."

"It's just the two of us," Shadow said numbly.

"Yes."

"And don't even think about leaving me at the Israeli Embassy," Shadow said.

"How'd you deduce that?"

"Your mother was a Mossad agent," Shadow remarked.

"Not bad, Realtor. Go on."

"The gun pushing against the side of your backpack leaves the imprint of an Israeli .22 LRS favored by the Mossad. The model was discontinued in 1986. The handle was worn down by a female owner with well-manicured nails. Mossad agents never surrender their weapons, so she's dead."

"Interesting, Realtor. Now, hurry along. Let's get you to the Embassy. You'll be safe there, while I track down Moriarty."

"Screw safe! You're wasted and obviously need my help. I'm coming with you."

"Please, I'm a consulting detective. No offense, my dear cousin, but you sell houses," Tuesday stated.

"Listen, you ghoulish gumshoe, I bet, like Mycroft and Sherlock, my deductive skills are better."

"Better than whose?" Tuesday asked indigvaltly.

"Everyone's," Shadow deadpanned.

"Fine. A wager then. If you can recount even five relevant details of my last few days, you can join me in the search. If you can't, you're locked away safe in the Embassy until I've found Moriarty."

Shadow yawned, then spoke in rapid fire fashion, "You departed a small airstrip in Sussex by private jet to Opa Locka airport, arriving 42 hours ago. The pilot, Enrique, was brunette, six foot, three inches tall.

He took you doggy-style at 31,000 feet, resulting in his, but not your, happy ending. Upon arrival, you rode a motorcycle to this hospital, stopping for a hot, glazed donut purchased at a drive-through window. Other than short bathroom breaks, you've been at my side since your arrival. You have a colleague at Scotland Yard who assisted in my revival. Despite your sweet tooth, you relish limes. You're twenty-seven, but the bacchanalia of drugs you abuse make you look thirty-eight. May we go?"

"Why you little … I won't be twenty-seven until next week! Do I really look that bad?" Tuesday questioned, examining herself in the camera of her phone.

"Like you were rode hard and put to bed wet. You need to get to rehab, but I know you won't go."

"You definitely have Mycroft's genes," Tuesday said.

"Knock, knock. Sorry, Ms. Holmes. I just need to chart your vitals. I hate to be nosy, but I was in the doorway and that was frigging awesome! The night nurse told me you were one of those Holmeses. I thought she was yanking my chain. How'd you do that?" said a mesmerized nurse who came to sit on the side of Shadow's bed.

About now, I'll wager you, too, are speculating how Shadow deduced all that. It all sounds easy once she explains it, because, it is, quite elementary.

"The indentation an inch behind the toe of my cousin's right boot is from the shift lever of her motorcycle. The smudge on her left bootheel is of a lichen unique to Sussex, and based on the breakdown in coloration, it's been no more than fifty-one hours since she trampled it on her way through the airfield for a nine-hour flight. The bottom of her right boot shows a mixture of mud and bird excrement caused by the digging of burrowing owls indigenous to the Opa Locka airport. They're most active at dusk during mating season, which was on the rainy full moon forty-two hours ago, and therefore most likely to have left the muddy souvenirs she slogged through. A Scotland Yard phone number assigned to the detective's division was visible on her phone's call history. The time of the call was one moment after my call to her. My cousin's donut smells like kerosene and sugar. There's a small, greasy bag in the trash that at best fits two donuts, however, based on her BMI, she's a one and done donut girl. The rapid movement of her eyes along with the slightly uncoordinated movements of her lanky limbs are likely due to a combination of cocaine and ketamine. And lime green is the only Jell-O that's been eaten on my hospital tray, and since I didn't eat it …"

"And Enrique?" the nurse asked.

"GET OUT," Tuesday shouted.

"Geez! I thought British doctors would be more polite. That was amazing, Ms. Holmes. Hey, can I get a selfie?" the exiting nurse said as Tuesday slammed the door in her face.

"Naturally, you heard me speaking with Enrique when you woke up," Tuesday remarked.

"The tone of your blabbing about your high-altitude escapades wasn't nearly as triumphant as it should have been, and your knees show traces of friction marks from your doggy-style dalliance, and your hips are tight. A decent orgasm loosens your gait. In terms of Enrique's appearance, there's a strand of light brown hair blended with yours on the crown of your head. The angle it rests suggests a man with a height two inches above your lanky six-foot one-inch frame. The fact that you didn't brush your hair since your plane ride is either due to poor hygiene or, I'd rather think, a testament to your dedicated care of me.

"Thanks for saving my life. If only I could have done the same for my parents. You do realize, if you were a cleverer detective, just knowing I was Mycroft's great-granddaughter would have saved you the two minutes and nine seconds you wasted testing me."

"Put these on, Cousin" Tuesday said, tossing Shadow her clothes and winking, "The game is afoot!"

4

The game was, indeed, afoot, however I imagine at this point, you might be perplexed as to how I became enmeshed in this adventure? Like lots of couples, Shadow and I met in a pub. As a point of clarification, not so much in it as behind it. I was rummaging through the rubbish heap at the aforementioned Jimbo's, when this lush lass joins in. Her attitude suggested she was the type who loathed jazz brunches and fancied blokes who reeked of wet leather. Her oddly familiar scent, a vast improvement over the trash, startled me, causing me to inhale abruptly, awakening the promise of that which evaded me—my memory.

I studied Shadow keenly, grasping for a window to my past. Other than her wardrobe, which appeared to have been procured via an ancient Church donation bin, she appeared rather ordinary. However, when Shadow Holmes looked at me with her piercing grey peepers, I nearly wet myself.

A tall, slender damsel was poking about the bushes. Her appearance was that of a Bonnaroo refugee. That was Tuesday. She smelled like owls, donuts, formaldehyde, the countryside, and the floor of a nightclub loo. She winked at me with those mischievous grey eyes the color of a Weimaraner's and I tilted my head a bit as I tend to do when I am amused, causing Tuesday to flash her naughty smirk. These events bewildered me. For a moment it felt as though we'd had that exchange a hundred times before, however, if we had, Tuesday failed to acknowledge it, as she turned away and continued her search. My desire to unlock my past was soon outdone by more primal needs. I hadn't eaten in days, thus I found myself in survival mode, merrily munching upon half of a perfectly good medianoche, and the bread was still warm—mostly. Tsk! Tsk! Don't get judgy, mate. It was in a bag and I was famished. Shadow Holmes, rooting about like a terrier, found a gold lipstick tube and sniffed it. I looked her way, and she spoke her first spellbinding words to me, "The fuck you looking at?"

Like I said, mate, the lass has a way with words.

Shadow appeared to be getting a rush out of the lipstick, thus I decided to give it a whirl. I devoured the last bit of pork in the bag, plodded through the debris field before me, and took a deep whiff of the cosmetic. Its smell was reminiscent of fish dip, beer, and a tad snakish, stirring something fierce within me, drawing me to her. More than a feeling, less than a remembrance. Still, it was something, thus I held her in my gaze. Shadow studied me closely, as if checking me for ticks.

I was not going to let the opportunity slip from my grip, additionally, the indignities of a beggar's life were wearing on me. I had to convince her I was worthy of salvation. I led the way, and the cousins eagerly followed me home. What can I say? I've got a way with the ladies. For the record, my home at the time being an abandoned shack behind Jimbo's. The second Shadow stepped inside, she commenced ogling everything so hard, it was as if she fused with the place. I was so lost in observing her observe everything, I neglected to observe the other one, Tuesday. She was gawking about as well, and still grinning, however her eye movements were sharp, yet concurrently clumsy, compared to Shadow's Yoda-like gaze. The two of them began speaking about me as if I wasn't present—and in my own dwelling!

"Blow me back to Baker Street, Cousin! You'll never guess his name," Tuesday said, smirking as she rifled through my belongings.

"Watson," Shadow replied matter of factly.

"Extraordinary! How'd you read this document from across the room?"

"I eat loads of carrots, and if you weren't so high you would have seen his dog tag," Shadow commented, shaking her head in a disapproving manner.

"Service dog. Belongs to a veteran. British. This uniform is ancient," said Tuesday, observing the tattered garment hanging from a nail on the wall.

"You mean, belonged," Shadow corrected.

"Ah yes, no human footprints in or out for months. Must have had something in my eyes," Tuesday replied, blinking.

"Yes. They're called drugs," Shadow said.

"Very funny. Poor creature, but he's made it on his own this long in this swamp disguised as a city. I'd wager he was in an accident, rupturing the outer fibers of his femoral nerve, which explains the pause in the old boy ascending the step on the way into this dump."

"Listen, Cuz! Miami is paradise, especially compared to that fog pit you call home. And how are we supposed to catch Moriarty if you can't even observe the obvious damage to Watson's sciatic nerve?"

I had no idea who this Moriarty character was at the time however, the mention of their name sent chills down my spine and caused me to dash to Shadow's side.

"Hmmm," Shadow exclaimed, looking quizzically my way. "Pull yourself together, Tuesday. Look at his limp. He was hit right in the ..."

How humiliating. Yet, for all their deductions, neither genius deduced the worst of my conditions—head trauma, which in fairness, is a challenging diagnosis to make on a dog.

Their chatter continued for some time, them putting me under the Holmes' microscope, until I felt invisible. These ladies clearly had boundary issues.

"We should get him out of here. Think he can keep up?" Shadow asked, looking at me, her mouth almost curving into a smile—almost.

Given these two held keys to my past I would have followed them over a road of broken glass. My excitement built. I had to convince them I would not be a burden. I stood on my hind legs and with paws dancing in the air, twirled to demonstrate my agility. Unfortunately, I was so overcome with nerve pain; a wee yelp escaped. Perhaps I had oversold the role.

Shadow didn't appear to be one of those, 'I didn't rescue the dog, the dog rescued me' folk, nonetheless she invited me back to her parents' residence, freshened me up, and allowed me to accompany her and Tuesday as we snooped about. The police had zero leads. But me, I always follow my nose—and something smelled dodgy.

5

Those two snooped about the Holmes' residence like a regular pair of Nancy Drews. Nonetheless, it was I who sniffed out the poison which killed Shadow's mum and dad in the bottled water dispenser in the kitchen. The scent, similar to that on the lipstick, alarmed me. I growled at the cooler. Shadow moved forward to examine it. I placed myself between her and it, barking loudly.

"Easy, Watson," Shadow said, patting my head.

Her touch was sharp at first, then slow and rhythmic, with just enough playful diversions behind my ears. It had been a long time since anyone had stroked me in such a manner. I must say it felt delightful. I gazed upward to express my gratitude, as I found this reinforces human behavior in these circumstances, increasing the duration of said stroking, and there, right there in Shadow Holmes' eyes, a memory twinkled. Those eyes. I had regarded them before.

"Good job, Watson," Shadow said.

Good job, indeed! Despite the glimpse at my evasive past being ripped from me, I knew one thing for certain. It felt good to be of service. It was my very discovery, along with Shadow's examination of said water cooler, yielding towel fibers unique to those distributed by the

County's homeless outreach teams, which caused her to sigh and smile simultaneously. Shadow stared into her cell phone, took a deep breath, and called the contact listed as 'The Man'.

6

"Miss me, baby?" a mellifluous voice breathed through the speaker on Shadow's phone like a late-night DJ on a blues station.

"I need information on a missing homeless man," Shadow said.

"You know I can't violate confidentiality, but if you're calling me, something must be terribly wrong?"

"The man's name is Humbert—"

"Nelson! I had a bad feeling when his parole officer reported him missing. Shadow, my love, what's happened?"

If you had been in the room, you would have felt her grief. "Just tell me where he is."

"I've never heard such pain in the timbre of your voice."

"Shut up, Eren! Where's Nelson?" Shadow demanded.

"Listen to yourself, Shadow. You're holding it together, but I can feel your insides spilling out and the only thing that would cause that. Oh, God! Something's happened to your parents, hasn't it?"

Shadow stood silent. I felt her heartache, raced to her side as if I had always stood there, as if I always would, and nudged her hand with my head. She patted me and raised a curious eyebrow. I was so overcome by emotion, to this day, I'm uncertain whether it was

Shadow's grief, my excitement at the anticipation of regaining my memory, or a confluence of both, which caused my tail, indeed my entire derriere, to wag in a most undignified manner reserved for long-time companions, yet we just met. Or had we? My confusion was maddening. Adrenaline coursed through my blood vessels. My brain buzzed. I shook my head vigorously, as if dislodging water from my ears after a bath, prompting something dormant within me to burst forth. It was then her thoughts rushed me.

It's my fault. If only I had recognized Moriarty sooner. I can't believe they're gone. They were the only people I loved, besides you, Eren. Don't make me say it, Shadow thought, but those were not the words which issued from her lips. What she numbly said as she ceased patting me was, "Murdered."

After I shook off the astonishment of my sudden acquisition of mind reading skills and following a brief bit of sobbing on the other end of the phone, Eren replied, "Oh my God, Shadow! I'm so sorry. I'm heading your way."

"No! I don't have time to explore my feelings."

"Don't worry, my love, I didn't think you were looking for a booty call, unless—"

"Shut up, Eren."

"See you in five minutes."

"Eren, wait—"

"Can't wait to see you either, my love," Eren said, hanging up.

Just what I need, Eren Adler decaying my orbit. God, I missed him, Shadow thought.

"Oh, do tell, Cousin? NO. Stop! Permit me," Tuesday said.

"Walk with me," Shadow said.

We exited the house and walked to Shadow's cottage, Tuesday speaking rapidly along the way, "The manner in which you address this man clearly indicates deep feelings, yet he's bested you in some way. Not a constable. He's in a position of authority in government. Hot, intelligent, complicated, and most certainly damaged."

"A mall security guard could have deduced that much," Shadow replied as we entered her cottage.

"Ouch! He jilted you."

Shadow gave her cousin a stern look, disrobed, tossed her clothes to the floor, washed her armpits in the kitchen sink, donned undergarments, and studied the contents of her closet, which captured Tuesday's attention.

"Curious wardrobe, Cousin. Old biddy meets London Fashion Week. I'd say you purchased them from a thrift shop but you'd never put in the time to hunt for these treasures. My word! You're so lazy you wear your mother's vintage clothing!"

"We're the …We were the same size," mumbled Shadow.

"Apologies, Cousin. I'm a tad high. Tell me about your boyfriend."

"Ex-boyfriend!" Shadow snapped, slipping on a skirt and top.

"Pleaseeeee."

"He was the closest thing to a woman I ever experienced. He always knows exactly what I'm feeling."

"Feeling? You?" Tuesday laughed. "Of course! He runs the County's homeless programs. I could have hacked their Management Information System. I'm quite handy with technology, you know. Sounds like maybe you needed a friend, or perhaps the aforementioned booty call? I could step out for a bit if I'm in the way."

"I liked you better when I didn't know you existed," snarked Shadow.

"Just when I thought we were going to be besties. Why did he break it off? Was it your delightful personality?" Tuesday snarked right back.

"Eren Adler was the only thing I ever desired—until now," Shadow huffed as she laced her boots as if attempting to throttle her ankles.

"And now you want Moriarty. Dead, of course. However, based on the change in your skin tone, you still want Adler, do you not, my dear cousin?"

"SHUT UP. He's here. How do I look?" asked Shadow, rushing to a mirror at the sound of an approaching vehicle.

"Like you've been on holiday—in hospital. That wasn't five minutes. Should I be concerned?"

"Depends how you feel about feelings," Shadow replied.

"I'd give him a feel alright. He sounds yummy."

I'll bet you forgot all about me. Still here, mate. Next thing I knew, a bloke pulled up to the curb and exited a classic Jeep. Tuesday and I peered at him through the doorbell camera monitor in the living room. He moved like the night air, gamboled to the door, and knocked with authority. He wore a slate suit, white button-down shirt, no tie, and grey suede quarter boots. Greying auburn hair sprung from the back of his outback hat. He had a wide-open face which drew one in. A smile so broad as to cause his brown eyes to squint, beamed through an ungroomed auburn beard. He smelled of the ocean, pizza, and last night's bourbon. I liked him right off, although something about the man, gave me the chills.

7

'Twas the third day of polar night. Snow whipped against the floor-to-ceiling windows of Jane Moriarty's fortress which, although situated in the coldest place on Earth, was so well-heated as to permit her to lounge topless on a chaise wearing her favorite, red-flowered bikini bottom. She hadn't had a murderous thought in sixteen hours.

Marvelous. Now all I have to do is wait for that stupid girl to lead me to it. Last of those blasted Holmeses, Moriarty thought.

She rose in the pitch darkness, walked to the freezer, poured a margarita, and returned to her chair, bumping her pinky toe as she sat. "Ttssssss," she moaned. Visions of slaughter overtook her. Then it all went black.

Awakened seconds later by her own aroma, she sniffed her armpits, contemplating, *Argh! It's getting worse. I have no choice, Great-Granduncle. Let's see if communications are back online. Can't wait to see what those media vultures are saying. Something along the lines of, 'Grandson of Mycroft Holmes, dead at the hands of Moriarty!' Would like to see that headline. No connection! Damn storm! Even the satellite phone is fucked. I hope that sniveling idiot Fahrenheit received my message.*

8

"I'm so, so, sorry, Shadow," the man in the doorway sniveled. He closed his eyes and gently embraced her. Now comes the eerie part. With eyes still closed, he said, "And hello to you, and you."

Preposterous! How in bloody hell did this bloke know Tuesday and I were there? His eyes were closed, and we were out of sight in the living room. I thought Shadow would tell him to shove off; instead, she melted into him like butter in an air fryer. I had only known Shadow for a brief period, therefore in retrospect, should have been happy for her. Instead, a great resentment commenced building in me regarding this gent. It took what seemed like an eternity before Shadow broke free of whatever trance he had cast upon her. As much as I wanted to hate him, he flashed a smile like bloody Buddha, and I was back to liking him. (What can I say? I'm fickle in matters of the heart.)

"So, will you tell us where Humbert Nelson is, or pretend to be a bumbling bureaucrat, citing regulations, and getting in the way?" Tuesday probed, entering the room.

The bloke got even spookier once Tuesday spoke up, thus, I kept a low profile.

"You never told me you had a cousin."

Good grief! Not another one, mate! How many geniuses was it going to take to find one vile villain?

"Interesting," Tuesday commented.

"I sense you're perplexed. I don't have Shadow's powers of observation, or even yours, I imagine from your cockiness. However, I am skilled at, let's call it reading people. Shadow looks at you with curiosity, concern, a scoop of love, and a dash of contempt, as people tend to do with family members. And even I can recognize those Holmesian eyes. Yours are lovely, by the way," Eren stated, tipping his hat.

"Dr. Tuesday Hudson. Charmed, although you touchy feely types are worrisome."

"Worries are highly overrated. Your humble public servant, Eren Adler. Pleasure," Eren responded with the well-practiced handshake of a vicar on Easter morning.

"Humble?" Shadow said with an eye roll.

"I'm terribly sorry about your parents, Shadow. And yours, Dr. Hudson," Eren said looking at Tuesday.

Like I said, this bloke was eerie. I mean, how could he possibly deduce Tuesday's parents were dead? Believe me, this spookiness did not escape Tuesday.

"How did you determine my parents were dead?" Tuesday probed. (Told you, mate—eerie!)

"It's written all over your aura," Eren joked.

"Auras! Oh God, you certainly have a type, Cousin," Tuesday moaned.

"May I?" Shadow grinned; her fingers mashed into the shape of a triangle.

"Only if you use the term feelometer sparingly," Eren replied.

"Feelometer? And you think I'm the one who's stoned," Tuesday japed.

"In the time of your grandfather, a German biologist introduced the concept of the umwelt. Familiar with the term?" Shadow queried.

"Naturally. It was coined to explain how different animal species in the same milieu are attuned to dissimilar environmental signals," Tuesday responded.

"That's a relief. I thought we were going to have to dumb things down for you. The umwelt is another way of saying, you observe but you don't see; at least not what Mr. Adler sees. For example, embryonic frogs can sense predatory snakes outside their eggs four days after conception. Octopi communicate using ultraviolet light frequencies visible only to other octopi. Songbirds follow magnetic fields during their migration. Whales, bats, and other animals use echolocation to send and receive soundwaves, some of which convey emotion. These creatures sense things humans and other animals don't."

"What do bloody bats have to do with my DEAD PARENTS? Enough! Tell me about your schmeeolometer," Tuesday slurred.

"My umwelt, or feelometer as Shadow deemed it, allows me to experience things others don't. For example, if you weren't so strung out, you would have noted the physical manifestations of your emotions when I said sorry for your loss. The little color you had in your face vanished. You closed your eyes, your lower lip descended slightly disrupting your grin, you swallowed and dropped your shoulders. All of which I perceived was due to some deep inner pain associated with death. Since Shadow never mentioned you, I assumed your pain was due to the loss of your own parents as you couldn't have been that close to hers. So, just how high are you?"

"Not nearly enough," Tuesday said removing a small brown vial from her pack, pouring a powdery substance onto her clenched fist, and inhaling said powder through one nostril, whilst holding the other closed.

"Why hadn't you mentioned her, Shadow? Oh God! You didn't know about her."

"Not bad, Feelometer Boy. She never mentioned me because we just met when my antidote saved her life," Tuesday said.

"You were poisoned?! I would have sucked it out … Sorry. I didn't mean it to sound … are you okay?" Eren said.

Okay? What do you think, asshole? My parents were murdered. I was poisoned—by a psycho oversexed Moriarty. I just found out I have a cousin— Sherlock Holmes' stoner granddaughter no less, oh, and you popped back into my life after wrecking me. Am I okay? Fuck you, Eren Adler, Shadow thought, however all she said was, "Fine."

Tuesday grinned, circling Eren with her hands behind her back, stumbling as she went, "Interesting. Your casual genius comes across as unintentionally arrogant, thus you speak in a tone that's apologetic about your intellect. Never apologize for genius, Mr. Adler. There is far too little of it in the world."

"You are too kind. Tuesday, but if I were really a genius, I'd be rich and sitting on a little island in the South Pacific with your cousin. I know we just met, but if I may make an observation?"

"Oh, you are the charmer. You may," Tuesday winked.

"Girlllllll, you're a hot mess! We have several excellent rehab programs I could refer you to, but I can tell you're not ready. Now, why would someone poison your cousin just when you show up?"

"We'll get to that, but first, let's get to the root of you and your feelometer. You're two years younger than my cousin although your prematurely grey hair suggests otherwise. You were trained as a psychotherapist and practice your craft shedding the layers of people and systems. You delight in pizza, Kentucky bourbon, and swimming in the ocean. You spend a minimum of six hours daily on your cellphone, as indicated by the small callouses on your thumbs. You sleep soundly on your right side. You're a proficient and generous lover and fancy having your bum squeezed. Speaking of which, may I?" Tuesday asked, reaching out her long thin arms towards Eren's backside.

Moriarty's on the loose, and you need a stint in rehab, Tuesday, but go ahead, play grab-ass with my ex. If I ever needed a good laugh, now's the time, Shadow thought as she retrieved a tin of toffee covered popcorn from the kitchen counter, seized a handful and popped it in her mouth, "Mmffff. Haven't eaten for days, Want some? It's got these tasty little chocolate almond chunks. Sorry. Go for it, Cousin. We have a murderer to catch, so make it quick."

9

"I'd promise to make it brief, Cousin, however it's obvious your boyfriend prefers boxers. May I, Mr. Adler?" Tuesday inquired, walking behind Eren, and playfully reaching her hands closer to his bum, her eyes struggling to focus.

"Feel free," Eren joked.

Tuesday stumbled, righted herself by way of cupping Eren's butt cheeks in her hands, leaned closely to his ear, and purred, "Deep breath into your belly please, Mr. Adler. Ahhh! How singular! Again, please, through the nose. Exhale ever so slowly through your mouth. As I suspected. The breath never lies."

Shadow rolled her eyes in a cantankerously superior manner.

"What? Just because I don't believe in auras?" Tuesday said and came round to face Eren. "Eastern medicine has been doing breathwork for centuries. I've made a study of the impact of trauma on breathing. It's not only your brain that's traumatized when something awful happens to you. Muscles, nerves, organs, all hold memories, and each of them are fed by the breaths we take. Your breathing reveals the slightest disturbance in your pelvic floor muscles. It is therefore elementary, my poor Mr. Adler, that you experienced horrific sexual abuse, likely in your early teens, leaving the slightest shroud over each of your endearingly joyous exhalations. Everyone likes you, don't they, Mr. Adler?"

"Not everyone," Eren chuckled.

"I'll have to have a think on how you exude such humble jolliness, however it's absolutely bewitching. In fact, if the love between you and Shadow weren't so nauseatingly palpable, I might give you a romp myself," Tuesday winked.

Touch him again and I'll break your arm ... Cousin! We don't have time for this crap. I need a bath. And a nap. And a half bottle of a nice 2001 cabernet, Shadow considered, but "Wrap it up," was all she pronounced, whilst popping popcorn into her mouth.

"It's quite elementary, my dear cousin. What we're dealing with is a delusional, if not admirably charming, superhero rising from the ashes to save the homeless narrative, whereby one convinces themself, others, and even you, Cousin, that they have some connection to your innermost emotions, as if they're channeling the bloody ghost of Carl Jung. Top it off with his choirboy-turned-cowboy looks, and I present to you, Mr. Eren Adler. How'd I do?"

"Bravo!" Eren clapped. "Although you forgot to mention, I floss. Sometimes twice a day."

Shadow pushed her hair over her ear, and smiled right at him, whilst speaking to Tuesday. "Listen, Ms. High and Mighty, but mostly high, if you spend any time with Eren, his otherworldly powers of perception will become abundantly clear, even to someone with your limited—"

"LIMITED. I'll show you limited, Realtor!" Tuesday said, shaking her hair back and striking a martial arts pose which caused me to tinkle. (Just a wee bit, I assure you.)

"Ladies, please. Let's not fight over little ole me."

"Get over yourself, Eren! My parents were murdered! Are you going to help or stand there pretending to be cool?"

"Can't I do both? Sorry, my love. Just trying to lighten the mood. As we in government say, I'm here to help. I spoke with Nelson's parole officer. He's missed his check-in, which makes this official police business. They've issued a BOLO. Lucky for you, I know where he was living, if you can call it that. I'll tell you in a minute, but not until you introduce me to the heavy breather lurking in the corner."

"Watsonnnnnnn!" Shadow beckoned.

See how she treated me, mate? It would've served Shadow right if I remained stationary. Who was I attempting to fool? I respond to her beck and call as if I were a greyhound sprinting the last furlong whenever Shadow Holmes speaks my name, however, not on that occasion. I didn't want to appear too anxious. Thus, I sauntered out, cool as a cucumber and made my way into the foyer. I presented Eren with the obligatory testosterone fueled bloke nod. Instead of nodding back, he smiled at me like an army nurse doing battlefield triage. Whilst my desire to learn my history was strong, I didn't want him conjuring up some deep-seeded secret regarding my mother telling me I'd never amount to much or some such drivel, thus I maintained my silence and begrudgingly sat next to Shadow, of course. And I need to make one thing perfectly clear. I am not a heavy breather. I suffer from sinus troubles due to the local climate. Naturally, I realize I could relocate, however, say what you want about Miami, but winter here, as is expressed in the vernacular, most certainly does not 'suck'.

"Hmm? You look like you're on the road to solving a mystery, Watson. You've got a special one there, Shadow," Eren remarked.

"He'll do," Shadow said, giving me a nod.

He'll do? Not exactly a Shakespearean sonnet, however something about Shadow's words, combined with Eren's, caused me to turn several tight circles, as if I were a circus dog. A pathetic pain inducing display which, ironically, the humans found endearing. I realized it was imperative to modify their view of me, thus, I ceased my rotations, barked, and delicately tugged the bottom of Shadow's skirt in the direction of the door. It was indeed time to solve a mystery. My mystery. And if time permitted, I would assist with theirs.

You're absolutely right, Watson, Shadow thought, looking down and patting my head. I wish she had said it aloud, thus prompting the others to recognize my worth. Why humans don't simply say what they are thinking is a mystery I'll never crack. Nonetheless, my actions were the impetus for Shadow to demand to get bloody on with it, "Enough of this crap. Spit it out, Eren. Where's Humbert Nelson?!"

"He was last seen under the Julia Tuttle Causeway..." Eren said, his voice trailing off.

At that point everyone became quiet as a mouse hiding from a Doberman, and despite my failure to fully comprehend the umwelt, it felt as though fleas were crawling all over me, filling me with dread black as the evening sky.

10

'Twas the fourth day of polar night. Jane Moriarty lay topless on a chaise, wearing her red-flowered bikini bottom. Her eyes glowed in the pitch darkness of the room. She sipped a margarita, whilst recalling every word of her soon to be published research article entitled, The Dynamics of an Asteroid: Applied. Moriarty was in the process of visualizing the formula in the second to the last paragraph on page six, and had made it far as $B =$, when her concentration was interrupted by the flash of the infrared motion detector illuminating the Sakha tundra for a kilometer in all directions.

Moriarty studied the grounds. Two dozen red eyes heading her way. Moriarty hissed, reached for the 44-magnum holstered to her desk chair, and upon observing a pack of arctic wolves closing in on a fast-moving herd of caribou, thought to herself, *marvelous!*

Moriarty donned her parka, boots, and gun in hand, stepped outside. The wolves had put upon a caribou, or as referred to in the colloquial, a reindeer, cut from the herd. Moriarty's head slowly oscillated. Her tongue peeked through her lips, until the frigid air forced its retreat. Her mind raced in anticipation of viewing the kill.

She'd seen prey resist before but never when the odds were this uneven. A typical pack of arctic wolves ranges from five to seven. This one consisted of twelve, their silky white fur specked with blood.

The wolves moved in, containing the beast in a tight circle. The reindeer lowered its rack and bellowed. The fierce wind shifted, knocking Moriarty off her feet. The frigid ground stung her bare thighs. "Ttssssss!" she moaned; visions of carnage filled her head. She blacked out, only for a few seconds, awakened by her own stink, thinking, *Argh! It's usually gone by now!*

The wolves picked up her scent and turned toward the source of their distraction. The reindeer, a large bull, seasoned from years of battle, saw its advantage and slashed its antlers wildly. A yelp pierced the polar night. Much to her dismay, the reindeer, which appeared uninjured, fled, bounding through the thick snow. The pack trudged after it for a few meters, and upon determining their efforts to be futile, ceased their chase.

"Blasted pheromones! And BLAST you, Rudolph!!!" Moriarty screamed, firing her weapon madly at the majestic bull. But the reindeer had already made its escape. The security lights faded. Moriarty's eyes glared red. The pack howled into the blackness.

11

Prior to continuing, dear reader, I realize not everyone will appreciate the descent of this tale into darkness. Nonetheless, this is a whodunit, and I'm the raconteur, so put on your grown-up panties and try to remember, mate, you can't have a truly good story absent the bad blokes.

Years before Shadow's parents were murdered, a Miami judge, frustrated by the residency restrictions placed on sex offenders and sexual predators released from the lock-up, (making it near impossible for them to find housing more than 2,500 feet from a school, playground, bus stop, or other designated areas), told some pervert to go live under a bridge. In this case, the bridge being the Julia Tuttle Causeway. The Tuttle is a beautiful span of concrete connecting Miami to Miami Beach. The causeway is named for this lass, Julia, who lured a rich chap named Flagler south to build a railroad all the way to Miami.

Speaking of luring, imagine a picturesque causeway leading to Miami Beach, with a bunch of trolls living under it, only in this case, they're worse than anything ever imagined in Grimms' Fairy Tales. And as it turns out, Eren's grim tale put him right back in the path of these monsters.

It began one day when Armando, the head of the homeless outreach team asked to meet under the causeway. As Eren drove to the western-most bridge, the hairs on the back of his neck tingled like mange on a stray. Armando led the way under the bridge to two small tents and a lean-to made of old palettes and cardboard. A small gas generator, hooked to an old TV and a charging cable attached to an ankle monitor on one man's leg, whirred under the bridge. The three residents were sexual predators on parole. The men explained that due to the County's residency restrictions, they were forced to live in no-man's land, under the causeway.

Eren took no pity on the predators, however he had a job to do, which was to provide housing to the unhoused, and these men, despite their atrociousness, were homeless. They had served their prison sentences and the criminal justice system released them to the streets.

The housing programs Eren funded served thousands of people a year from all walks of life. Doctors, lawyers, bankers, cooks, single parents down on their luck, families, teachers, tradespeople, people suffering mental health issues, addicts, thieves, murderers, no matter; they all were entitled to housing—even the trolls under the bridge. Eren left the causeway, neck hairs still erect, drove to Government Center, and took the elevator past his floor, to the office of the County Manager. An overinflated sense of justice put Eren in the doghouse with the upper echelons at County Hall on more than one occasion, this however, was purportedly his finest hour of disobedience.

County Manager Bill Brown was a force of nature. He held the office for an unprecedented 12 years, and outlasted the terms of four mayors, a recall election, six hurricanes, and one race riot. The typical county manager, or as I refer to them, the ultimate pack leader, is a rare breed indeed. No matter their intentions and how careful they are, few last more than two or three years in political climates which will eventually ooze nastiness all over them, and once oozed upon, they're through. Remarkably, after a dozen years on the job, Bill Brown was ooze free and he wasn't about to let the bloke in charge of what Brown publicly touted as his saintly homeless programs, but secretly despised as a waste of money for the dregs of society, get even a drop of ooze on him. When Eren made his case for placing the predators into housing, warning that the situation would become dramatically worse, his request was promptly denied.

Eren went about performing his job most admirably and as predicted, the causeway situation became much, much, worse. A year and a half after Eren's first visit, the place looked like a bloody kennel with more than a hundred sexual predators crammed under and around the bridges of the Julia Tuttle Causeway. Wrap your brains around this, mate. Picture a Miami highway, cutting a path over balmy Biscayne Bay, to the tourist-fueled economy of Miami Beach. Imagine the sun shining over blue waters, palms swaying in a light breeze. Now imagine it lined with the tents and ramshackle shacks of sexual predators. Not exactly the cover of the Chamber of Commerce brochure. Can you see parents explaining the sight to their children in the rental van, "No, Timmy, that's not a campground." Even the international media got involved. Community leaders and elected officials called for solutions. Eren had one, and he shared it with everyone who would listen. It was the same solution he proposed all along. House them. This time the community, concerned for the safety of their children with a commune of predators nearby, demanded action. Eren was given the green light and began placing the predators into housing within the residency restrictions. It went as well as expected. Until it didn't.

Horace Cobb was the 28th predator housed. On his third day of residence in a South-Dade neighborhood, Cobb lured a six-year-old child into a restaurant bathroom. And just like that, Bill Brown finally got oozed. And Eren, poor Eren. Even his feelometer couldn't prepare him for, as they say in the vernacular, 'that shitstorm'. From what I heard, Eren was nearly banished to work at the County animal shelter. It wasn't Brown's reaming or the media bashing that got to him. He was tougher than that. It was Eren's guilt over what happened to the child, by an animal his team placed. And yet, in order to close the encampment, he continued to place more predators every day, praying against all odds none would reoffend. The internal conflict was overwhelming. Nonetheless, I had to give the bloke credit. Even in the face of personal challenges, his team placed nearly all of the original 140 causeway-dwelling predators into housing in a little over a year, yet 106 bastards still resided there when our adventure first commenced. I'll bet you're thinking I'm bad at maths? I am. That, however, is irrelevant. You see, mate, as fast as Eren's team placed them, the justice system kept setting these rogues loose without discharge plans. Word got out that if you lived under the bridge, the County would provide free housing. In no time, the Julia Tuttle Causeway became the entry point to an endless flow of predators, including the one we were searching for, Humbert Nelson. Thus, into Eren's Jeep we went and journeyed to the infamous causeway.

12

Shadow leapt from the Jeep and made her way through the crowd as if she were a botanist in a field of poison ivy. She studied each person, each tent, shack, blade of grass, until settling on a high point on the slope of the causeway, retrieved a pouch from her purse, flashed a wad of cash the size of a Chihuahua, and shouted, "$10,000 for the person who can tell me where I can find Humbert Nelson."

In a heartbeat, those blokes were scrambling up the side of the bridge like a litter of rats. Consensus was nobody had seen Nelson for days, despite this, three people provided information which proved helpful. John Stock, a predator who catfished young boys until he was found out on an investigative show live on the telly, offered Nelson's sibling's name. Turned out the sister's ex-boyfriend owned a bottled water company, which was the only way that twat got a job with access to people's homes, including Shadow's parents' residence. Georgia Scott, a former Girl Scout leader, who would hopefully never get near another box of Thin Mints, shared the address of a cheap motel she and Nelson 'vacationed in' when they needed a hot shower. Finally, Seymour Sludge, came forward with the most promising lead.

"I saw Nelson talking to a lady in a boat one night," Sludge said.

"What kind of boat?" Shadow asked.

"A fast one. Nelson swam out to meet her. Wouldn't catch me in that water at night."

"Did you see the bag?" Shadow asked.

"How'd you know about the bag?" Sludge asked.

"Go on," Shadow prompted.

"Nelson held it over his head, kicked back to shore, and made a beeline for his tent," Sludge offered.

"That was the last you saw of him, before you passed out drunk," Tuesday, who had staggered up the hill, added.

"How'd you know?" Sludge asked.

"Lucky guess," Tuesday said.

"That's his tent. The blue one, near the shoreline," Shadow stated.

"Yeah," Sludge replied.

Shadow peeled off a $100 and handed it to Sludge, commenting, "Don't drink it all in one place."

"Hey! You said $10,000!" Sludge demanded.

"That was for telling me where to find him," Shadow said.

"I know where he is," a bloke shouted from a shack at the base of the bridge.

Now here's where there was an interesting turn of events. Shadow and Tuesday walked down the slope of the bridge, studying this wee man, as if about to diffuse a bomb. Eren was already at the side of the bloke's tilted shack composed of old pallets.

"Where is he, Kent?" Eren asked.

GREAT SCOTT. It was Peter Kent! The predator who molested Eren!

"I'll tell you where he is, and I don't want your money. I just want to talk to Eren. To apologize," Kent said sheepishly.

"If you want to make amends, Kent, tell us where to find Humbert Nelson," Eren stated.

"Not until we talk. In private," Kent said.

"That's not happening, Kent. Let's go, Eren," Shadow demanded.

"It's fine, Shadow," Eren said, crouching down and entering the predator's shack. Kent followed behind and closed the pallet door.

"I'm right outside," said Shadow.

"Me, too," Tuesday surprisingly chimed in.

Shadow stood and Tuesday paced outside the shack, their Holmesian ears struggling to tune to the conversation within. They couldn't hear a word; however, I heard everything. My hearing happens to be one of my best senses. Honestly, mate, I hear like an elephant. I'd wager you were unaware elephants have excellent hearing. I may be unable to shoot water from my nose, however I'll have you know I can make out squirrel chatter 60 feet up an oak on a windy day. I heard their entire conversation.

"I regret the pain I caused you and the other children. I changed in prison. I knew I could never control my urges, so I took matters into my own hands and castrated myself," Kent said, adding quickly, "I'm sure you would have gladly done it for me."

I must say just one word came to mind here, and not that the bastard didn't deserve it, nevertheless, OUCH.

"Hating you nearly ruined me," Eren said.

"I'm sorry," Kent said.

"I forgave you long ago, Kent. I've released my pain. You are what you are, but know this, if I ever sense you so much as think about abusing another child, I will end your existence in an unimaginably painful way that will make castration seem like a spa day."

I didn't think he had it in him, however at that moment, Eren made me proud.

"You'd be doing me a favor," Kent said.

As they stepped outside, Eren's demeanor suggested he was unscathed. In fact, he was grinning. I could sense the relief in Shadow's previously tense posture, and even though Tuesday considered Eren a wee bit looney, her conduct conveyed she was relieved as well.

"Nelson's at Mack's Fish Camp," said Kent.

Shadow started peeling off hundreds when Kent stopped her, "I said I don't want your money. Good luck and be careful. I got a good look at the lady in the speed boat. Believe me, she's more dangerous than any of us down here."

"Why'd you say that?" Shadow questioned.

"Because some of these idiots became so aroused, they swam after her boat begging to be taken along, until—" Kent said.

"Until she put her boat in reverse and tried to mow them down," Shadow interrupted.

"How'd you know?" Kent asked.

"The destruction to those flats caused by her engines," Shadow stated pointing to small white channels in the seagrass.

"She hit eight people. They were banged up pretty bad. But it's not like anyone here would call the cops," Kent said.

"Goodbye, Kent," Eren said.

I must tell you; I was nearly touched by the scene until I reminded myself this Kent bloke was a bloody child molester. Nonetheless, we had a lead, so back into the Jeep we went, off to the very soul of Florida, an enchanted place full of other beasts.

13

Spellbinding. Subtle. Stunning. Spanish explorers called it, 'Laguna del Espíritu Santo'. It's English translation, 'Lake of the Holy Spirit'. Indigenous people, named it 'Pa-hay-okee', meaning Grassy Water. Marjorie Stoneman-Douglas, Mother of the Everglades, deemed it 'The River of Grass'. To me, it's a muzzle full of mosquitos. Trust me, the insects in the Everglades are fiercer than any alligator, however we were on the hunt for a different fiend. A child molesting monstrosity whose side hustle was parent poisoner.

Driving with Eren was an unworldly experience. He had an old ragtop Jeep, which presented more rag than top. The warm breeze pummeled my whiskers like an invisible swarm of tiny wasps. The noise from the wind precluded conversation, furthermore, even though Shadow and Tuesday were likely contemplating the slowest, most agonizing form of death for each of those bridge bastards, we all needed some quiet time to reflect on Eren's act of forgiveness. Personally, I never wanted a bath so bad in my life (and I hate baths!).

Due to her giraffe-length legs, Tuesday occupied the front passenger seat, which permitted a welcome opportunity for a period of semi-solitude with me and Shadow in the backseat. It was a long drive. I nodded off, awaking mid-snore as we bounced in and out of the first of many, many potholes. The rough terrain aggravated my nerve pain. I was spent, yet I sensed danger was at hand and was determined to remain alert in the event Shadow required my aid. I studied her face, hoping she might open her lovely peepers and give me a gander. Her windblown hair revealed a tattoo on the back of her neck. A violin and bow. A quaint, if not mundane tribute to Sherlock Holmes. The design was unremarkable. The ink, however, was a most singular shade of violet which gleamed in the setting sunlight reflecting off the sea of sawgrass which enveloped all but the road before us.

Shadow sensed me watching, as with eyes still closed, she faced my way, placing the tattoo out of sight. With fingertips softly mashed together, her hands formed the shape of a triangle in front of her face. Her mouth was flat and stiff, as if her face long ago forgot where it concealed her smile. Her eyelids, like those of a dreaming child, quivered at infrequent intervals. At first take, I theorized her eyes were shut to block out the wind, however over the years, I understood this to be her crime solving posture. I deemed it her 'I'm most certainly going to apprehend you' look.

Tuesday was in a drug-induced stupor. As to Eren, for a bloke who most recently ventured into a shack with the perv who perved him, he seemed remarkably calm. Indeed, other than his death-grip on the steering wheel which due to the road, if one could call it such, leapt about like it was trying to make a break for it, he appeared to have recently returned from a three-hour massage. As to my condition, my stomach growled. I was becoming hangry. About that ...

Nobody considers bringing snacks on these detective adventures! Likely because none of them have children. People teach kids to find a constable if they need help. If one observed, they would take note that parents always have snacks. Take it from me, teach youngsters if they're hungry, find a parent. You're welcome, mate.

The Jeep bounced us down a dusty lane, north of the Miami-Dade County Line. If Nelson were present, he had violated parole, however that was the least of his worries with this lot after him. As we approached a small cabin, Eren slowed enough for me to get a whiff of the place. Muck, rotten fish, shell casings, beer, and the unwashed, and I didn't like it.

"Charming. Is this where you take all of your out-of-town guests?" Tuesday joked as she awoke.

"Only the special ones. Isn't it stunning?" Eren responded, as he turned and shot Tuesday an ice-melting smile.

"Reminds me of the Grimpen Mires. You don't happen to have any canine beasts running amok out here?" Tuesday japed.

"Gators, and pythons, and armadillos, oh my! Just a modest fish camp, Tuesday. People have been coming out here to escape for decades," Eren responded.

Tuesday shook her head, ran her fingers through her hair, and jumped from the moving Jeep, landing on the road in a Ninja-like fashion, causing Eren to apply the brakes with such force I collided into the back of his seat. Shadow was propelled through the air as if a clown shot from a circus cannon. I barked urgently. Mercifully, Tuesday grabbed hold of Shadow's arm and guided her to terra firma, where she gracefully settled on her feet as if she meant to exit the vehicle in such a manner.

"Sorry. You scared me to death, Tuesday. Is everyone okay?" Eren questioned urgently.

No, moron! This blitzed bitch and your driving almost killed me, Shadow thought, admonishing her cousin, "Are you out of your drug-addled mind?!"

Shadow snatched Tuesday's pack from the Jeep, retrieved the drug vial and tossed it in the adjacent canal.

"Noooooo!!!" Tuesday anguished, flopping to the ground.

What a spectacle. I was glad to see Tuesday rid of her demons; however, I realized this was just the first step in her long painful journey. Speaking of which, I must admit, these ladies had moves, however Tuesday's theatrics cost me dearly. Nerve pain lit every fiber of my being. I gathered my strength and exited the Jeep, letting gravity nurse me to the ground, sticking my landing in that classic yoga pose—the constipated panda.

"Your disembarkment was unique but effective, Watson," Eren said.

Of all the nerve. I would have liked to give him one, right in his disembarkment. I was snarling mad. Thankfully, Shadow came to my defense.

"Take it easy on him, Eren. He doesn't snore half as badly as you," Shadow interjected.

She told him, all right—sort of. And I've been told my snoring is adorable. Adorable!

"And there it is!" Shadow said, pointing to a car, which was all but submerged in the canal. "Nelson stole a car, headed out here in the dark, didn't see the canal, and drowned."

"The swerving tire pattern in the dirt indicates the driver was far from sober," Tuesday added.

"You should know," Shadow snarked. "There's only one set of tire prints No one was following him. From the amount of vegetation on the hood, I'd say the car's been here for three days."

"Please. I can't do this without drugs. You know people, Eren. Hook me up," Tuesday pleaded.

"You only think you need them, Tuesday. Don't worry, you have a few hours before you crash," Eren said.

It was at that point, Eren removed two torches from his glovebox, tossing one to Shadow. He grasped a hook and cable from a winch mounted on his Jeep and pranced to the side of the canal. The cable made a dreadful whizzing noise, which I attempted to ignore. Whilst attempting to ascertain what this bloke was up to, he kicked off his boots, tossed his hat into his Jeep like a Frisbee, and removed his shirt.

"WhiiWheew!!" whistled Tuesday.

"I see three alligators, one's easily ten feet," Shadow said.

"Don't worry, my love. I'll take it easy on them," Eren said, grasping the flashlight in his mouth, as he dove into the water and vanished.

Alright, mate. I'd seen some stuff; however, I was starting to feel as if I was in a bad episode of Scooby Doo. First, this Eren bloke claimed to have a feelometer, next we cozied up to an entire colony of perverts, and finally, he dove into a canal filled with crocodilians—at nightfall. In his absence, Tuesday swallowed a pill plucked from her pack, and paced the camp in an abrupt, ungainly fashion, pursuing the unanswered, arms drawn behind her back, every so often frantically shaking her long locks about, giving the appearance of a rabid Afghan. Shadow leaned against the Jeep, monitoring the bubbles released from Eren's underwater movements with her torch, and observed her cousin's display in a slightly amused, yet concerned manner. Just as

Tuesday was about to, as they say in the Colonies, blow a gasket, Eren reappeared atop the car. I'm sorry, but this bloke was either David Copperfield's brother, or despite his gentle demeanor, a Steve Irwin wannabe.

"Miss me?" Eren asked.

"Not unless you located my drugs," Tuesday said.

"Shadow, my love, turn on the winch, please," Eren requested.

Shadow did as instructed and following additional whining and popping sounds associated with the tightening of the cable, the car came to rest along the canal's edge. Shadow opened the door. Water poured out. Nelson's body was wedged behind the wheel. He smelled worse than the swamp.

"Phew!" Didn't you say something about the dead being articulate?" Shadow remarked.

"Drowned after striking his head on the steering column. Well, that was bloody fruitless, wasn't it? We're no closer to Moriarty," said Tuesday.

"Ah, but we are, Tuesday. The car told us exactly where to look," Eren said.

"Now he's talking to cars. You know how to pick them, don't you, Cousin?"

"The bag of money Moriarty gave Nelson has the initial's, J.M. on the right-hand corner. Nelson tossed it under the back seat. Are you so screwed up you can't see it?" Shadow said, flashing her torch on the bag.

"I saw it. So, Jane Moriarty has monotone trowels. I mean monogrammed bowels," Tuesday slurred. "Towels! Monogrammed towels. What of it?"

"Those aren't Jane Moriarty's initials, Tuesday. Try to keep up," Shadow said with a wink.

"The Jolly Mermaid," Eren added.

"Of course! I'm a ninny! How'd you know about the Jolly Mermaid in your line of work?" Tuesday teased.

"My line of work? I'll have you know I've been to lots of fancy spas and had more than my fair share of facials. Given some too."

Despite Eren's attempt at humor, something about the mention of the name Jolly Mermaid made me jumpier than a kitten at the Westminster Dog Show. We journeyed in silence to our next stop, an invitation only spa on Fisher Island with a reputation for fulfilling dreams. An island where they make your fantasies come true. Reminds me of an old program on the telly. What was the name of that show?

14

Eren drove our party to a ferry terminal across from a fantastical island occupied by a handful of residents with the highest per capita income anywhere in the Colonies. Shadow sent a text, and whoever was on the receiving end replied faster than a retriever fetching a duck from a shallow marsh.

"Shadow Holmes and guests for Dolly Jolly," she said to the Fisher Island ferry attendant, and, just like that, we were in.

It was but a brief journey across the channel. One could swim there if it weren't for the boats, and sharks, and jellyfish. In no time, our windblown crew was deposited on the island. An oversized golf cart bearing a BMW emblem arrived. It was driven by a woman wearing a loosely filled Barbie-pink bikini barely concealed under a mermaid-patterned sarong, her delicate feet adorned in blue-green sequined heels. She smelled of wet swimming attire and cannabis.

If you have yet to put two and two together, try to keep up. That was Dolly. She took a step toward Shadow, as if attempting to administer a hug, however after astutely observing Shadow's stiff body language, she experienced a change of heart and backed off. The lass knew how to read a room, just one of Dolly's yet to be revealed, formidable skills.

"Shadow Holmes. I've been worried sick about you. I'm so sorry about your parents, dearie. I loved them like family," Dolly said.

The fuck you say?! Shadow's mind seethed. *How she'd know my parents were killed? So much for Tuesday's discreet medical examiner friend. If someone leaked news of their murder, why haven't the police questioned me? And nothing from the media? Even if Father wasn't a famous detective, he was the last male in the Holmes line. And Mother. A double, almost triple homicide if you count my near-death. That's worth a soundbite. What were my parents involved with? The poison and whatever Dr. Dopehead cured me with must have screwed with my head. Maybe it's from being so close to Eren again? Stop it, Shadow! Focus on catching the bitch who killed your parents. Show those middle school bullies you really are related to Sherlock Holmes. Think it out. Why would Moriarty give Nelson a bag leading us here? Was Dolly working with Moriarty? I've known her since I was a kid. She adored my parents. Give her a chance. She loves to talk. Let her.*

"Sorry kids, I do go on. I'm Dolly Jolly. And you two look scrumptious. Don't look at me like that, Dr. Tuesday Hudson. I know I'm not supposed to, but I know who you are."

How the fuck does she know about Tuesday? Obviously, Father told her. He was my best friend. Why hide family from me? Seems Dolly knows what's going on. Look at her. Even at 72 she still struts like a webcam girl and talks as much. Go ahead, blab away, Shadow thought.

"Aww. And look at you," Dolly proceeded to study me, like she was judging best in show, dropped to her knees, extended her hands, and called, "Come here, boy. Who's a good boy?"

I find the term 'good boy' disturbing on multiple levels. I am neither good, nor a boy, nor do I to this day comprehend why humans use the term with such frequency to summon my species— even the females. Nevertheless, something about her voice? Inexplicably, I ran to greet her and licked her about the face, which tasted faintly of kippers. She fed me kippers! I remembered. And I recalled something else—a flash of gunfire. My brain buzzed, less severely than on the prior occasion, causing me to shake my head. It was then I heard Dolly's thoughts, which unlike Shadow's, were disorganized, a wee bit mad, yet free as the wind and hopeful, *Watson! Blimey! Couldn't be. But his name is right there on his tag? Watson. Damn dementia. Focus, Dolly. He's the spitting image of Arthur's dog. Saved me from a bullet. That was over 40 years ago.*

My he's aged well. Huh? Focus, Dolly. Dogs can't live that long. I imagine there's oodles of red and white border collies with green eyes. Where's my vape pen. I want to play dominos. Where did I park my car? Incoming! What a cute doggie. Who are these people? Oh, right. Shadow and her friends. Shake it off, old girl. One last mission. For Arthur!

Tsk, tsk, dear reader. I realize my account may sound farfetched, (although I do enjoy a good game of fetch), so forgive my failure to this point in discussing a crucial concept in fiction. Suspension of disbelief, otherwise known as poetic faith, is an unspoken arrangement the audience makes with the raconteur to suspend logic and believe whatever, pardon my tongue, shite they're being shoveled. For example, we all know dragons, elves, and orcs, aren't real, nonetheless you likely dashed to the cinema opening day for every Hobbit movie ever released. Or for example, in this tale, when you believe I'm some omnipotent bloke who knows exactly what's happening everywhere and relays the character's innermost thoughts and desires. Simply put, when you suspend disbelief, you agree to believe in—MAGIC! You're welcome, mate.

Dolly composed herself and turned her sights on Eren, beholding him as if she discovered a brand-new tennis ball right out of the can and wanted to give it a squeeze. "And, The Man, as you call him, Shadow, needs no introduction. Eren Adler, I have a six-inch dossier on you."

"Well, hello, Dolly! Pleasure, however, your intelligence is flawed. My dossier is well over eight inches," Eren grinned.

"Dossier! You're a freaking spy!" Shadow bayed into the night.

15

'Twas the fifth day of polar night. Communications were still down. Jane Moriarty drink in hand, walked in pitch darkness to her chaise, contemplating her cellular division algorithm as she went, until stubbing her big toe on a table. *Marvelous! No reaction, and I haven't had a murderous urge in 1,901 seconds.* Moriarty sniffed her armpits. Her breath quickened. She dashed to the full-length mirror. Her right nipple brushed the glass. *Call yourself a genius. Stumbling around here like a bloody mole woman. You should have every micron of this place memorized by now.* She opened her eyes wide to the looking glass. They glowed pink. *It never took this long before. On the bright side, it should give that stupid Shadow Holmes time to find it. Chill, Jane. Chill!* Moriarty thought, gulping her margarita.

She swabbed her armpits, swirled the swabs into a test tube, and injected the contents into the portal of a mastiff-sized machine. She pushed several buttons, returned to her lounge, thinking, *had to inject that cobra venom, didn't you, Great-Great-Grandfather?*

16

"The great-granddaughter of Mycroft Holmes and I didn't know! I'M AN IMBECILE. You taught me to swim here, Dolly. You told me all those high-tech cameras and two-way glass were for your shows! How could I have been so blind? You're a SPY."

Now Dolly Jolly was not just your everyday spy, mate. Dolly worked for MI221b. In the event, you've never heard of MI221b, you're not alone. Affectionately deemed 'The Bee' by Her Majesty herself, due to Sherlock's fascination with apiculture, MI221b is the most clandestine spy agency on Earth and Dolly was once their top agent. She also held the honor of being the second ever webcam girl. That was back in 1996 when humans were still pleasuring themselves to magazines. (Eh, eh, eh! Don't get judgy, mate. Most humans toss off now and again.) Now Dolly wasn't what you'd call a looker, nonetheless, she exuded the perfect mix of naughty to nice, was imaginative, and loved to entertain. Additionally, she had the British government footing the bill for tons of fancy camera tech, which drew the crowds. When Dolly performed her weekly underwater shows, wearing nothing but her sequined mermaid tail, her viewership was so massive, she crashed The Bee's server—317 times. It didn't end there. Dolly got inside her customers' heads (the big and wee ones) and like any seductive spy, deduced their fantasies, playing them out online. Don't get the wrong idea, dear reader. The Bee isn't run by a bunch of degenerates. They set Dolly up with two-way web cameras to spy on other spies, some of whom happened to enjoy a good fantasy. Dolly, and The Bee, made a killing, in more ways than one, as people caught on tape begging sea sirens to shove sea cucumbers up their orifices whilst dressed in dolphin cosplay outfits with multiple blowholes, tend to be loose lipped, and even when they didn't say a word, Dolly was adept at tracking down the enemy's home addresses should she need to, as they say in the spy business, whack them. (And not the fun kind of whack either, mate.) Dolly sold over $11 million in web services in six months. Three years and $108 million later, Dolly was Miami royalty. She bought a building in the swankiest zip code in Miami Beach and opened the Jolly Mermaid, #cumwatchourscalytails. And come they did.

"A spy! Which means Father, the kind, funny man who chatted up every child and dog in our neighborhood, was a spy too. And he convinced me my deductive skills were second to none!" Shadow exclaimed, her mind seething, *never told me you were a spy, Father. Never told me I had a cousin, an aunt and uncle I never met, and never will. You spent your life gaslighting me. Best friend! More like best fraud! Realtor! Realtor!! While I was busy showing houses, Daddy was playing SPY.*

Hang on, mate! I nearly neglected to reveal information of great import regarding Shadow's father. As they say at the cinema, Daddy had a particular set of skills, which in this case meant from his comfy home in the tranquil Miami suburb of Biscayne Park, far, far from the hustle and bustle of chilly London, Arthur Conan Holmes ran British Intelligence.

Shadow knew nothing of her father's role as head of MI221b. The guise of Realtor checked many boxes for a spy. Meetings and calls at odd hours at ever-changing locations with a vast array of people from all walks of life. Truth was, Arthur Conan Holmes was a fabulous Realtor. He made tons of money. He also ensured Shadow knew nothing about his actual work. Despite, or perhaps as a direct result of being raised in the family business, Arthur understood the hazards of his profession, as did his wife, Guinevere, who happened to be one hell of a stay-at-home spy. Arthur and Guinevere wanted to keep the world safe, however their love for Shadow was like no other. From the second they heard her heartbeat, her parents wanted to protect her from all the evil they fought in their lives, thus weeks after Shadow's birth, Arthur and Guinevere Holmes relocated from London to Biscayne Park and resigned their service to Her Majesty. Only they didn't.

Shadow grew up carefree in the tropical climes of Miami, sluggishly pursuing two doctorate degrees, completing her coursework, yet lacking the rigor at the time to complete her dissertations. Her parents knew their daughter had the brain power to become anything if she applied herself and loved herself. Arthur was convinced she would become a renowned astrophysicist, yet was ecstatic when Shadow, bored with the pursuit of science, followed him into the real estate business. Arthur was so proud, he changed the name of his company from Homes by Holmes, to Homes by Holmes & Holmes. Being successful Realtors led the Holmeses to having numerous remarkable acquaintances. One of whom happened to be Dolly Jolly.

"Sorry, dearie. Your parents, bless their souls, hoped you would never find out. Must come as a real kick in the teeth," Dolly said.

Tuesday staggered to the golfcart, leaned against it, and ranted in a grating manner, "You didn't know? Neanderthal! Your father wasn't a spy. He was THE SPY—director of The bloody Bee! His true identity was only known to a handful of people, including the Queen. Dolly was his right hand, until her brain turned to pudding. I would have mentioned it, Cousin. I was certain you knew. How dense could you be? Better deductive powers than anyone. Ha. You're not even stoned. Least I'm enjoying myself. Didn't know your parents were spies, you stupid bi—"

"Tuesday!" Eren said sternly, to which I growled; a response I was uncertain was to defend Tuesday, Shadow, or nay Dolly, as I felt a kinship to them all.

"Better watch out, Mr. Adler. Watson's onto you. He looks jealous. Should be too. Go on and kiss her, Feelometer Boy. You know you want to. As do you, Cousin. You practically ovulate every time he's near. Didn't know your parents were spies! I can't wait to tell Lestrade. You're even more clueless than him. Hullo! Since you knew nothing of your father's work, how did you get my phone number and the code phrase?"

17

"The game is afoot," Shadow remarked, leaning against the golfcart as if waking from a dream. "I was six. Father was everything to me. He loved to play …. and snack. My favorite childhood activities. I stuck to him like his shadow, which wasn't easy on my little legs. One day we played The Mycroft and Sherlock Game."

"I would have called it The Sherlock and Mycroft Game. After all, my grandfather was the famous one," Tuesday said.

"Mycroft was older and wiser," Shadow retorted.

"Mycroft was lazy and dull. Sound familiar, Cousin?" Tuesday responded.

"Why you slow-witted stork!" Shadow exclaimed.

"Dearies! Please," Dolly interjected.

"Oh, let them have at it. I love it when Shadow crinkles her nose just before she screams. Look out! Here comes a big one," Eren said, as Shadow's nose crinkle disappeared and she almost smiled. Almost.

"We know this is a lot. Go on, dearie," Dolly said.

Shadow deliberately pushed her hair behind her ears, paused, and glanced at Eren. GREAT SCOTT!! She was flirting, yet again.

Shadow proceeded in a trancelike tone, reliving a piece of her childhood, "The game took place in our yard. The object was for me to find a hidden cylinder. I could ask Father ten questions, but I would only win if I found the cylinder in one. The first day I located it in three questions. It was hidden in a hollow below a woodpecker's nest in a palm. The next day, two questions and the cylinder was mine. That time, it was in Mother's car's muffler. The following day, one question led me to the cylinder, which was buried in the yard.

"One question?" Dolly asked.

"The previous hiding spots demonstrated a pattern based on the location of citrus trees in our yard. If you followed the path of the swallowtail butterflies in the morning light, you—"

"You deduced that at six? But you didn't know they were spies? You're right. You are an infantile. You're a bicycle. No, imbecile! You're an imbecile," Tuesday slurred.

Dolly's mind raced, *Wanker! Tearing into the only family she has left. And look at her. All those powers of observation and she can't take a second to check her face in the mirror? Is she ever going to cut that mop? Such a pretty face, but that dreadful hair makes her look like the secret lovechild of Big Bird and Cousin Itt. A little lipstick wouldn't hurt either. And remember, Tuesday, you're not always the smartest one in the room, especially in this room. Listen to your cousin. You might learn something. How high are you? Do you have any to share? What a cute doggie. I think I left a burner lit on the stove. Where's my car? Lalalalala, lalalala dadada. Focus, Dolly. Focus. For Arthur.* Dolly composed herself and spoke, "The Bee has an excellent rehab program, Tuesday. Lots of folks get in over their heads. Go ahead with your story, Shadow."

"After I found the cylinder, Father told me to dig it up, but he stopped me before I could open it. He explained Mycroft and Sherlock played the game and if anything wicked ever happened, I should retrieve the cylinder, dial the number, and say the phrase, 'The game is afoot'. We buried the cylinder in a spot known only to us, and never spoke of it again. He told me it was our secret … I … I thought it was a silly game … until I found my parents dead. I didn't know whose number I was calling. Under the circumstances, it was the only logical option."

"How quaint. Now, get on with it before I crash! Did your father say anything else about the game, Cousin?"

"No! Damn him!!! Why didn't he tell me the truth!!? He and Mother might still be alive. I'm so STUPID. Father told me Sherlock killed James Moriarty in Reichenbach Falls. Although his body was never recovered, Great-Grandfather Mycroft postulated there was a 1 in 174,294,801 chance Moriarty survived. The odds were impossible he lived, no less had children who have a hard-on for our family. Father joked not even the mathematical genius Moriarty could beat those odds, and I believed him. I even verified his calculations! I'm not even a decent mathematician," Shadow groaned.

"Permit me to shed some light while I'm still able, my dear cousin. Unless your boyfriend can score me a refill from one of those rough sleepers he tends?"

"Ex-boyfriend, and no! You were saying?" Shadow said.

"Sherlock did kill James Moriarty; however, he had a brother, a station master in the west of England. He was Jane's great-grandfather and took over the Moriarty criminal enterprises. Presently, Jane runs the show. Under your father's direction, Dolly recruited Jane Moriarty. Isn't that so, Dolly? What I don't understand is, how could The Bee possibly believe Jane Moriarty could ever be trusted? But what really slays me is how Arthur allowed you to stay in the game? Were you this stupid before the dementia?" Tuesday slurred.

"Tuesday! I know you're suffering, but please show some regard for other people's feelings," Eren said.

Dolly's muddled thoughts and speech merged and spilled out, "It's alright, Mr. Adler. Tuesday's spot on about the dementia. Arthur diagnosed me before the doctors. Sent me to every specialist. I'm not an active agent anymore, but Arthur, rest his soul, didn't have the heart to remove my security clearance so I still know everything that goes on around here. And I'm not as stupid as you think, Dr. Tuesday Hudson. For your information my mother's father was Inspector Baynes of the Surrey Force, the only constable to match Sherlock Holmes in investigative skills. As to Moriarty. She was … Moriarty was … Where did I leave my car? Aww. What a gorgeous animal. Spitting image of Arthur's dog. Saved my life. Shadow Holmes, what are you doing here? Do your parents know you skipped school again? You came for another dip in the mermaid tank, didn't you? Alright, young lady, but if you think you're escaping your homework you have another think coming."

18

Inspector Lestrade could not escape the feeling something was amiss. During the length of the one-hour, twenty-seven-minute train ride from Victoria Station to Eastbourne Station, he checked his phone 47 times. He hadn't heard from Tuesday since her call.

Following a brisk walk, Lestrade let himself into the Hudson residence at 11:24 a.m., four moments earlier than his customary time of arrival for their weekly meeting.

At 11:32 a.m. Tuesday had not arrived. Further, she failed to call, text, or respond to his myriad messages.

At 11:33 a.m. a clump of dread formed in Lestrade's brain, journeyed through his clenched throat, reaching its final destination in his lower intestines; or perhaps, he hoped, the feeling was due to his new probiotics.

Despite her epic drug abuse, with the exception of two occasions, one involving the curious incident of food poisoning from a listeria-ridden hot 'dog in the night-time', the other, involving the overconsumption of ouzo with a 'Greek interpreter', they met religiously every Sunday at 11:30 a.m. at the Hudson residence since they were 18 years of age.

A day of conducting an exhaustive search of the residence for signs of foul play, which whilst exposing a fascinating collection of bongs and latex lingerie in Tuesday's sleeping chamber, revealed nothing of significance.

At 11:59 pm. Lestrade sat on the couch, took out his phone and recorded a case note, as always, notated with the date and time, 'Hudson- no show' Lestrade's right leg twitched, causing his foot to jerk, overturning the coffee table, bringing to light, a personalized clue from Tuesday. Lestrade inhaled deeply, sending his lump of dread off on holiday. He thought of Tuesday, smiled, and drew another breath. His father always told him to breathe as if each breath might be your last, for one day it might bloody well be.

Archie Lestrade came from a long line of Scotland Yard inspectors, dating back to his great-grandad, Greg Lestrade, a proud, barely competent detective. Greg had a complicated relationship with Sherlock Holmes who constantly outdid him and broke the law along the way. In the process of solving a crime, Lestrade discovered Sherlock Holmes engaging in, amongst other criminal acts, breaking and entering, thievery, assault, blackmail, and countless felonies. Holmes even went so far as having Dr. Watson shoot suspects with his service revolver! Despite this, Sherlock Holmes achieved the fame and fortune Greg Lestrade would never come to realize. Greg's only refuge was his cottage near the sea in Sussex, until Sherlock Holmes retired there and ruined that for him too. The cottage lay dormant for years, until Archie's father, Leslie Lestrade got hold of it.

Inspector Leslie Lestrade was an ego-less, somewhat bumbling, yet successful investigator, who relished time in Sussex, where he met his best mate, Dylan, and where the Lestrade family spent weekends and holidays.

Archie Lestrade always suspected something peculiar regarding his father's friendship with Tuesday's father, Dylan Hudson, who was, of all things, a dentist. The two laughed together, fished, swam in the sea, went to pubs, played darts, screamed at footballers on the telly, got hammered on Guinness; basically, stupid stuff lads do. It was on these occasions, following his mother's death in a tragic cycling accident, Archie found himself deposited at the Hudson household.

They were 12 that first time. Tuesday bounced into the room, barefooted, headphones blaring a Stones' tune, munching salad from a bowl, her index finger and thumb serving as utensils. She sported an ill-fitting sleeveless Beatles tee-shirt, a tartan schoolgirl miniskirt, and a smirk which caused Archie Lestrade to tremor. He introduced himself in a rattled, but formal manner. Tuesday grinned, threw her arms behind her back, paced about, looked him up and down, and abruptly offered her unsolicited, highly accurate analysis of the budding Lestrade.

Tuesday told Archie he was a decent rugby player, had recently taken up guitar and his finger placements were off, that he snuck off twice a week to bike the streets of London to feel a sense of closeness with his recently deceased Norwegian mother, that he aspired to be a detective, that he obsessed over numbers, that he was designing a video game in his basement, that he coveted fancy attire, that he suffered bouts of dyspepsia, that his right leg twitched when he became unnerved, and that he had never kissed a girl, at which point, Tuesday Hudson, who was a head taller than Archie Lestrade, and remains so to this day, grabbed him by the collar and snogged him—hard. It was their only kiss. She tasted of Caesar dressing. He loved her, and anchovies, ever since.

It wasn't as though they never had the opportunity for that and more over the years. Tuesday's mother was a constant traveler and Dylan and Leslie were usually off getting bashed. I mean honestly, how could responsible adults leave two teenagers alone? Perhaps they deduced nothing was at risk, except for Archie's heart, which Tuesday had torn into like a chainsaw, and she bloody well knew it.

Archie Lestrade grew up, developed into a fine detective, and relished his career, until the Queen took a fancy to him. Oh, it's not like that, mate. Lestrade's a golden-haired looker, with such a sincere and graceful demeanor that even when reporting on gruesome crimes, it has the effect as to cause lasses, and some lads for that matter, to feel that all is right in the kingdom. Archie, with the clandestine assistance of Dr. Tuesday Hudson, had recently solved a triple homicide and was being interviewed on the telly when he caught the eye of Her Majesty who was so stricken with Lestrade, she made him the voice of the New Scotland Yard.

Whilst his promotion to Chief Public Information Officer came with a significant salary increase, an expense account at Harrod's for those tailored suits he fancied, a staff of 16, and rock star fame, Lestrade was miserable. His life had evolved into an endless series of interviews about crimes other detectives had solved, and photo shoots. The last one being the topless cover of the Lads of the Yard wall calendar. Lestrade longed for two things—to return to sleuthing and Tuesday Hudson.

19

Tuesday attempted to wrestle her shirt over her head, whilst still wearing her backpack, "a swim sounds delightful."

Swimming. Is that Shadow Holmes? And who are these people? Aww. What a cute doggie. Looks just like ... pull it together, old girl. For Arthur! Dolly thought. "Bollocks! I've gone off again, haven't I?" Dolly asked, holding her head.

Dolly's definitely a few sandwiches short of a picnic. She used to be so sharp, Shadow thought, prompting, "You were telling us about Moriarty."

"I'm sorry, dearie. Your parents wouldn't want you involved. Let The Bee handle that sicko."

"Remember what you told me when you taught me to swim, Dolly?" Shadow asked, hoping to reach her.

"Oh my, yes. You were a natural, and you looked so cute in that little mermaid swimsu–"

"Dolly. Focus, please!"

"Sorry, dearie. I remember. Trust me. I said trust me."

"I missed a lot about Father, but I know he trusted you," *apparently more than me,* Shadow thought. "And I trust he'd want you to help us find his and Mother's killer."

Dolly sniffled, cleared her throat, and spoke, "Thank you, dearie. In our line of work, trust is transactional. In exchange for immunity for Moriarty's criminal enterprises in certain areas of the world, she was more than happy to sell out her competition, and Arthur made sure her freedom was predicated on her winding down her criminal enterprises."

"A ruse! You twits at The Bee thought you had Moriarty reined in. She wants to rule the bloody world, and you allowed her to expand operations in twenty-five countries and murder dozens of innocents, right under your noses!" Tuesday yelled.

"You knew? You knew and you didn't tell Father about your discoveries, did you, CUZ? No! You disdain government agencies and working with other people. You think you know more than everyone and it cost my parents their lives!"

A bout of uncustomary silence overtook Tuesday, who looked down and shuffled her boots, which she tripped over. Well, well, the great consulting detective missed more clues.

"I thought I was protecting you and your parents. I had proof of her villainy, and I wasn't going to turn the task of justice over to some bumbling bureaucrats. They'd just lock Moriarty up. I was going in for the krill. Chill. Ahem! I was going in for the kill. I was too late. I'm sorry."

"Moron!" Shadow screamed, reaching for Tuesday's hair. Thankfully, Dolly had quick reflexes for a boomer, and pushed Shadow's hand aside.

"Ladies! You two are the only Holmeses left. You're bloody national treasures, so let's not off each other, least for now. Allow me to fill in a few blanks before I'm off searching for my car or talking puff pastries. I do love those ... Shadow Holmes, what are you doing here?"

"Having a nice visit, Dolly. You were telling us about Father and Moriarty," Shadow urged.

"Blimey!" Dolly exclaimed, head in hand.

"Maybe this will help," Eren said, taking Dolly's hands. "Breathe with me. That's it. In and out. In ... out ..."

I'd show him in and out, alright. Reminds me of an Italian double-agent I knew. He was a master of in and out. The things we did. That man's skin tasted like olive oil. Kept company with him for six years. Can't even remember his bloody name. He shot me in the bum. I stabbed him, twice. Good times! Where did I leave my car? Focus, Dolly. For Arthur, Dolly thought as she breathed with Eren. "Thank you, dearie. That was helpful. Sorry, I think I can continue. Everything was going swimmingly, until a month or so ago when Arthur came back from a meeting with Moriarty. I could tell he was worried about her."

"Of course he was, you ninny. She was planning to murder him," Tuesday said.

"No, Tuesday. He was worried for her."

"The fuck you say?" questioned Shadow.

"Understand, Jane Moriarty is brilliant, cunning, and ruthless, not unlike your father, dearie. Arthur respected her, even cared for her. They shut down three crime organizations together, but I knew things had changed after their last meeting. Arthur had a moist look in his eyes; nearly the same look as when you had mono, dearie."

"Nice to know Father gave a shit about the psycho who tried to kill me."

"Don't take this the wrong way, dearie, but have you considered why you're still alive?"

"Because my antelope saved her!" Tuesday slurred.

"It couldn't have, dearie. The Bee analyzed the poison used on Arthur and Guinevere. They had ten times the amount in their system than Shadow had. If it's any consolation, they likely didn't suffer much," Dolly added, grasping Shadow's forearm.

"Nonsense. It was my artichoke—"

"Shut up, you stoned excuse for a sleuth! I should have read the toxicology report myself. Obviously, Moriarty didn't dose me with enough poison to kill me. Moriarty wanted to draw me into the game. Father had something she needs. Something she thinks I'm stupid enough to lead her to."

"You're likely right, dearie, but your parents didn't want this life for you. I can get you somewhere safe, Shadow. Let our agents handle this, please."

"Perhaps you should heed her advice, my love," Eren added.

Heed her advice? Shut up, Eren. What century are you living in? It is kind of sexy though. Stop it, Shadow. Remember he left you. You don't get a say in my life, asshole! Shadow thought, but what she said was, "As I told my clueless cousin, fuck safe!"

"Slime cream photos?" Tuesday slurred.

"Pardon?" Dolly said.

"Crime scene photos? Do you have them?" Shadow asked.

"Didn't think you'd want to relive that, dearie, but yes. I took them myself and kept them off the main server, just in case Moriarty hacked us. Never can be too careful. Come along and have a look before I fade. Follow me," Dolly said, pulling a palm branch causing a tunnel to appear under our feet. Impeccable timing on her part as I felt the *pip, pip, pip, pip, pip* of gunfire in the dirt around us.

20

That's right, mate, 'five pips', followed by three pings. If you haven't already deduced, those were gunshots deflecting off the tunnel doors, which sealed behind us as I brought up the rear. GREAT SCOTT! That was close. Shadow was fabulous and our connection was undeniable; however, I had been in her company but a few hours at that point, and no lass was worth getting my bits blown to bits. Despite my exuberance regarding peeks into my past, I was contemplating returning to my safe little shack behind Jimbo's and having a nice lie down. After all, Virginia Key was directly across the channel. If I waited until the shooting subsided, I could swim there. I only needed to paddle faster than the bull sharks. I was about to take my leave, however one look into Shadow's shining eyes and oxytocin flowed between us as current moves through a wire. Additionally, this spy stuff was, as the young people say, cool AF. A mermaid sex resort! Bullet proof doors! A secret tunnel! Let's not forget the thrill of the chase, although at the time, we were the ones being pursued.

"I'd imagine Moriarty, or her people, would have better aim. Dissatisfied customer?" Shadow questioned.

"Vlad Gorbachecov. Afraid right before your father took me off active duty, I slipped up and released some photos of him dressed as the prime minister," Dolly said.

"Doesn't sound so bad," Eren said.

"It was Margaret Thatcher," replied Dolly.

"No wonder he's trying to kill you," japed Tuesday.

"Oh no, dearie. Just a bit of spy fun. He vowed to scare me to my dying day. Now, hurry along before I forget where I'm off to."

We followed Dolly down a passage to a glistening underwater lagoon which smelled like last week's yoga pants. Dolly peered into a swim mask hanging from a hook, thus opening a rock wall, and we found ourselves viewing a chamber fantastical enough to provide fodder for Carl Sagan's nocturnal emissions.

"Welcome to The Bee," Dolly said as we entered.

Shadow studied the place, "Father couldn't have worked here. Too many shiny gadgets for his delicate eyes. And no immense wooden desk, but that out of place recliner in the corner bears his bounteous butt print. This is your workplace, Dolly."

"Honk!" Dolly blew her nose and sniffled. "Just like Arthur. He should be around any minute. Shadow Holmes, what are you doing here?"

"Hello, Dolly. You were just about to show us the crime scene photos."

"Blimey. Sorry, dearie. 007, be a dear and show us the classified crime scene photos."

"You named the computer 007? This is going to be a hoot! Whoopsie," Tuesday said, tripping, falling to the ground.

"Oh no, dearie. It was Guinevere's idea. She designed the thing."

Et tu, Mother! She said she was designing a recipe website! She even cooked the dishes for us. That coq au vin was scrumptious. Liar. Why didn't you tell me? Maybe, I could have saved you ... maybe, Shadow lamented silently.

"Voice and facial recognition accepted. As requested, Special Agent Jolly," 007 responded.

Images of the inside of the Holmes' residence projected from the plate glass wall. Eren flew to Shadow's side and took her hand. *Get off me,* she thought, however, the first image, that of Arthur and Guinevere dead on the couch, their mouths crusted, caused Shadow to grasp Eren's hand tight.

"Do you need a minute?" Eren asked.

"No! Next picture," Shadow said, breaking her grip.

Shadow sat in her father's recliner with fingers mashed, breathing in his scent, her grey eyes burrowed into the pictures, *I'll show those schoolyard brats what a Holmes can do*, she thought. "Next one. Next. Next. Next. Stop! Can you Zoom in on the newspaper in Father's suit pocket?"

"Affirmative," 007 responded.

"There. Zoom in on the crossword. Even with his dying breath, Father would never leave one word missing no less, two. Seventeen down, group of crows."

"That's easy ... zzzzzzz," Tuesday emitted, as the drugs along with whatever adrenaline had been fueling her for days, finally took their leave of her.

"Murder!" Dolly said.

Obviously, you were murdered. What else are you trying to tell us, Father? Shadow pondered. "12 across, advertising houses. Of course, listings!" Shadow exclaimed, thinking, *good job, Father. Of course, you could have just left a note.*

"Just like Arthur. He'd be so proud. Honk!" Dolly expressed, blowing her nose. "Why Shadow Holmes! What are you doing here?"

"Just leaving. Thank you, Dolly," Shadow said, hugging her.

"I'm coming with you," Eren said.

Coming with me. If only. God, he looks good. Stop it, Shadow. He's distracting you. Be firm. Give him something to do. You know Eren, he must feel useful, Shadow thought, responding, "I need you here. Please, Eren."

"I see."

"How do you feel about babysitting?" Shadow queried.

"Which one?" Eren joked, looking about, his gaze stopping at me.

Of all the nerve! Did this touchy-feely bloke think Shadow deemed me in need of minding? And her amorous thoughts stirred my protective instincts. Nothing against true love, but Eren had hurt her before. The fiend! I fixed my gaze upon him, growled, and circled, coming to rest at Shadow's calf. My message seemed to register on his feelometer.

"Take care of her, Watson," Eren said.

"And watch out for her," Shadow replied, looking at her cousin crumpled on the floor, who with copious hair framing her entire form, very much resembled a Puli of my acquaintance.

"Don't worry," Eren said.

"It's not her I'm worried about," Shadow retorted, squeezing Eren's arm.

What a lovely young couple. Wonder if they'd fancy a threesome. What's that big yellow heap on the ground? Blimey! Did I shoot Big Bird? Where did I leave my car? Shadow Holmes! What's she doing here? Oh, no! Moriarty. That sicko killed Guinevere and Arthur. For the Holmeses! Dolly thought, uttering, "You take care of yourself, Shadow Holmes. Moriarty is pure evil. And don't worry about us. I've still got a few schemes up my sarong."

"Come, Watson. The game really is afoot," Shadow said, patting my head.

Those words, said to me in such a fashion, along with Shadow's touch and her eyes fixed upon mine, triggered a memory. A grey-eyed man. A stout one.

21

"These huge, gray monstrosities shouldn't be allowed, Abner," Glady said.

"I don't get it, but people want these big box houses, Gladys," Abner replied.

"Can't even take a walk without raising my blood pressure. First thing in the morning, we should go down to Village Hall an—"

"SQUAWKKKKKKK!!"

The woman jumped and grabbed the man's arm, "For fuck's sake, Abner! What the hell was that? I nearly threw my back out. And what are those kids doing on the recreation center field this time of night? They know the park closes at sunset. Look at that cop! Sitting in his car with the windows up staring at his computer. He probably doesn't even know the rules. I'm going to talk to him. I'll bet he's watching porn, or worse, cat videos!"

"You should have done stand-up, Gladys. The squawk came from that night heron. Those kids spooked him from his usual spot," Abner said, pointing his flashlight from the bird perched above the bleachers, toward the middle of the field. "Look, Gladys. Those kids are wearing domino masks. Maybe it's a flash mob?"

"Nobody does flash mobs anymore. Try to keep up. Why are they wearing masks? ABNER. What if they're terrorists?" Gladys said, shoving Abner's firm bicep.

"I wonder why they're doing that same little routine, over and over? Nobody's moving their feet? It looks like they're signing?" Abner said.

"Signing, like sign language? That's crazy, crazy person! Who are they signing to? They're all facing the same direction. Besides, it's dark, crazy person."

"That's sign language, Gladys. Remember when I worked at—"

"Nobody gives a shit about what you did last century, big shot. So, what are they signing?"

"Hell if I know. I can only sign my name and letters," Abner laughed, "Wait! I think they're spelling something."

"Alright genius, what are they spelling?"

"It's dark, Gladys. I can barely make it out. It's the same letters, slowly, again and again. It's been a long time since I signed, and I can't see the last letter. I can make out L.E.S.T.R.A.P."

"Les Trap! Must be a gay bar on South Beach," Gladys said.

"You're a riot, Gladys. Hang on. That wasn't a P, and there's another E on the end. L.E.S.T.R.A.D.E."

"Lestrade? Maybe it's the name of a band?" Gladys said.

"A band? For the deaf?"

"Listen, crazy person, it's after 11. They shouldn't be out there. I'm going to talk to the cop," Gladys said storming off.

"To complain about a bunch of deaf kids?" Abner called after her.

"Don't give me that face, Abner."

"You mean this one?" he replied with a dopey smile.

"Ha-ha. Same stupid smile since you were twenty. Men don't know anything about aging. Not a wrinkle on you and nothing sags."

"Have you seen my balls lately, Gladys?"

"Not if I can help it."

"Like I said, Gladys. Stand-up. You missed your calling."

"You know the only reason I never left you is because you're great in bed," Gladys replied.

"That's the nicest thing you've said to me in forty years, Gladys."

"I didn't mean it, crazy person," snarked Gladys, taking Abner's hand and walking off, as the police officer transmitted an encoded video to Bee Headquarters—subject line, 'The Biscayne Park Irregulars'.

22

Thanks to Dolly's car, which we were indeed able to locate, we returned to Shadow's humble mission style cottage in Biscayne Park. It was cozy, packed with books and papers, and painted a warm terracotta throughout, thus enhancing the richness of the wood-beamed ceiling and oak floors. A brown leather couch bearing two pillows and a zebra pattern throw appeared to be the perfect respite for my aching form, thus I climbed aboard and settled my head on a pillow.

"Good idea, Watson," Shadow said.

She poured a glass of prosecco, prepared a plate of coastal cheddar and whole wheat crackers, and flopped by my side, reviewing the most recent Homes by Holmes & Holmes ad copy, pondering, *as much as I tried to get him into the 21st century, Father printed this out and proofed it every week before Mother sent it off to the paper. He was such a control freak, for all the good it did him. Let's see what we have. He changed the order! For the last three years, every ad started with waterfront homes with deep dockage for the boaters. Growing market. This ad starts with waterfront canal … and we never list homes in some of these neighborhoods. Hmm.*

I eyed the plate of food and sighed.

"Sorry, Watson. I'm a terrible hostess," Shadow said, feeding me chunks of cheese, which I (as humans often express in a blatant act of canine cultural appropriation when referring to their own dietary habits), wolfed down. Shadow rose, filled a bowl of water, placed it on the ground, and returned to my side. I was indeed parched; however, I was too drained to move, nonetheless with great effort, I relocated my head to her thigh and continued my mental voyeurism, *first listing. El Portal. Peacock Street. Canal front. I know this address. Beautiful wood home demolished to make way for another hideous mansion. What do these schmucks see in these big white rectangles? Concrete house. Concrete drive. Appalling landscaping. Father would never list a house with zero curb appeal. Why the game, you lying, spying prick? And you were no better, Mother. God, I miss them,* Shadow thought, finishing her beverage, pouring another glass, assuming her 'I'm most certainly going to apprehend you' posture. *Couldn't even see your parents were spies, but you've calculated the orbital pattern of half the celestial bodies in the Milky Way. 'Head in the stars, Shadow? Think it out, dear girl,' Father's words of inspiration whenever I stopped applying myself to the task at hand. How are these homes tied to Moriarty? What does she want? And why would Father have been worried about her? Is she ill? I hope so. And I hope it's a horrific disease that's painful AF. Best revenge is finding her and stopping whatever she's planning. What the hell is she planning? Think it out. Half dozen listings. Easy peasy.*

House number two. Miami Beach. A six-bedroom, seven-bath on Pine Tree Drive. Let's see the file. Joint owners. Hmm. Wife didn't sign the listing contract. Father would never make that rookie mistake. What are you trying to tell me, Father? "Aaahnn," Shadow yawned, thinking, *I'm burnt. Time to get off my ass and make espresso. I have one of Mother's holiday coffee cakes in the cupboard. Yum. Too tired.*

What's that? She was thinking of cake. GREAT SCOTT. I could always go for a piece of cake. I rolled on my back and pawed her forearm to convey the import of retrieving it.

"Does someone want a belly rub?" Shadow asked.

Belly rub! Belly rub! Naturally, I wanted a belly rub. Unfortunately, unlike me, Shadow could not read my mind regarding the cake, however rubbing my belly proved to be a fair exchange in lieu of filling its contents, thus I woofed to acknowledge my consent, as these days, dear reader, it's all about consent. Shadow raised an eyebrow over one watery grey eye, which served to resume my previous recollection. A stout man with watery grey eyes—Shadow's eyes, in an armchair in a place which felt … like home.

This dog slays me, Shadow thought as she rubbed my tummy with the perfect amount of force. *Next listing. Morningside —right down the block from my favorite bakery. Charming three-bedroom one-bath. Charming. Real estate lingo for small. Nobody wants tiny bedrooms and one bath. You don't have to sell it, just find Moriarty. Father socked away so much money. It's not like you have to work anymore.*

Fourth listing. Miami Shores. I know this house. Grace Abernathy lived next door. Made fun of me all through middle school. 'You're not related to Sherlock Holmes. Too lazy to finish the Tropic Scavenger Hunt. Fell asleep in the bookstore. We should call you Shadow Lazybones. Haha! Shadow Holmes, Shadow Holmes, she's a stupid lazybones. Look everyone, it's Shadow Lazybones.' I heard the little witch got herpes, Shadow thought, smiling.

Fifth house. North Miami. Odd little fourplex. Since when do we list multi-family? Sixth house. Homestead? That's an hour away with no traffic. Why would Father list a house down there? Remember, these clues weren't meant for me. He was leading his agents to Moriarty. I'll probably get myself killed. On the bright side, if Moriarty kills me, at least I won't be alone, Shadow thought looking my way.

Never! In order to demonstrate my commitment and put her mind at ease, I turned on my side and hugged Shadow's thigh tight with my paws.

That did not just happen! Border collies are the most intelligent breed, and this one was trained as a service dog, but Watson responds like he understands everything I'm saying … and thinking. Earth to Shadow! Get some sleep. You're shot out. A mind-reading dog and a feeling-reading ex-boyfriend. If Eren were here he'd tell me my attachment to Watson is compensation for the loss of my parents. If Eren were here … He looked good. Bastard! Maybe we still have a chance? If I don't wind up dead.

I was dead tired, nonetheless, I saw my opportunity to convince Shadow that I could indeed hear her thoughts. I thrust my paws in the air and played dead. Unfortunately, Shadow was unable to bear witness, as her glorious brain had drifted off to that magical place between sleep and slumber where one may think freely. *Six houses. Is there a pattern? Do they have anything in common? Order of listing? Distance between homes? Prime numbers in street addresses? Sum of zip codes? Cross street numbers squared? GPS coordinates? Paint colors? Bedroom configurations? Number of toilets? Septic or sewer? Landscaping? Asking price? Celestial coordinates in reference to addresses? Types of trees? Or is it the homeowners Father's pointing me to? Think it out, Shadow. You're not going to solve it from the couch like Great-Grandfather. Get off your ass and go see those houses. That's the only way you're going to find Moriarty. Zzzzzzzz.*

23

'Twas the sixth day of polar night. Jane Moriarty lounged topless on a chaise in her red-flowered bikini bottom, sipping a margarita. She sniffed her armpits. Her heart raced. She rose, dashed to the full-length mirror and studied herself. Her eyes did not glare red. *Marvelous*, she thought.

Moriarty swabbed her armpits, swirled the swabs into a test tube, and injected them into the portal of her machine. She pushed several buttons, returned to her lounge, lifted her margarita to her lips and gulped it down.

Didn't think about how that cobra venom would affect your female descendants, did you Great-Great-Grandfather? Twat! And you didn't think I could do it without them, did you, Daddy? Didn't think I'd kill you either.

A ding emitted from the machinery. Moriarty leapt up and charged to the device. Her tongue slipped through her lips, "Ttssssss." *MARVELOUS. I'll show him.*

24

I'll show them, Shadow thought, as we approached the first home in our investigation, a 7,800 square foot, six-bedroom, five and a half bath rectangular monstrosity, resembling a dental office. The cement driveway bore concrete statues of two lions, both stained with rust, a byproduct of a poorly aligned sprinkler system and a well-visited marking spot for neighborhood canines. Given the aforementioned irritative effect of rust fragrance on my bladder, and my being a dog, I took the opportunity to relieve myself.

"Exactly how I feel about the place, Watson," Shadow whispered as she faltered toward the door, wondering, *why didn't Moriarty come back and finish me? She knows where I live. She must have people following me. I haven't noticed anyone. What does she want from me? And what the hell do I know about being a spy? Dolly has her lucid moments. Someone at The Bee must be hunting Moriarty. I should go home and call Interpol. Let them handle this. Have some wine. A nice long nap. NO. For once in my life I'm going to finish what I start. Time to be a Holmes!*

Shadow's heart raced, her breath quickened and I, too, found myself in an anxious state as she knocked on the door of the hideous mansion.

"Geez! I told you people not to come for the stuff until next week," a 40ish year-old woman dressed in black said, opening the door.

Crap! She thinks I'm from Goodwill. Maybe it's time to buy my own clothes? Screw that! I'm going to own this look, "Hello, Mrs. Sharp. Shadow Holmes of Homes by Holmes & Holmes. Lovely home," she lied.

"Sorry. Love the outfit," the woman replied disingenuously. "Dorothy Sharp. My friends call me Dot. Aww. Gorgeous dog. What's his name?"

"Watson," Shadow replied.

"No way!" Dot said.

"I found him with the nametag," Shadow said, thinking, *why did I tell her that?*

"No way! What are the odds?" Dot asked.

Approximately 7.648 million to one. Did Father mean for me to find him? Shadow thought.

"Who's a good boy? Here boy. Come," Dot said, crouching and tapping her knees.

As we've previously established my feelings regarding the term, 'good boy', I did not obey.

"Well, aren't you a lucky girl. He won't budge from your side. Looks like you were meant for each other. Bwaaaah."

I did not mean to cause this woman such pain, thus I ran to her and licked away her tears. She smelled of patchouli and incense. I sneezed. Robustly. Whilst I busied myself with consoling the poor creature, I followed Shadow's eyes, tuned to Dot and every detail of her surroundings. *Dot's listed as the sole owner. What the hell does this hottie need with such a mammoth eyesore? Stop thinking like a Realtor ... And there it is!* Shadow thought, expressing, "Sorry about your fiancé, Dot. How tragic. Especially with a baby coming."

"Bwaaaaaaaaah!" Dot continued with vigor. "How'd you know? My boobs. They're huge, right?"

"Enormous," Shadow lied, thinking, *those tiny things? It was the prenatal vitamins on the counter. Duh!*

"Bwaaaaaaah. Sorry. Hormones and grief. But how'd you know about Bruce?"

"The phone number on your kitchen counter is for the Perez Funeral Home on West Dixie Highway, and the way you're crying and twisting your engagement ring."

"The wedding was next wee ...week ... Bwaahh! Oh God! I'm gonna yak. Make yourself at ... errrpp," the woman replied, dashing off to the half bath in the hallway.

Here goes nothing, spy girl, Shadow thought taking the place in, thus, I took the opportunity to do the same. The hideous mansion's cement walls were polished, sealed, and yielded a singular aroma: vanilla. Perhaps someone was baking a lovely cake, or more likely an attempt to infuse a homey smell to drive up the sales price? Of course, a bit of extract wasn't going to cover up the stench of the old bloke who died here, perhaps one of the reasons Shadow decided to commence our tour of the property in the backyard, where we were greeted by a resonating "meooooowww," emanating from the branches of a Gumbo Limbo tree in the adjacent yard; the call of one of the innumerable peacock denizens of the Village of El Portal.

As we paced the grounds, I studied Shadow's technique, which was a combination of intense observation, pontification, and walking about as one might do on a pub crawl. Our tour of the property halted on several occasions, first in the backyard where Shadow stopped to sniff a flowering tree, which smelled not unlike cake. Our second stop took place on the pool house patio where Shadow observed several items of swimwear drying on chairbacks, before quickly moving onto the patio table featuring the remains of drunken debauchery; empty liquor bottles, lipstick-stained glasses, and a variety of trash, including discarded napkins, one of which she lifted, studied, and sniffed, causing her to smirk, thinking, *it's oleandermentary!*

Upon reentering the house. Shadow paused in the great room, paying particular attention to a shelf in the bookcase which held a well-used leather medical bag bearing the monogram, Dr. B. Shadow examined the contents. Next to the case, a framed, faded black and white photograph of a man, two small boys, and a glowing hound in front of a pub. Shadow grinned, thinking, *you must be shitting me, Father? A veterinarian named Ba—*

"Sorry. Can't even hold down crackers. I only came here to meet you. I'm staying in our condo on South Beach. Makes me sick being here. Where Bruce ... Bwaaaaah," blubbered Dot, rejoining us.

"Sorry. I realize how difficult it is to lose a loved one," Shadow offered, thinking, *especially when they've been murdered.* "Will your guest in the pool house, relative of Bruce's with an interesting taste in lady friends, be vacating soon ... so we can show the property?"

"How'd you know?"

"Two sets of footprints on the path to the cottage with similar gaits, and the various shades and lipstick patterns on the shot glasses on the patio table, bikinis drying in the sun," Shadow pronounced.

"That would be Freddy. Did too much acid in the '60s. Half the time he doesn't know what day it is. He didn't even show for the funeral. What the hell am I going to do with that degenerate now? I don't care if he is Bruce's brother, I won't let Freddy Baskerville anywhere near my baby. Footprints and lipstick, huh? You really are related to Sherlock Holmes."

Dot's comment caused Shadow to straighten her posture and raise an eyebrow, causing my head to buzz, bringing forth another memory. I dug at it as if extracting marrow from an unyielding bone, until all at once, tasty morsels sprang forth. Another mansion. Another time. Another Baskerville. The warm Miami air turned bitter cold. I stood upon the moors of Dartmoor. Bits and pieces teased. Sir Charles Baskerville, dead of fear whilst fleeing a man-eating hound which glowed in the night. His brother, Sir Henry Baskerville, inherited the estate rumored to be haunted by said hound. A rogue passing himself off as a bloke named Stapleton, was in reality Rodger Baskerville, Sir Henry's cousin, who stood to inherit the estate. Stapleton trained a giant hound to kill and painted it with phosphorous to produce an ominous glowing effect as the beast roamed the moor. Sherlock Holmes in disguise deciphered the plot and saved Sir Henry. Stapleton, aka Rodger Baskerville, attempted to escape across the moors, where he died. Only he didn't. Turns out Rodger Baskerville was secretly recruited by the military for his knowledge of phosphorus incendiary devices. After the war, he retired to Miami, married, fathered two sons, and opened a pub in downtown where he died under suspicious circumstances. My neck fur rose. Nasty stuff, that phosphorous. How could I know this? It was as if I were there. Preposterous! I gave myself a stern full-body shake and shrugged it off to head trauma— the gift that keeps on giving. My behavior did not go unnoticed as Shadow turned an eye to me, considering my demeanor.

What's up with this dog? Looked like he saw a ghost. Sure, Shadow. Just like he can read your mind. Head in the stars. Why would Father send me to a Baskerville, a veterinarian no less? Of phosphofreaking course! Sins of the father, Shadow thought, blurting, "your boyfriend's father was—"

"A piece of work. He tortured animals, and Bruce spent his life caring for them. Bruce had such a kind heart. It gave out right there," Dot continued, pointing to a spot on the living room floor. "Bwaaaaah!"

It wasn't a heart attack, Shadow thought. "I know how hard it is losing a loved one. And you being pregnant, I can't even imagine," said Shadow, dispensing an A-frame hug to Dot as if fitting her for a tin corset, thinking, *the fuck was that? Since when am I a hugger?*

Following a period of further sobbing, "Thanks. You're sweet like my Bruce. After he sold his practice, he spent his time doing the two things he loved most, animal rescue and me," Dot laughed. "No little blue pills for Bruce. Nobody would ever guess he was 92 ... Bwaaahh!"

Lying to the bereaved may be a new low, but here goes, Shadow thought, "I'm so sorry, Dot. Thank you for meeting with me during this difficult time. Just one more thing. Are you familiar with that tree with the pink flowers? I'd love to get one for my yard," Shadow lied again, pointing out the window.

"Sorry. Not a tree person. Pollen allergies. Errp," Dot belched.

No reaction. I'm sure it wasn't Dot, but just to be safe, Shadow thought, asking, "Maybe a cup of tea will settle your stomach?"

"Tea? Oh, God. I hate the stuff. Errrp," Dot belched. "Sorry. Bruce was the teetotaler. Poor ... Bwaaaah."

Most uncharacteristic! You know how us Brits love teatime, however, Shadow although born in London, was raised a Yank and preferred espresso. As such I knew she wasn't requesting a cuppa, thus, whilst she chatted with Dot I popped into the kitchen in search of the teapot. As I grasped the handle in my mouth, a vanilla scent wafted into my muzzle. Despite my disappointment as to the lack of cake to accompany it, I delivered the teapot to Shadow.

What the ... He understood me. One mystery at a time, Shadow. Dot didn't kill Bruce. She's clueless. Other than Watson's theatrics, she didn't give a shit about the teapot, Shadow thought, as I placed the kettle by her feet.

"That's one crazy smart pooch. Want to see if he's chipped?" asked Dot, removing a device from a drawer.

GREAT SCOTT. A microchip scanner! A means to my past locked away in modern technology. My heart was aflutter. I pranced to Shadow's side and nudged the scanner with my snout. (As previously stated, it's all about consent.) I barely contained the movements of my tail slapping against Shadow's calf as she ran the device over my body.

Odd? You'd think a service dog would be chipped, Shadow pondered, causing my tail to cease its hopeful gyrations mid-wag and for my sad puppy face to appear. In human terms, to say I was dismayed would be an understatement of great proportion.

"No luck," Shadow said.

"Maybe you're the lucky one?" Dot smiled.

"Funny thing is I'm not sure I could do without him," Shadow replied, surprising herself, whilst stroking my head, thinking, *no such thing as luck. Poor thing was abandoned in a shack. Or was he? And since when am I all touchy feely? I don't open up to anyone like this. Must be the shared loss.*

"I get it. Nobody wants to be alone. Bwaaah. We still have each other, don't we?" Dot said, patting her stomach.

I can't tell Dot her fiancé was murdered. What if I'm wrong? But if I'm right, and I tell her, I'll be putting her at risk. And her baby! New life amongst all this killing. A baby. Wouldn't that be ... Head in the stars. Make small talk and get rid of her, Shadow thought, asking, "When's your due date?"

"May 15th. Four more glorious months. Eerrpp. Do me a solid. If you see Freddy, tell him to pack up his crap. Eerrp. Sorry, Shadow. I gotta get out of here before I dehydrate my kid. Not again, eeerrpppp," said Dot, dashing out the door.

"Take care, Dot. I'll call you with the first offer," Shadow shouted after her.

Shadow opened the teapot top, exposing minuscule remnants of leaves and pink flowers, and grinned. *If Sherlock were here, he'd ... you'd sound like a moron. You used to say it when you were a little girl pretending to be Great-Granduncle Sherlock. Nobody's around. Go ahead, embrace your inner Holmes*, Shadow thought, exclaiming, "Hullo!"

Shadow flopped on a modernistic wicker couch which appeared to have been designed by a committee of anorexic beavers. I took my place beside her. (For the record, the couch was even more uncomfortable than it appeared.) Shadow assumed her 'I'm most certainly going to apprehend you' posture, her neurons popping off so fast I could barely keep up with her inner churnings, *oleander trees produce a deadly poison, the effects mimic a heart attack. Killer got a smidge of it on their fingertips when brewing the tea, wiped it on the napkin, then blotted their lipstick. Even if the brother wears lipstick, never know these days, wasn't him. He would gain nada, and Dot would throw him out on his ass. Moriarty wasn't here. Her stink is burned into my brain. She sent some bimbos to get to the brother. One of them killed Bruce ... likely killed Freddy, too. The father left something worth killing for. What does Moriarty want from a phosphorous munition's expert like Rodger Baskerville? It's so old school. If Bruce had whatever it was, he wouldn't put his fiancée and baby at risk. He hid it somewhere*, Shadow opened her eyes, fixing them once again on the bookcase, thinking, *Baskerville Hall. They tore the place down to build a storage facility.* Shadow dashed to the picture and examined the date on the back, exclaiming, "And hullo to you!"

We drove to the storage facility near the Miami River, located the unit corresponding to the date on the Baskerville Hall photo, entered 0515, the baby's due date into the combination lock, and voilà! We searched through the collection of, shall we say, antiques, until discovering, hidden in of all places, an urn bearing the remains of a poodle who went by the name Dragonbreath, a faded document. Shadow dusted it off and studied the title 'Increasing phosphorous yield extraction from human bone,' by Rodger Baskerville, thinking, *this guy was one sick puppy.*

25

Something hounded Inspector Lestrade. He wriggled in his middle coach seat, watching the video from the Fisher Island security camera for the umpteenth time. His gut was telling him something was amiss, or perhaps he considered it might be the result of the bangers and mash he ate for breakfast. He knew he shouldn't be relying on a video sent from an untraceable source in the first place, no less heading to Miami on holiday to rescue her, or heaven forbid, identify her remains. When it came to matters concerning Dr. Tuesday Hudson, logic seldom had any bearing.

He replayed the video once more, studying the faces. Lestrade couldn't determine why Tuesday was in my company nor Dolly Jolly's, nor could he identify the man or the other woman in the video.

Lestrade studied the bearded bloke in the outback hat, contemplating his connection to Tuesday, *just her type, dark, dank, and dashing*. It nagged at him, as did something else. The other woman's familiar grey eyes. *Tuesday never spoke of relatives, no less Yanks. Perhaps, the woman was a distant cousin, thrice removed*, he thought.

Lestrade hadn't slept since he first viewed the video. He closed his eyes, and as things tend to do when nodding off, an unsteady memory crept forth. He was thirteen, half-asleep at the Hudson's. His father and Tuesday's were several pints passed pissed after their football team was crushed in a fierce match. Tuesday's father said something about the weight of the Crown weighing heavily upon his family. Lestrade's right leg shook him awake.

He replayed the video in slow motion. He hit pause on the frame displaying the group fleeing from gunfire, considering, *Tuesday would never run from a fight; especially when she's high, and she was practically holding the bearded bloke's hand.* Lestrade zoomed in and clicked a screen shot. The ruffian's eyes told a story. He knew they were headed for trouble and ... he was in love.

Lestrade always told his mates he was a good copper due to four things: being methodical, his father's teachings, his instincts, dumb luck, and a fifth he would only admit to himself; to overcome the stigma that he wasn't simply another bumbler in the Lestrade line. He was hoping beyond hope his dumb luck would hold out and he would locate Tuesday, preferably alive. He looked at his phone. Six hours until landing. It felt good to be back to detective work, even if he was feigning being on holiday and might get sacked, or worse.

Lestrade was spent. He shut his eyes, thought of Tuesday and drifted off until the plane hit an air pocket, jolting him right back on the case. *What's she doing with that dog? And Dolly Jolly? She put on quite the show in the day. What's the old girl up to?* Lestrade searched the web and located Jolly Mermaid videos on his favorite porn site. His right leg twitched, waking the matronly woman seated next to him, who looked on and chuckled.

"Oh, it's not like that, madam," Lestrade said, quickly swiping the mermaid video from his phone's screen.

"That's alright, Inspector Lestrade. I watch you all the time on the telly. Tell you what, luv, you just aim your lovely voice my way for a bit and this will be our little secret."

Lestrade fidgeted uncomfortably, wishing he had sprung for a business class seat that turned into a proper bed, "Yes, madam. Our little secret."

"Oh dear! We're not losing you, are we Inspector?"

"Pardon?"

"Don't play dumb, Inspector. You're moving to the States."

"Madam, I assure you, I am not. I'm on holiday."

"Then why are you studying that picture?" the woman asked, tapping the screenshot on Lestrade's phone.

"Am I to understand you know this woman, madam?"

"That's Shadow Holmes. Sold us our winter flat on South Beach. Oh, you're working a case, aren't you? Her great-grandfather was Sherlock's brother Mycroft you know. How exciting! Lestrade and Holmes back at it. I can't wait to tell the girls at the nail salon."

"Madam, if you could please—"

"There I go popping off again. Official police business, innit it? Not to worry, luv. My lips are sealed. I'm sure you'll have a good 'holiday', Inspector." The woman leaned over in her seat and whispered, "Good luck with your investigation, luv. Whoever you're after, I'm sure you'll catch 'em cold."

26

Jane Moriarty hiked the snowy trail to Reichenbach Falls. It had been a harsh winter, with voluminous sunny spring days of late and the resultant melt produced unprecedented torrents of water cascading spectacularly into the black abyss below.

Moriarty's smartwatch tinged. A video arrived, subject matter, 'Holmes'. Moriarty thought, *Marvelous! Finally, phone service. News of their deaths, no doubt. Fitting to be in the very spot Sherlock Holmes killed Great-Granduncle James to watch the reports of my murdering his brother's grandson. Unfettered by his eternal interference, I can finally retrieve my birthright.*

Moriarty reached down and excitedly tapped the play button of the video from the Fisher Island Ferry. Her tongue slipped from her mouth, "Ttssssss!" *Those eyes! There's another Holmes! Noooooo!!* Fueled by failure and adrenaline, Moriarty smashed the replay button and took a quick, misstep forward.

Hikers call it post-holing—a vertical drop into a snowy trap. One voluptuous leg, followed by the other, plunged through the snow.

In her 20s, tired of catcalls and back aches, Moriarty considered breast reduction surgery. Now, with hands and arms trapped at her sides, her bodacious breasts were the only things buoying her above a snowy abyss. Trapped like a champagne cork, there was no sense struggling. *Blasted Holmeses! How could there be another? No matter, I'll kill her too*, she thought.

Shocked by the cold, her brilliant mind took twelve seconds to reset from thoughts of retribution to survival. Moriarty knew she had to be extracted from over a meter of snow before hypothermia set in, and the only way out was straight up. She shouted to her submerged smartwatch, "R1, Deploy help." Eventually, her operatives would come looking. Eventually.

Her legs stung. She knew better than to wear short shorts in this weather, however they made her look taller, and she never could resist the Laura Croft look when adventuring outdoors.

Agony gave way to numbness as her second-to-second countdown filled her head. Counting soothed Moriarty, and her cadence rivaled that of an atomic clock. 2,189 seconds passed. Hypothermia and frostbite loomed. Her breasts descended further into the snow. They tingled, and not in a good way. The pain! Moriarty's mind reeled with images of wrapping her legs around the other Holmes girl's neck, constricting the last breath from her lips. Moriarty passed out, coming to seconds later, thinking, *six days in total darkness and its back already. How am I supposed to think, to rule, with this going on? This is why you must do it, Jane. Shadow Holmes. Stupid girl. Didn't know I was a Moriarty, or her parents were spies! She'll lead me to it. And the other one. Did Arthur Holmes have a child out of wedlock? I heard he was wild in his youth. My nipples feel like popsicles. They better come soon. Breathe, Jane. Breathe.*

The ice tightened. Jane felt faint. She took a shallow breath, and she heard it. Another and she saw it. Her heart raced. "BLASTED HOLMESES," she screamed as the helicopter bearing The Bee insignia circled overhead, opened a hatch, and lowered a robotic harness on the end of a thin cable.

"Ttssssss," Moriarty hissed as the harness tightened around her throbbing chest. The chopper remained stationary as a winch yanked her upward. Her frost-bitten body lifted from the icy chasm. Images of knifing Shadow and the other Holmes over and over again consumed her until it all went black. She awoke in the air, the key to world domination remained buried meters below.

As Moriarty numbed to the rush of wind against her frost-ravaged body, she practiced her visualization techniques; a skill learned from her last therapist. She felt badly about killing that one. She had great nails. Moriarty envisioned herself in her favorite chaise, on the balcony of her Miami Beach flat. She was wearing her red-flowered bikini bottom. No top. The sun felt good against her perfect skin. Her scent was absent. She brought the drink to her lips. A frozen margarita.

"Frozen," Moriarty muttered aloud. Freezing pain shotgunned her happy images aside, replaced by the hideous sight of her frostbitten legs below. Moriarty's eyes glimmered red. *I'll be wearing that bikini bottom when I slay them*, Jane thought, before passing out.

27

I'm slaying it! Or did I just get lucky? The Baskerville listing was too easy, and that paper was gruesome. Imagine using human remains to produce weapons of mass destruction. What does Moriarty need the paper for? Why all the subterfuge, Father? You didn't want me in the spy biz, so these clues were meant for your Bee agents. Where the hell is the cavalry anyway? Here we are. House number two. Joint owners. Wife didn't sign the listing contract. Hmm. Another murder? I'm in over my head. Go home. Nap. No! I can do this. I must do this, Shadow thought, tousling my fur, saying, "Hate to interrupt your nap, Watson."

For the record, I was merely resting my eyes. We exited the vehicle. Although Shadow's heartbeat was elevated, her breath was unaltered, and I found myself noticeably less anxious than when we knocked on the door of the first house. We were greeted by three redheaded young ladies, approximately 19 years of age, each clutching a cell phone. They were identical in appearance and wore dark dresses bearing thin black ribbons. They smelled of candy-scented perfume one might wear to a boy band concert.

"You the Realtor?" the young ladies asked in unison.

"Shadow Holmes of Homes by Holmes and Holmes."

"Scarlett," one said.

"Ruby," another replied.

"Ginger. The oldest," the third said.

"By sixty-three seconds," Ruby replied.

"I can't believe Papa didn't list the house with Uncle Max," Scarlett said.

"Papa told us it's because your family is related to Sherlock Holmes," Ginger said.

"Yeah, right! He's so gullible," Ruby replied.

"What's with the clothes?" Scarlett asked.

"Don't you get it, dummy? She's trying to look like the olden days. Like when Sherlock Holmes was around," Ginger clarified.

"Oh! I think they're cool!" Ruby said.

"Thanks," Shadow replied, thinking, *triplets. This should be fun.*

"Cute dog. What's his name?" Scarlet asked.

"Watson," Shadow said.

"You people really milk this Sherlock Holmes act," Ginger snarked.

Shadow studied the young women up and down, observing their slit ribbons, a symbol of loss in the Jewish faith, commenting, "Sorry for your loss."

"Thanks. Follow us," the girls replied in unison.

The triplets led us through a modest hallway, into an office containing a large desk upon which were no less than seventeen messy stacks of handwritten letters, an open box containing five partially eaten donuts, and behind it, an odd red-headed man wearing a skull cap and a white shirt also bearing a slit black ribbon, who remained in his overstuffed leather chair, scowling.

"I changed my mind," the man announced.

"Shadow Holmes, Mr. Wilson. I'm sorry for your loss. I certainly understand if this isn't the time to sell," Shadow said, observing Wilson gaze at a wedding picture on the wall, thinking, *that's why the wife didn't sign the listing. Another murder. What kind of life did my parents lead? And I thought real estate was a cutthroat business.*

"You're not Spaulding. Oy! Never mind. We need to sell, Ms. Holmes. With my Susie gone, and all these kids crammed in here, we need a bigger place so my parents can move in and help. I have work to do. Show Ms. Holmes around, girls," Wilson said.

With the triplets as our guide, we commenced our tour on the second-floor walking through a ghostly hallway of sheet covered mirrors (yet another sign of mourning), leading to a multitude of adjoining bedrooms lined with bunkbeds as one might see in a barracks. While the rooms were absent children as they were attending school, clothes, toys, sippy cups and snack wrappers were scattered about as if the aftermath of a hurricane party. Shadow took note of a wall of family photos, bearing the father, mother, an additional set of triplets, a set of quadruplets, and two sets of twins, all of whom bore red hair. We walked downstairs to the back door, where the girls abruptly halted.

"Bella's out back," said Scarlett.

"She's in heat—like every other day. I'm surprised Watson isn't going nuts," Ginger remarked.

"Now that Mom's gone, we're going to have her fixed. She loved that dog. Wouldn't even let Papa kiss her on the lips, but that dog ... it was disgusting," Ruby said.

I caught sight of her in the afternoon sun. Another redhead. A dachshund, nose in the grass, on the hunt for food. The breed is insatiable, in every sense. My tail thumped against the windowsill. I barked a casual greeting.

"Stay, Watson," Shadow said, stepping into the yard.

My neck fur rose. My ears perked. We had not been parted since we met. I stood uneasily, observing through the window. Shadow strode to the boat dock, bent to examine a board, and walked across the yard toward her. "Hello, Bella," she said, crouching, holding the dachshund's face close to hers.

I was overcome with jealousy of a somewhat bipolar nature. On one paw, I coveted the affection Shadow was paying to Bella. On the other, I was desirous of Bella's company, purely in a platonic manner, as despite Ms. Scarlett's comment, I did not 'go nuts'. In fact, my nose failed to detect any trace of Bella's cycle whatsoever, which I found rather odd, as an American bulldog mix whose appearance was such as to suggest he recently escaped the pound, was digging under the fence.

"Get! Get!" Scarlett shouted, turning the garden hose on the failed Romeo, thus causing his retreat.

"Bad girl, Bella. We're taking you to the vet—today!" Ruby said.

"What a mess. We have to fill in that hole," Ginger said.

"Meet you inside," the girls chimed.

Shadow observed the scene, turned her sights on me through the glass, raised an eyebrow, entered the house, and with me at her side, walked through the unremarkable living and adjacent dining room to an area of spectacular culinary enterprise. As is often the practice in orthodox homes, there were two kitchens, one smelling of milk and cheese, the other, the scent of that which produced the former. Shadow paced briskly and repeatedly between the rooms, paying particular attention to drawers which she opened and closed. She plopped on a stool in the dairy kitchen and assumed her 'I'm most certainly going to apprehend you' posture, pondering, *Zombie Blood. Who names these things? I saw that shade of nail polish on the kitchen drawers and the mother in the family photos. So many multiple births. All those children—without a mother. At least they have each other. Sad. Stay on task, Shadow. The mother died here—alone. Trying to get something in one or both of those drawers. Couldn't find it. A gun? She didn't die violently. Hmm. What was she after? Boat dock had traces of peanut butter on one of the planks. Peanut allergy! She needed an EpiPen! One of Moriarty's operatives came by boat, fed Bella peanut butter and removed the pens from the drawers. Bella licked the peanut butter, then the mother's lips. The husband is hiding something. I can sense it. Sense it! Eren is rubbing off on me. Rubbing ... Wouldn't that be ... Head out of the stars, Shadow! A woman is dead.*

"Damn dogs! Not you, Watson," Scarlett said, patting me as the girls joined us.

"Would you like to talk in the next room?" Shadow asked.

"How'd you know?" the girls chimed.

Not related to Sherlock Holmes. Hate to do this, but I need to confirm my theory, Shadow thought, stating, "Sorry to be insensitive, but since you asked. There are stretcher marks on the floor leading to that spot, where you mother passed while searching in vain for her EpiPen."

"That's sick!" said Scarlett.

Crap! I went too far, Shadow thought. "I didn't mean to upse—"

"She meant sick in a good way. How'd you know?" Ruby questioned.

"There are high-heel scuffs between the kitchens leading to two drawers with traces of Zombie Blood nail polish, which is the same shade your mother was wearing in your family photos."

"You really are related to Sherlock Holmes. Hey! Can we get a selfie?" Ginger asked, as the girls mobbed us like paparazzi.

"I'm a mess," Shadow responded, unconsciously beaming with pride, fixing her hair, as the girls snapped away.

"Mom kept an EpiPen in every room in the house," Scarlett sniffled.

"Crazy thing is I saw the pens last week," Ruby offered.

"Terrible to die like that. At least she had Bella with her," Ginger said.

"Gross. Bella was licking her mouth when we ... you know," Ruby said.

"They were two of a kind. Bella had as many litters as Mom," Scarlett, sniffed.

A woman with multiple multiple births. 'Changed my mind'. Of course. Wilson didn't mean the house! What the hell does Moriarty need with a human cloning machine. First a Baskerville, now a Wilson conned by a Spaulding, Shadow thought, raising an eyebrow toward me, which triggered another memory. Another league of redheads.

I stood in a damp London tunnel. Mr. Jabez Wilson, a pawn broker, duped by a thief named Spaulding who built a tunnel under his shop to get to a bank vault full of gold. Naturally, Sherlock Holmes solved the case and thwarted the robbery. The bank compensated Wilson to repair the damage to his shop, instead he took the money, moved to Miami Beach, married a nice Jewish girl and bought a house which his grandson Sammy inherited. My memory retreated. I was left flummoxed—and I wasn't the only one.

"You still here?" Wilson asked, joining us in the dining room.

"Just leaving Mr. Wilson. When's the funeral? I'd like to send a platter," Shadow lied, to which Wilson commenced bawling.

Crap! I've done it again. I need to be more sensitive in these situations. I should apologize ... but I don't think it's me he's upset with, Shadow thought, studying the man, however before she could offer an apology, the triplets laid into the bloke.

"Papa! Why are you waiting for someone named Spaulding?" Ginger asked.

"What did you fall for now, Papa?" Ruby said.

"Not again!" Scarlett exclaimed.

"Spaulding said she was only going to scan her and bring her right back. We were so blessed. Think of all the women who can't have children," Wilson blubbered.

"Spaulding! You're so naive, Papa. Didn't you recognize the name?" Scarlet asked.

"Sure, Spaulding, Wilson. Like the sporting goods companies. She's from Eggs R Us, the international fertility research firm," Wilson said.

"Vincent Spaulding was the alias used by John Clay to trick great-grandpa to rob a bank. Any of this sounding remotely familiar, Papa?" Ginger questioned.

"He didn't see the irony," Ruby whispered to us.

"YOU GAVE THEM MOM'S BODY," Ginger screamed.

"You still don't get it, do you, Papa?" Scarlett questioned.

Wilson most certainly did not get it, as with the exception of his puffed-out eyes, the red-headed bloke remained motionless, bringing to mind a budgie attempting to view itself in a broken mirror.

"I see you have a lot to discuss. I'll call you with the first offer, Mr. Wilson," Shadow said, as we took our leave, thinking, *that poor woman. Even autopsies are frowned on in the orthodox faith. Too bad. I'm sure Tuesday would love to get her hands on the body.*

28

"Keep your bloody hands off me," Tuesday shouted, kicking Eren repeatedly.

"I'm trying to unfasten your restraints," Eren replied.

"Didn't take you for the bondage type, Mr. Adler. Your eye. Did I do that?" Tuesday asked shakily.

"In fairness, you yelled something about me hurting your cousin and clocked me."

"Apologies. Drugs often blur the lines between angels and assholes. So, which are you?"

"Depends on who you ask. Stay put and drink this," Eren said, unbuckling Tuesday, handing her a Gatorade.

"Am I still tripping or are we in Atlantis?" Tuesday asked, looking out the glass ceiling.

"Technically, we're under Atlantis."

Given it's Miami, the Peter Pan metropolis which will never grow up, there's nothing irregular regarding naming a place Atlantis; an underwater graveyard, three miles off the coast of Miami Beach, where the dearly departed's ashes are mixed into cement and dropped to the ocean floor, forming the perfect substrate for corals to grow.

Corals attract fish, crustaceans, and, well, you get it, circle of life, and that sort of muck. Brilliant idea for an eco-friendly exit from life as we know it, wherein people's ashy avatars are embodied in kitschy structures, such as sea turtles, starfish, and mermaids, and a perfect location under which to hide a safe house.

"I went free diving here during Ultra one year when I was training with deep water divers. I can hold my breath for three full minutes."

"Dolly dropped us. You missed the submarine ride," Eren said.

"Shadow?" Tuesday asked.

"No communications in or out," Eren replied.

"How long?" Tuesday asked, leaping off the stretcher, falling back shakily.

"Not long enough. You need rest. What's it going to take to keep you in bed?"

"Kind of you to offer Mr. Adler, however I thought you loved my cousin," Tuesday japed.

"Shadow is the love of my life."

"Love of your life? What a load of dung! I confess, I am mystified by your relationship. Your pervasive passionate proclamations in combination with the manner in which you gaze upon my cousin, indicate your deepest affection, and likely a raging hard-on. Further, any nincompoop may observe Shadow's pining puppy dog face when she looks your way and deduce that although you broke her heart, she feels naughty in the knickers every time you're near. Sure, she's cheeky, but she's a flipping genius with, I might add, a bum dreams are made of. You're clearly intellectual equals who make each other randy as rabbits, so why abandon her?"

"I'll tell you, but only if you promise to stay put and tell me if Sherlock Holmes diddled his landlady?"

"Eww! And no, he most certainly did not diddle her. I'll tell you everything, but this would be much better if I were still high," Tuesday said, smiling.

"The trauma you astutely observed in my breath, Dr. Hudson was indeed caused by Kent's abuse when I was twelve. I told my mother. She didn't believe me. By the time I was fourteen, the shame was too much. I hung a rope from a mango tree in our yard, stood on a ladder, and jumped. Mercifully, termites had eaten into the branch, and it snapped. I landed on my feet, in more than a physical sense. My humiliation waned, and for the first time in two years, I felt hopeful. My grandmother took me to therapy where I began to experience my umwelt. I was fine until the causeway. Until Horace Cobb abused that poor child my team placed, and I found myself, rope in hand, under another tree. I couldn't do that to Shadow."

"And now?"

"I've completed over a year of somatic therapy. You saw me with Kent. I was unphased. Shadow said she understood, but she doesn't trust me. How could she?" Eren said placing a cold compress on Tuesday's forehead.

"Thank you, Mr. Adler," Tuesday smiled. "She shouldn't trust you. However, love leads us to strange places, doesn't it? I mean look at us, stuck in an underwater graveyard swapping yarns."

"You haven't told yours yet."

GREAT SCOTT, MATE. An origin story within an origin story! About time you learned the mating habits of the world's most famous detective, eh?

"Most people are unaware, Mrs. Hudson, Sherlock's landlady at Baker Street had a young brother, Rock. Upon her death, Rock Hudson, a dashing army intelligence officer, inherited her estate. One wouldn't imagine the estate of a landlady who waited on my grandfather hand and foot to include a grand property in Sussex, a hefty bank account, and a hand-scribed collection of Sherlock Holmes stories. Mrs. Hudson however was a savvy investor and had the means to do so thanks to Grandfather who rewarded her dearly for placing her life at risk on many occasions.

"My grandmother, Vivian Churchill, was the rebellious daughter of a diplomat. She traveled extensively, spoke eight languages, loved mystery novels, made a hobby of flirting, and was drop dead gorgeous—not that that mattered to Grandfather. It did however matter to Captain Rock Hudson, who following a whirlwind three-day courtship, married Vivian before shipping off to war, leaving the 27-year-old Vivian bored and lonely in the Sussex countryside.

"Earlier when I said Grandmother loved mystery novels, what I meant to say is she lived for them. She read every single Sherlock

Holmes adventure, studying his methods, even dare I say, dressing up on occasion in a deerstalker hat, cape, and little else."

"I see where you get your sense of style," Eren said.

"Thank you, Mr. Adler," Tuesday replied, flourishing her hand in front of her face. "As I was saying, one sunny day, after reading 'The Adventure of The Empty House,' featuring the bravery of her deceased sister-in-law, Vivian felt so inspired as to permit her horse to lead a sojourn into the surrounding meadows in hopes of locating Sherlock Holmes. Horses being naturally curious creatures, and upon considering a remote apiary, trotted over for a closer look. It was there, she first encountered him. Like everyone in Sussex, Vivian knew of Sherlock's desire for solitude, yet she couldn't resist dismounting her horse to converse with the legendary man.

'Good day, Mr. Sherlock Holmes. I am — '

'No need for introductions, Mrs. Vivian Hudson. Your sister-in-law was a singular woman,' Sherlock said bowing.

'What they say about you is true, Mr. Holmes. Guess what I had for breakfast.'

'I do not engage in parlor tricks, madam.'

'Fine, I'll begin. Your breakfast consisted of one salted poached egg, a hunk of brown bread hastily torn from the loaf, and a pot of lapsang souchong tea with honey from the third, no make that the fifth hive on your left. Now, *do me*, Mr. Holmes, *do me*,' Vivian winked.

'You have extraordinary powers of observation, madam, however, I do not *DO* anyone. If you'll pardon me, I must tend to my bees. Your beast upset them. Good day, Mrs. Hudson,' Grandfather replied.

"Vivian returned day after day, set up her easel, and painted Sherlock tending his bees. She spoke very little and when she did, Grandfather found her company tolerable. One day, she set up her easel in silence and proceeded to cry.

'My deepest sympathies, Mrs. Hudson,' Sherlock offered.

'Thank you, Mr. Holmes. Rock died doing what he loved best, I imagine. Honestly, I barely knew the man. Indeed, I know and care for you much more than I did my own husband, Mr. Holmes. Looking back, I only married him to annoy Father. As your contemporary, Dr. Freud might say, I have daddy issues, she winked.

'Madam, grief has a funny way—'

'I assure you Mr. Holmes, I am not grief stricken. Indeed, I have a singular proposal for you, if you'll permit me a moment to complete it?' Vivian tested, picking up her paintbrush, dipping it lightly on the palette, adding a single stroke to the canvas, smiling, and expressing, 'THERE.'

"Father told me when Vivian presented the beatific painting of Sherlock tending his bees, a young heir at his side, her dog frolicking near the hives, herself in the foreground, mouth adrip with honey, my 89-year-old virginal grandfather was so taken with her genius, he took her— right atop an active hive. The dog! It's Watson!" Tuesday screamed, bolting out of bed, falling to the floor.

"It's okay, Tuesday. Hallucinations are one of the withdrawal symptoms, *but that seemed very real*, Eren thought. "At any rate, let's get you in bed."

"I'd wager you say that to all the girls, Mr. Adler."

Eren smiled as his mind stewed, *only one, and I'm stuck below an underwater cemetery nursing you, while a murderer is after her.*

29

The drone came out of nowhere, latched onto the cable, and retrieved Moriarty via the very harness The Bee utilized to ensnare her. Having secured her, the drone shot down the chopper with a single missile. Unfortunately for Moriarty, an untimely gust of wind caused the protuberance of her right nipple, which extended one millimeter further than the left, to shear the top branch of a spruce as the drone sped off.

"Ttssssss!" Moriarty screamed into the air. Prior to blacking out, her mind clouded with murderous thoughts. *Blasted Holmeses! They'll see what it feels like. Knives! Yes, knives will do nicely.*

30

"Cutting through these clues like a hot knife through butter, huh, Watson?" Shadow said, thinking, *fuck me. I've become one of those people who talk to their dog.*

I did not wish Shadow to believe her efforts at communicating were in vain, additionally, her possessive use of the term 'their dog' filled me with happiness, as such, I barked vociferously and licked her face.

Silly dog, Shadow thought, as she sprang from the car in front of house number three, a diminutive white mission home, its yard awash in purple bougainvillea flowers. Unlike her uneasiness when approaching the first two houses, Shadow was, as the young people say, stoked, and pounded on this door as if delivering pizza she feared would soon cool.

"You Shadow?" a bespectacled 70ish man, who smelled of nicotine asked.

"Hello, Mr. Frank. Shadow Holmes."

"What's with the getup? I thought you people were rich?"

Nasty old bastard, Shadow thought, replying, "They're vintage. It's all the rage these days," she lied.

"What's with the dog?"

"This is Watson, my service dog," she lied again.

"Service dog. Modern day bullshit. He better not piss up the place. Come in," Mr. Frank replied turning, thus providing an unobstructed view of his derrière crack peaking above his sagging suspendered trousers.

Despite his demeanor, and not wishing to be rude, I wagged my tail in greeting as we followed the bow-legged man who ambled with aid of his cane to the living room. Although a faded white throughout, the home's immaculate interior was the most noteworthy of the lot we had seen with arched hallways and a built-in window seat, splendid displays of early 20th century architecture.

"Take a load off," Mr. Frank said, lowering himself into a chair, cane between his legs.

Shadow accepted the offer and sat on the only other chair in the living room, which I leaned upon. She took in the room, as did I. The floors were original oak, well-maintained, and clean enough to eat from. (Regrettably, nobody had bothered to drop any food.) Assorted black and white photographs lined the walls. A variety of succulents rested upon a glass shelf, thriving in sunlight which gleamed through French doors. A cypress coffee table bearing an empty ceramic vase and an overflowing ashtray rested between us and Mr. Frank. The entire residence smelled of smoke which caused me to sneeze. Repeatedly.

"Charming home," Shadow said, on this occasion, being truthful. "Must be hard to leave after spending your life here."

"How'd you figure?"

"The pencil marks in the foyer with the initials B.F, marking your height since you were two."

"Pass those things so often I forget they're there. Mom bought the place new in 1939. Haven't changed a thing. I was born here. Never lived anyplace else, and as soon as you unload this rathole, I'll be free of it," Mr. Frank sighed.

Shadow gazed at one of the photos on the wall containing a group of people standing about a multitude of vertically arranged railroad ties, crisscrossed by horizontal beams, all strung together with cable over a long stretch of pineland, giving the appearance of the underpinnings of an uncompleted bridge. *Dead mother. He doesn't strike me as a killer. Let's see his reaction when I bring her up,* Shadow thought, remarking, "Your mother was involved with the Koreshan Unity."

"Who the hell told you?"

"The picture of your mother next to the rectilineator used by the Koreshans to measure the curve of the Earth," Shadow said, pointing at the picture.

"Mom was one of the last. How'd you know about the idiotic rectilineator?"

"I read a lot. Cellular Cosmology, the Koreshan Unity's treatise espousing the spiritual and scientific belief that the Earth's surface is concave, and the entire universe is contained within its hollow sphere, is … fascinating," Shadow lied yet again.

"Fascinating! Load of hooey! The Koreshans were a crazy cult who believed the Earth was hollow. They also believed in celibacy. Lucky for me, Mom couldn't keep it in her pants. Crazy old broad. Have a look around. I'll be out back," Mr. Frank said, retrieving a pack of unfiltered Camels from his pocket, rising precariously on his cane, wobbling toward the back door.

We strode into the master bedroom, which in today's real estate market, would barely qualify as a guest room. The four-poster bed was covered by a quilt featuring cross-sections of globes, which Shadow yanked from the bed. She peeled back the sheets, studied the mattress in detail and sniffed, thinking, *solitary urine stain. Smells awful, and fresh. She died here.*

Based on the odor, I concurred. Shadow remade the bed and paused to read the inscription on a photo on the nightstand—that of a bearded man, signed, 'To Mabel, I'll be back. Cyrus.' Shadow smiled, thinking, *I'll be back. Maybe the Terminator but not you, buddy. Dr. Cyrus Teed. Physician, pseudoscientist, self-proclaimed savior, charismatic nutcase. Died too long ago to be Mr. Frank's father. Some messiah. His body washed out to sea in a hurricane. Land was donated to the state for a park and historic site. Great spot, right on the Estero River. Father caught lots of redfish there. Eren and I canoed to the Gulf … well, he paddled most of the way … even saved some paddling for me. Eren … Head in the stars!*

Shadow walked briskly to Mr. Frank's piffling bedroom, taking in its barren walls, twin bed, and nightstand bearing an ashtray, lamp, and pile of tattered National Geographic magazines. The closet held a meager quantity of clothing and a toolbox, which Shadow examined, thinking, *pipe wrench, hacksaw, hand auger, thread seal tape. Toss in the bowlegs and butt-crack … plumber.*

We crossed an open pocket door frame into a spotless outdated bathroom, Shadow contemplating, *we'll never get asking price for this minuscule place. There I go thinking like a Realtor again.*

We journeyed to the adjoining bed chamber, barely large enough to house a papillon. The space was illuminated by a picture window, contained a rusty filing cabinet, and a wooden desk and chair one might find in an old schoolhouse. Shadow rested in the chair, opened the cabinet, examined the yellowed file folders, and drew one from the middle. The activity of late provoked my nerve pain, thus I curled by her feet as she read. After a brief period, she tossed the file back in the cabinet, closed the drawer and assumed her 'I'm most certainly going to apprehend you' pose, *the Flaming Sword … Teed's Hollow Earth periodical. Mabel published it for decades after his death waiting for his return. From her notes, she was working on the final issue right before she passed, but it never made it to print … or did someone steal it? Hollow Earth. The son's not a believer. He's miserable, but why kill her at their age and for what? Some crackpot journal about civilization existing inside the Earth. Think it out. Could Moriarty have gotten to him? I don't smell her. Just smoke, but it's not stale … and the house is immaculate. Hmm. Son can barely walk. He's not cleaning the house. And the mother was ancient.* Shadow dashed to the bathroom, admonishing herself, *damn it! Walked right through and didn't process that it's cleaner than an operating room. Stop thinking like a Realtor!*

She flung open the medicine cabinet door examining the contents as if she knew exactly what she was seeking. *Empty bottle of amiloride! Diuretic for blood pressure. Prescription filled last week. An overdose can cause fatal hyperkalemia, potassium overdose. Empty bottle of toilet cleaner in the trash. The housekeeper murdered her. Almost got to say the butler did it,* Shadow chuckled to herself, rushing out the French doors to the backyard. I followed closely behind. Mr. Frank, burning cigarette in hand, dozed in a lawn chair.

"Agatha?" Mr. Frank startled as we approached, his cigarette falling from his tobacco-stained fingers.

Agatha and a plumber. Seriously, Father? Shadow thought, raising an eyebrow, which caused my head to buzz, shaking lose another recollection. Another Agatha. Another plumber.

I stood in the servant's entrance of a large gas-oil lit home. A squealing housemaid smelling of lavender, cleaning products, and sweat, vigorously shook her head up and down. Reflected in her eyes, I saw him—a plumber on bended knee, a wrench in one hand, an engagement ring in the other. Sherlock Holmes, in disguise, proposing to a housemaid to gain access to the home of a blackmailer, Mr. Charles Augustus Milverton. After deceiving the woman, and concluding the case, Holmes never returned. I shook my head in disbelief. What could these olden-day images have to do with me?

"Sorry to disturb you, Mr. Frank. Is Agatha your housekeeper?"

"You're awfully nosey."

"Sorry. Your house is immaculate. Our clients are always looking for a good housekeeper," Shadow lied again.

"Yeah. Her name's Agatha. Hasn't been around all week," Mr. Frank took an embroidered hanky from his pocket, sniffed it, smiled weakly, removed his spectacles, and dabbed them.

A familiar scent reached my nose. Sweat, cleaning products, and lavender! Fun fact, mate. Each human gives off a particular odor, many passed down through family lines. The lady who gave Mr. Frank the hanky—a descendant of Agatha sworn to revenge! My neck fur rose. I growled and stationed myself between Shadow and Mr. Frank.

"Watson!" Shadow yelled, thinking, *what got into him?*

I quieted but did not budge.

"Service dog, my ass!" Mr. Frank said.

"Sorry, Mr. Frank. He's not usually like this."

"Don't bring that animal back. Get out and call me as soon as you get an offer."

"I will, Mr. Frank. Sorry again about my dog," Shadow said, the words 'my dog' joyfully reverberating in my head as we seated ourselves in her car.

What the hell was that? Could this Agatha be related to the Agatha from Great-Granduncle Sherlock's cases? A Baskerville, redheads, and now a plumber and a housemaid. I must be losing it. Three houses to go. Next house has a lockbox so no rush. I must be a mess. Who cares? On the other hand, never can be too careful ... Shadow who typically avoids mirrors like a vampire, thought, checking the car's rearview. *Fuck! I knew it! Somebody's following me. Maybe I can draw them out. Someplace public.*

David Raymond

I'm starving. Haven't had a decent meal all week. The cafe down the block has a decent wine selection and chicken breasts juicier than Dolly Parton's.

31

Jane Moriarty scrutinized her breasts in the dimly lit mirror of her guestroom in the Florida Governor's mansion as if viewing a failed science experiment. From the top they could grace the perfect tits section of any porn site. To Moriarty alone, the right was far from flawless. That spruce clipped off a minuscule bit of nipple tip, which stung against her bra—fortunately, she seldom wore one. Moriarty dipped a creamy concoction from a jar, gritted her teeth, boosted her boobs, and applied the balm to the undersides, which were a ghastly shade of purple. Her blistered legs were even worse and could easily be featured in a heartbreaking GoFundMe appeal. She drew her shoulders back, took a breath, bent over, slathered cream on her legs and shuddered in pain. Her mind darkened with images of slashing those blasted Holmeses into wee bits. She was awakened seconds later by a chime.

"Hudson!" Moriarty screamed into her cellphone, thinking, *so, Sherlock Holmes screwed his landlady. Didn't think he had it in him. Though I imagine it was she who had it in her. Pity. I always supposed he and Dr. Watson were gayer than me. I mean really, two grown men of means sharing a flat.*

"And the bearded man? He could prove useful. Fetch them. What do you mean you lost them?! They were on a bloody island! Ttsssss! FIND THEM—ALIVE, or you won't be!" Moriarty threatened, hanging up.

"Everything okay, Professor?" Fahrenheit sheepishly called through the door, as Moriarty's pheromones wafted into the hallway.

"No, you blithering twit! Get in here! NOW," Moriarty ordered.

Fahrenheit inhaled a deep whiff of her through the keyhole and became erect straightaway. Flustered, he gingerly knocked on the door, opening it with a fiendish grin.

In the event you're wondering who this bloke is, Florida Governor Fester Fahrenheit is to fiends as King Kong is to apes, as Godzilla is to lizards, as Hitler is to Nazis, however in the Sunshine State these qualities seem to be just what one needs to become an elected official as some Floridians relish banning books, not saying gay, and having their reproductive rights stripped. (And just think, you people bitched about getting taxed on your tea.)

Fester Fahrenheit came from a family of immigrant farmers. Not the boo-hoo, poor, penniless type, mate. They were filthy rich! Following the Second World War, Fester's grandfather, Gestapo Colonel Friedrich Fahrenheit, exploited a hungry nation's needs, purchased cheap acreage in war-torn areas, and started the largest wheat farm in Germany. Upon Friedrich's death, his sole heir, Klaus Fahrenheit took over the company.

Klaus had an even keener business sense than his father, who he abhorred for his role in the War. After three years of expansion, restructuring and acquisitions, Citrus Industries was birthed, its South Florida headquarters far from the coldness of Berlin. Klaus loved everything about Miami Beach. Shorts in February, fishing the Gulf Stream, and the bounty of beauties on the beach. It was there Klaus met Fester's Cuban mother, Harmony Havana, a tatted yoga instructor, with the mind of a Greek philosopher, the heart of a monk, the flexibility of a circus contortionist, and a mouth that could suck a coconut through a garden hose. Klaus and Harmony married, had two children, Fester and Tiffani. Upon Klaus' demise in a dubious fishing accident, Fester inherited the family business.

Surprisingly, Fester, who previously showed little interest in anything but womanizing, grew Citrus into the largest chemical manufacturing operation the world had ever seen. Unlike his proper father, who abided by rules and respected the environment, Fester only cared about two things. Power and as they say in the vernacular, vajayjay. He obtained the latter aplenty by having an endless supply of money, cocaine, and Molly; the former by ferreting out regulatory loopholes permitting him to pollute the planet and grease countless hands to cover it up.

Bored with the conquest of business, Fester took on the challenge of politics, which he had a unique take on. Instead of promising what he would do, Fahrenheit ran on a platform of anti. Anti-abortion, anti-gay, anti-woke, anti-science, anti-books, anti-liberal, anti-vax, anti-this, anti-that. He won in a bloody anti-landslide. Upon concluding his victory speech, wife and children at his side, a woman approached him backstage. She was short, stacked, and smelled like the bedsheets in the Playboy Mansion. Fahrenheit became indescribably aroused. It was then, before he was even sworn into office, Jane Moriarty's spell was cast, and it became abundantly clear who would be running the state of Florida.

"Sorry, Professor. I heard you scream. Are you alright?" Fahrenheit questioned, entering like a vagabond sneaking into a hotel laundry room.

"Do I look BLOODY ALRIGHT?"

"Like a goddess," Fahrenheit stammered, gawking at Moriarty's nakedness.

"Write this down and don't muck it up," Moriarty demanded.

"Yes, Professor."

"First, triple production in the phosphate mines."

"But, Professor, we're already up to two dozen a day. Plus, the environmentalists will go nuts."

"Boo-hoo. Next, a lease. Crystal River, all the way to the Gulf."

"Crystal River? You know that's impossible, Professor. Parts are federal, and we're decommissioning the nuclear ... power plant," Fahrenheit gulped.

"Shouldn't be a problem for someone about to be elected president."

"President!!?" Fahrenheit quivered with excitement.

"The press release is being issued as we speak."

"President Fahrenheit. I only dreamed of it. Do you think it's possible, Professor?"

"With my criminal organization's backing, it will be impossible for even you to lose. Are you writing these down, Fester?"

"Yes, of course. I'll figure out the Crystal River lease, Professor, I just have to manage the optics."

"Optics! How's this for optics?" Moriarty blurted maniacally, lifting her enormous breasts by their nipples, exposing their purple undersides, until the pain caused her to scream out, "ARGHHHHHHH." Her mind filled with images of blood spurting from Shadow's neck, until it all went black.

"You okay, Professor?" Fahrenheit asked, stirring her.

"Where's that frostbite expert?"

"She just arrived," Fahrenheit trembled.

"Fetch her. Now!"

"Anything you want," Fahrenheit drooled, as Moriarty's amplified pheromones sent him off with a ragingly painful erection.

Moriarty hated being the smallest person in the room. Excruciating pain, murderous thoughts, and an explosion of pheromones accompanied each of her steps up the rolling library ladder. She awoke seconds later, clinging to a rung. "ARCTICCCC," Moriarty bellowed, shoving her hand against the wall, propelling her and the ladder across the bookshelf rows, her bountiful backside greeting Fahrenheit and a tall, striking blonde, at eye level as she whizzed by. The ladder came to a stop in front of a first edition of her great-granduncle's book, 'The Dynamics of an Asteroid'. The red of her eyes reflected off the book's well-worn spline as she snatched it from the shelf. "Marvelous!"

"Professor, this is Doctor Angelina Arctic the—"

"I know who she bloody is, you knob, I sent for her. Now go play in the corner like a good lad," Moriarty demanded without turning around.

Moriarty's fragrance burst into Arctic's sinuses. Arctic blushed, placed a laser device in her jean pocket, and fashioned her long blonde hair into a bun, "Anyone else feeling warm?"

"Get on with it!" Moriarty barked.

"My laser will restore blood flow, regenerate tissue, muscle fibers, even damaged nerves, within hours," Arctic replied, unconsciously unbuttoning her blouse.

"It better, or I'll use that device on your blasted head!"

"The success rate is 99.8%," Arctic replied, tearing off her bra.

"Do me," Moriarty said and turned to face her.

"Pardon?" an increasingly randy Arctic replied, removing the laser from her pocket, mindlessly sliding out of her jeans.

Moriarty placed her bum on a step, splayed her legs, and yelled, "Do me!"

Dr. Angelina Arctic, licked her lips, let loose her hair, tore off her panties, bolted up the ladder, shone her laser on Moriarty's thigh and came. Both women moaned—the tall one in ecstasy, the short one in relief.

Looking on from the corner of the room, presidential candidate, Governor Fester Fahrenheit, who always was a premature ejaculator, whimpered in an ungodly manner, and creamed his pants.

32

The majestic tree trunk greeted Lestrade like the hand of God. He would have never broken the rules like this back home. Trespassing on private property was bad form. Lestrade hated bad form. In his position at Scotland Yard, he would have done the proper thing and obtained a warrant. But he wasn't in London and he wasn't officially working. For once, the idea of behaving outside the confines of the law as Tuesday did appealed to him. His thoughts of her had the effect as to amplify her absence. The image of her ever-smirking face consumed him, *WWTD? What Would Tuesday Do? She certainly wouldn't be distracted by thoughts of me. Work the case, Lestrade.*

Despite the darkness, Lestrade took in the oak. It was a grand specimen—the biggest he'd seen. He was struck with what the tree must have witnessed since sprouting from an acorn centuries ago. Indigenous people living in harmony with nature, resting beneath its branches like sleeping infants, fast-forward to today's developers of behemoth concrete McMansions who would feign oak allergies to fell it and its kin. *Not this yard*, he thought, marveling at the well-established landscape, bursting with native pollinator plants woven under a canopy of massive trees. In fact, the entire Village abounded with trees. Lestrade read in a recent police journal, the residents of Biscayne Park so revered their trees, a small band of crackpot zealots had taken to calling in bomb threats at neighborhood construction sites which involved the removal of large specimen trees. He took out his phone and recorded a case note, 'Arthur Holmes-fancies trees'.

Working up the courage for breaking and entering was harder than Lestrade imagined. He had never been to Miami. It was bloody hot. He was exhausted and parched. He flopped into a hammock chair suspended from a branch, pulled his water bottle from his pack and took a long swallow. *WWTD?* Just the thought of her rattled him. His leg twitched. Lestrade kicked something under the deep leaf bed which rolled from his shoe. He unzipped the outer pouch of his rucksack, retrieved his torch, turned it on, pointed it at the ground and discovered—nothing.

Lestrade knew he had booted something of substance. Using dental floss and twigs, Lestrade divided the grounds into quadrants. He painstakingly dug through the wet leaf bed, section by section, from the house to the cottage, straight down to the edge of the canal, until he felt something smooth and round. He picked the object up, pointed his torch and saw—nothing. He did however observe something. Glare. His hands wandered deliberately over the object. A clear, empty 22-centimeter-long cylinder, as measured by Lestrade's tape, which along with a marker and several evidence bags, he had retrieved from his pack. *Old. Likely acrylic. One side sealed. The other, threaded to a depth of approximately 1.5 centimeters, missing its top, if one existed. What secrets did you hold?* Lestrade thought, placing the cylinder into an evidence bag, marking it, and tossing it into his pack.

The air was rich. Lestrade took four belly breaths and resumed his search. It was a substantial yard. He wasn't certain what he was looking for. One hour, four minutes later, trouser knees, cuffs, shoes, and hands covered in mud and what he later determined to be iguana excrement, Lestrade finished, discovering amongst other things: thin tire tracks, an IV tube wrapper, two small conch shells, an empty packet of orchid food, a recently filled hole which was so poorly dug as to have an undeterminable diameter, the bottom half of a plastic doll, a spoon, the cylinder top, and a yellowed piece of paper, upon which was written, the number of the phone at the Hudson residence. The paper was found face-down, crumbled and damp in the northwest section of the property. The newly faded numbers indicated it had been freshly retrieved, likely from the cylinder. The hasty manner in which the paper had been discarded suggested the retriever had been either careless or stricken ill. Lestrade retrieved the evidence bag containing the cylinder, placed the paper within, fastened the top and tossed the bag back into his pack.

Lestrade shone his flashlight at the house, a handsome five-bedroom, three-bath, mission abode, carefully searching for the most discreet means of ingress. He was filthy and tired. *WWTD?* he considered; his face pressed to the glass of the French doors. The very idea of breaking and entering unnerved him. Lestrade's leg twitched, causing his right foot to overturn a flowerpot, revealing a key.

After entering the home, scrubbing his hands, clothing, and shoes, Lestrade spent one hour, twenty-two minutes examining every room and found—nothing. And it was precisely what he didn't find which troubled him. The house was comfortable, well designed, and immaculate. Not a bread crumb on the counter. For that matter, no bread. No mail. No trash. The fridge stocked with food. Not a speck of dirt on the floor, in a house surrounded by wet leaves. The precisely made beds hadn't been slept in. The only other anomaly in his investigation to that point being, of the nine flowered couch pillows, seven were slightly faded, two brand new. Lestrade snapped several pictures, wrote a case note on his phone, 'new pillows (2)'.

Lestrade entered the kitchen to refill his water bottle and heard a noise. He directed his attention to a scurrying gecko and noted something he had failed to notice before. The newly washed floor appeared less worn in an area representing approximately 32 by 32 centimeters. Lestrade wrote a case note on his phone, 'water cooler-recently removed'.

Lestrade headed out the back door toward the guest house. He was sufficiently tired as to have neglected to remove a single strand of dental floss strung between two twigs, upon which he tripped, causing him to topple into the trunk of the massive oak. Lestrade righted himself against the tree, causing the bark to unpeel, revealing a chamber.

It all came flashing to Lestrade. Poison in the absent water cooler, new pillows, the IV, the antidote, the Crown weighing heavily upon Tuesday's family! Her male relative was a spy! And the younger, grey-eyed woman. A spy as well? Didn't feel right. He googled Homes by Holmes & Holmes on the plane. Lestrade had solved many mysteries in his career, but imagining Holmesian minds engaged in the selling of houses stupefied him. Still, his instincts and the expression on Shadow Holmes' face in the video told Lestrade Tuesday's relation was new to all this.

Like every Scotland Yard detective, he had dismissed the rumors, but *what if*, he thought. Fear bubbled in Lestrade's belly, or perhaps he imagined it was the six empanadas he consumed whilst exiting the Miami Airport. Lestrade gasped as the last piece of the puzzle struck him like a rugby ball to the face. *MORIARTY!*

It felt good to be on the scent of a case again, and perchance a step closer to Tuesday Hudson. It was almost dawn. Lestrade breathed in the morning air, held it, and exhaled a deep huff. He snapped several pictures of the tree's entryway, bounded inside the chamber, and stopped dead in his tracks when he saw the insignia on the floor. A bee.

33

"Save room for dessert, honey?" the waitress asked, rousing me from my steak induced slumber.

"Slice of Key lime, glass of brut rosé, and the cheese plate for my friend, hold the grapes," Shadow replied.

"Filet mignon for his main, cheese for dessert. Lucky dog," the waitress said.

Based on the lateness of the hour some time had passed since our visit to Mr. Frank's house. I rose, stretched, and shook myself to full consciousness as Shadow's thoughts bombarded me, *that woman, one of Moriarty's agents tailing me. Tailing ... do spies really say that? Sounds stupid. Talk about stupid. She hasn't budged for two-hours, brand-new baby stroller, wheels clean as a whistle, and not a peep from that baby ... must be a doll in there. She could have killed me in my sleep last night. Why didn't she? What does Moriarty want? Why the bizarre connections to Great-Granduncle Sherlock's cases? Phosphorous from people's skeletons, a human cloning machine, civilization inside a hollow earth? All the makings of a cheesy mad-scientist flick.*

Cheese! The heavenly aroma waltzed into my nasal cavity. The waitress placed our food on the table and Shadow delivered my plate to the ground. Cheese! An entire room temperature plate stacked deep and wide. I vacuumed the scent into my drooling form. Torn between gluttonous ecstasy and the proper display of gratitude toward my benefactor, I am not proud to report, civility did not win out. After demolishing every morsel with the grace of a Labrador puppy, I managed to lick Shadow's hand in appreciation, although, in the name of full transparency, a wee bit of pie rested on her ring finger. It was scrumptious.

Shadow paid the bill, left a generous cash tip, and drove to the next home, checking her mirror every few blocks, thinking, *idiots. They're not even trying to hide. I'll lose them— when the time is right.* "Time to work off that meal, Watson," she said, pulling into the brick driveway of house number four, a stately Mediterranean revival, painted a warm salmon.

Shadow viewed the house to our left with contempt. *Grace Abernathy. I heard she became a school crossing guard—with herpes. Talk about a crime. Wonder if any of Great-Granduncle Sherlock's cases will be linked to this one?*

We exited the car. Shadow retrieved the key from the lockbox on the red front door and opened it. The scent of serpent assailed me. A fierceness arose from deep within. I growled loudly, circling Shadow in tight circles, my concern for her safety foremost in my mind. She shooed me off and stepped across the threshold. I sprang into action, tugging the bottom of her skirt in protest, causing her to backup into my snout, placing us in a most inelegant stance.

"Shadow Lazybones, too lazy to wash your own ass?" a woman traipsing up the moonlit walk called.

I relinquished my hold to fix a stern eye on this creature.

The little witch still lives with her parents, Shadow cursed to herself, responding, "Graceless Abernathy, how's the herpes?"

The woman touched her mouth, scowled at Shadow, and replied, "Nice outfit. What'd you do, rob a thrift store?" Grace replied.

"Nice sequined halter. Heading to an audition at the strip club?" Shadow retorted.

Grace drew back as if Shadow's words were weapons, uncomfortably blurting, "Hahaha. Just like old times."

Old times. Did the little whore think that was fun for me? If anyone was murdered around here, Grace is top on my suspect list, Shadow brooded.

"Why's your dog giving me the stink eye?"

"He's a good judge of character," Shadow replied, thinking, *don't say it, Shadow. You're better than this*, but the words slipped from her lips, "you miserable skank."

Tears flitted in Grace's eyes, as she choked out the words, "I've got to run home and feed the cat."

Word of advice, mate. Never trust a cat. I did not, however, smell a cat in the vicinity. We stepped over the threshold, and whilst my compassion for my partner's emotional state triggered by this Grace woman was sincere, I felt Shadow's behavior was unwarranted, as such I directed my disapproving gaze Shadow's way.

"Well, she is!" Shadow said, meeting my stare, thinking, *crap! Gone from talking to my dog, to explaining myself to him.*

Hearing the words my dog once more, melted my coldness, thus I directed a warmhearted smile her way. Alas, she was too acutely focused on the living room to take note. The smell of snake kept me so close I was practically tripping over Shadow's feet. It was a grand room furnished in a manner reminiscent of the gilded age. A large burgundy silk couch with intricately carved wooden legs sat opposite similarly adorned chairs of navy blue. In a disgusting spectacle of man's dominance over nature by way of firearm, the head of a large elk was mounted over the stone fireplace. Shadow gazed at a portrait of a regal couple hung on the opposite wall, thinking, *far cry from the vegetarians with the grow-house who lived here when Grace and I were in school.*

We passed through to the dining room, which housed a large table made of fine walnut with seating for twelve. Shadow examined the wood floors under the dining chairs, imagining, *well-worn path, fresh gouges under the chair at the head of the table. Much less-worn path opposite chair. Couple in that portrait. Man and woman of similar size. One of them hasn't eaten at this table in five, maybe six years.*

We entered the kitchen, which unlike the rest of the downstairs, was fully modernized right down to the matching high-end stainless appliances. Given our investigative history, I sniffed about for signs of poison. None were found. After examining the downstairs bath and finding everything in order, we ascended the staircase, the smell of serpent growing stronger with each step. My ears perked. I remained close.

The master-bedroom held two ornate nightstands, a dresser, armoire, and a shabbily made king size sleigh bed. *Pillow on the right hasn't been fluffed for years. No housekeeper,* Shadow deduced.

At the foot of the bed sat a large trunk, smelling intensely snakelike. Shadow sat on the floor, studying the vestiges of the claim ticket fastened to one handle. She opened the trunk and examined: a pair of boots which had seen better days, a khaki suit as one might wear on safari, six burlap sacks, and tucked beneath a soiled sock, a water-stained postcard bearing the photo of a statue of a large cobra which dwarfed an ornate building in the background. On the back, under the Miami Serpentarium heading, amid ineligible scribblings, the word debt, followed by the letter M. The addressee to which the postcard was mailed was covered in blood, however a postmark was visible. Shadow assumed her crime solving pose, *based on the price of postage, postcard was mailed London to Calcutta in 1985, but the trunk arrived via plane last week? Day before the owner listed the house for sale. What would make him split so fast? Think it out!* Shadow tapped the card to her forehead. That's when it hit me. That repulsive scent.

My head buzzed. A memory rattled me. A tall man, oddly shaped oscillating head, eyes aglow, wielding a walking stick. He stunk of serpent. The vision, the aroma emboldened me, enraged me. The sharp voice of a British man filled my head. Protect! Protect! Protect!

I can't share what occurred in the moments which followed as to this day they are lost to me, however when my lucidity was restored, the postcard was all but gone, remnants of it lodged between my paws and teeth.

"Bad, Watson!" Shadow said, shaking her head at me, as if admonishing a puppy for failing to hold its wee bladder and ruining one's precious Persian rug, thinking, *the fuck was that? It's not like that dog didn't have enough to eat tonight. He's been acting crazy since we got here. What triggered him? Of course,* she supposed, sniffing the air. *Snakes. Border collies are known to guard against snakes ... kill them even. Must be his service dog training. Or instinct? But this entire place smells like a snake pit. Why did Watson obliterate the postcard? And he's been guarding me like a sheep since we arrived. Hmm.*

I, too, was bewildered by my actions and despite my befuddlement over yet another voice in my head, I moved to Shadow's side, ever vigilant, as we checked the closet. On one side, a variety of men's clothes, suits, dress shirts, trousers, two lab coats in need of wash, and dozens of atrocious ties hung from metal hangers. On the dusty floor beneath them, sat three pairs of dress shoes and two pairs of gently worn running shoes. On the opposite side, a solitary dress hung in a dust-covered garment bag. *Hmm. He couldn't part with her wedding dress. Based on the dust on the bag and those gouges under the dining chairs, wife's been dead for years. No missing men's shoes. Husband hasn't left the house.*

We passed through the master bath to the hallway, into a lifeless bedroom, *guestroom, they never had kids,* Shadow thought, running her hand along the flowered wallpaper. The next room contained a full-sized unmade bed strewn with dirty clothing, two nightstands, a dresser with an empty open drawer, and a doorway. Shadow examined the crumpled clothes on the bed, pondering, *same perspiration pattern on the lab coats in the master closet. Same size clothes. He's been sleeping in this bed to be close to … Hmm.* Shadow walked to the door and tested the doorknob, which proved to be locked. She moved to the casement window, fought it open, and lifted her foot to the sill. I ran to her, gripping her skirt, tugging her back so forcefully, she fell to the ground.

"Watson!" Shadow yelled, viewing me as if I had chewed up her best pair of shoes.

I wished to convey my intentions were in her best interest, thus, I licked her face with great vigor. She smiled at me, and tussled my hair, "Stay," Shadow said, slipping out the window, thinking, *silly dog. I'll be fine … I hope.*

This was the first occasion Shadow had been out of my sight since we met. Concerned her balance was equal to her bravery, I paced in worrisome circles, stopping dead in my tracks upon reading Shadow's thoughts, *the fuck is this!?*

34

"How do you stand this fucking place?" Governor Fester Fahrenheit whined.

"I love the glow of the reactor at sunset, El Jefe. How'd you escape your guards?" asked the enormous, sweaty, mustached man wearing a guayabera and Panama hat, sitting atop a cooler on a dock near the Turkey Point nuclear plant. A cat circled his feet, playfully swatting a red laser light the man shone at various spots on the dock.

"They think I'm visiting one of my mistresses. What's with the cruise wear, Ricardo?"

"Sorry, El Jefe. It's casual Friday," the man said, as he continued taunting the cat with the laser.

"There is no casual anything in my administration. You! You better have my frigging lease!" Fahrenheit demanded, pointing to a woman in a navy-blue suit who looked on.

"Dr. Fiona Fission. Of the Nuclear Regulatory Commission, and we have some frigging concerns, Governor!" the woman responded.

"Those were addressed in the Executive Order granting the lease. Surely, you've frigging read it, Fission," Governor Fahrenheit scoffed.

"That's Dr. Fission. I've read it, and my concerns stand."

"You're in an appointed position, aren't you, Fission?" Fahrenheit probed.

"That 'someone appointed you, so someone can unappoint you' crap doesn't work on me, Governor. I'm the world's undisputed expert on nuclear energy. I don't care if you are running for president. I'm on my sixth president, buddy. Count 'em, six! If you do get elected, which I doubt, you'll need me, just like the rest of them. The United States government can't afford to function without my expertise. If you think the Nuclear Regulatory Commission is going to grant some shady corporation in the Cayman Islands access to a nuclear reactor, you must be even stupider than I thou—"

"Check your text," Fahrenheit interrupted as Fission's phone chimed.

'Lease executed,' the text from Fission's board chairwoman read.

"I don't care what's been executed, FESTER. Who names their kid Fester, anyway? I'm going to the press! They'll eat you alive," Fission said.

"Sorry, lady," Ricardo said, crossing himself, pointing his laser at a lever on the dock, which the cat struck with its paw, causing a trapdoor to open. Fission plunged into the canal, where five ravenous reptiles ripped into her. (As I said, mate, never trust a cat.)

"Crocodiles?" Fahrenheit asked over Fission's screams.

"They like the warm water from the cooling canals," Ricardo responded.

"Hehe Hehe. How'd you train them to do that?" Fahrenheit asked, reveling in Fission's last shriek.

Ricardo proudly observed Fission's body jutting from the thrashing jaws of a croc in the water below, opened the cooler full of bloody poultry, and flashed a boyish grin, "Tastes like chicken."

"What's that glowing in that small crocodile's mouth?" Fahrenheit asked.

"A foot," Ricardo replied.

35

I heard footsteps. My trepidation heightened. I dug furiously at the door, the smell of serpent rising, thankfully, a familiar scent approached.

"Worrywart," Shadow said, throwing open the door.

I was so overcome with relief at the sight of her, I rushed into the room and found myself overtaken by snake stink. I pounced hard on the floor, over and over and over again, until my pain induced yelp quieted me.

"Easy, Watson," said Shadow, examining the room which resembled the reptile house at the zoo.

Glass tanks each bearing a venomous viper occupied the floor around us, with additional serpents housed in tanks on rusty metal shelves, stacked two meters tall. Shadow's pulse raced. She assumed her crime solving posture, her mind ticking madly, *what the hell, Father? Cobras. Place smells like warm piss. Is this where Moriarty got her venom? The homeowner with the lab coats ... herpetologist ... dead? Why? Think it out?*

I shepherded Shadow through the maze of tanks, positioning myself between her and the snake enclosures, staring down the vipers as she rattled off their common names in her mind, *monocled cobra, Samar cobra, forest cobra, king cobra, Philippine cobra, Cape cobra, Indian cobra, Caspian cobra—deadliest in the world. What do we have here?* Shadow pondered, kneeling to examine a rod with a metal hook on the end, which lay on the floor in front of a tank. *Hmm. Indochinese spitting cobra—blinds its prey by spitting venom.* The serpent slithered up a piece of driftwood toward the screen top of its enclosure. The cobra reared, raised its hood, and as it prepared to spit, Shadow shoved the tank aside, sending the snake's expectorated venom toward the opposite wall, and revealing a stairway. She raised an eyebrow. My head buzzed, shaking lose another recollection. Another passageway. Another serpent. I crept silently about a Sussex manor; the scent of baboon and cheetah filled the night. A rope over a bed. A snake. 'The Adventure of the Speckled Band', wherein Sherlock Holmes foiled the fiendish Dr. Roylott's plan to murder his stepdaughter by way of viper. Ultimately Sherlock drove the snake back through an air vent, where it killed Roylott. Only it didn't. Turns out Roylott, a veteran snake handler had been bitten so many times he developed an immunity to snake venom. He came to in a funeral home, fled, and moved to Miami under the assumed name Apple, (I assume a nod to the serpent's temptation in Eden). Whilst I was grateful for this memory, pray tell, any memory, what these long-ago Sherlock Holmes tales had to do with my past was a mystery in and of itself. And what of my overpowering instinct to protect Shadow? Was it merely the unique bond between a rescue dog and their rescuer? Was my head-trauma creating an elaborate fiction? Or … had I somehow been there? Now whose head's in the stars?

With the viper out of the way, Shadow made her way toward the stairwell. I dashed to her side. The smell of strong irritant caused my eyes to sting. I sneezed. Robustly and repeatedly, unconsciously stepping onto the first stair.

"Back, Watson!" she cautioned, securing me by my collar, me stepping backwards onto the landing.

From the top of the stairwell, we peered into semi-darkness at a most disturbing scene. A rope hung from the rafters. It was attached to the far side of a metal examination table which sloped to the bottom of the stairwell where a plastic kiddie pool full of, by the smell of it, hydrofluoric acid bubbled. On a step alongside the table, a large empty syringe, smelling of heroin. Shadow's mind raced, *yuck! Still, ingenious way to kill yourself. But why? What could he want to keep away from Moriarty badly enough to murder himself in such a gruesome way? There's nothing left of him but goo. Did Apple's body produce the poison she used to kill my parents and poison me? No, if Father knew about it he would have had his spies come up with a cure. Apple must have developed an immunity. Is that what Moriarty needs? But why? Think it out. Of course! I thought I was delusional from the poison. Right after Moriarty kissed me, she hissed like a snake. Just like Great-Granduncle Sherlock's description of James Moriarty in The Final Problem, 'He is extremely tall and thin, his forehead domes out in a white curve, and his two eyes are deeply sunken in this head. He is clean-shaven, pale, and ascetic-looking, retaining something of the professor in his features. His shoulders are rounded from much study, and his face protrudes forward, and is forever slowly oscillating from side to side in a curiously reptilian fashion.' And if Jane behaves like a snake too, somebody in the Moriarty family tree, likely Jane's great-great-grandfather, who passed it onto James and her great-grandfather, had an interaction with a viper. Knowing that family, they probably screwed one, bunch of snake screwing ... Stop! As entertaining as it is to think a Moriarty had their way with a snake, it's more likely one of them used cobra venom. There are reports of some Indian cultures who inject snake venom to produce effects similar to opioid highs. Better not tell Tuesday, or she'll be shooting the stuff. That explains Moriarty's boosted pheromones. So, why did she want to drain Dr. Apples blo—.*

"Yoo-hoo, Lazybones" came Grace's grating voice from outside.

Will she ever go away? Just like herpes, Shadow fretted, locking the reptile room door behind us, exiting the house.

"Look what I found," Grace said, waving an old newspaper. "Remember Tropic Hunt?"

Shadow's brain stewed, *you mean the day you humiliated me in front of the entire seventh grade and gave me the nickname that haunted me through high school? Don't say it, Shadow. Don't give her any more power over you! Screw it,* "Vaguely, you stupid, miserable, herpes-oozing bully," Shadow exclaimed, thinking, *in your face, Grace!*

Grace's eyes flooded with tears, her face turned crimson, she leaned in, shrieking, "You were the bully, Shadow Holmes!!! Calling me Disgraceful, Graceless. Always correcting me in class. Making fun of my grades. You slept through school and got As. You promised our team would win Tropic Hunt and quit before the last clue. And, and, and you knew I liked Billy Weiner!"

Shadow stood on the lawn, watching this wailing Grace creature, thinking, *this bitch thinks I was the mean one. I did love calling her Graci-ass. I was only friends with her because she thought I was cool. She even looked up to me … until … Billy Weiner. She had a crush on him. I partnered with him on that science project. Billy didn't know shit about science, but he was cute as shit. Dumb as it, too. He tried to go to second base. I broke his finger. I only partnered with him to make Grace jealous. That was way before Tropic Hunt. Hullo! I WAS THE BULLY.*

Shadow's shoulders slumped, from deep within, a place beyond thoughts, I experienced her paralyzing remorse. I nudged the back of her knees with my snout as if herding a wee lamb, causing her to fold forward and latch onto Grace, hugging her tight for some time.

"I … I didn't realize. I'm sorry, Grace," Shadow said, a tear caught in her eye.

"Thanks, Shadow. Fucking Billy Weiner. He said you let him go to third base."

"Not even second."

"You were lucky. I dated him all through college, until he gave me this," Grace said, touching her lips. "And a concussion."

"You didn't deserve any of it, Grace. From him, or me," Shadow said, taking pen from her purse, she scribbled something on a notepad, tore the page out, and handed it to Grace. "Try this for your lips. I really am sorry, Grace."

"Why'd you do it, Shadow?"

"Bully you?"

"No. I get it; middle school is worse than the Middle East. Why'd you quit Tropic Hunt? We would've been the youngest team to win."

Shadow's head throbbed with visions of her father intercepting her as she approached the winning clue, *'what did I tell you about Holmesen-off? You'll become nothing more than a sideshow! Come to the bookstore, dear girl. I'll buy you that new hardcover on Interdimensional Physics. And you must promise to relinquish your dreams of becoming a detective, Shadow. Too dangerous a life. Promise me, dear girl. You must swear to it,* Shadow recalled, replying, "Daddy issues. Please forgive me, Grace."

Shadow stepped to her car, awash in remorseful insight, *poor Grace. I was the little witch. No wonder Eren left. He didn't think I had the emotional bandwidth. I should have been there for him when that poor child … I even told him to butch up. Beyond my poor choice of words … God … I am mean … mean and stupid. Couldn't deduce my parents were spies. Were they that good at hiding it or was I that good at being clueless or was it pure laziness, or a goddamn smorgasbord of all of the above? This is on me. I'm a clueless cretin. Thought I knew everything, was smarter than everyone. I couldn't see I was a resentful witch because my passion was stolen from me. You robbed me of my greatest gift, Father!!! And I didn't even realize it. Some detective! Maybe that's why you did it, Father? Maybe you thought I wasn't … No! You knew I'd be a brilliant detective, you lying, spying prick, and what's worse, you knew I'd love it. It's in my genes, my soul, my every fiber. All these wasted years. I wasn't lazy, just uninspired … and empty … empty and dark. No wonder you named me Shadow.*

36

"Come in from the shadows, Inspector Lestrade," a distorted voice drifted through the air of the high-tech chamber as the bark of the tree closed around him.

"Where's Tuesday Hudson?"

"Welcome to The Bee, Inspector. Please remove your shoes," the voice replied.

Lestrade removed his shoes, retrieved an evidence bag from his pack, and tossed them in. His leg twitched, causing his foot to strike a button on the floor, revealing a lift.

"Very good. You've found the turbo-lift," the voice said.

Lestrade stepped into the lift. Upon his ascent, he hit the stopwatch function on his phone, stopping it when the lift came to rest. Based on the estimated speed and time in transit, he estimated he was at a height of approximately 25 meters. He wrote a case note, 'Bee headquarters. Bloody high up, brilliant ride!'

Lestrade stepped off into a circular transparent chamber nestled within the oak's upper branches providing striking 360-degree views ranging east to west from Miami Beach to the Everglades, and north to south from Ft. Lauderdale to Homestead. Lestrade didn't wish to be so rude as to measure the chamber, however he estimated its circumference to be 30 meters. Lestrade recorded a case note on his phone, 'Helluva tree house.'

The chamber was a marvel of technology. Sophisticated surveillance equipment projected images onto transparent displays in a manner which dwarfed anything the folks at Apple ever dreamt up. Lestrade opened the compass on his phone, faced due north, and commenced viewing the images in clockwise order, beginning at 12 o'clock.

The first 17 displays flashed street scenes from the United Kingdom. The 18th-38th featured strategic allies and enemies: Paris, Pyongyang, Berlin, Beijing, Moscow, Havana, Vientiane, Hanoi, Budapest, Arctic Circle, Miami, Caracas, Sydney, Washington, D.C., Stockholm, Auckland, Singapore, Disney World, a certain major service station chain, the Saturday Night Live writers' room, and the Vatican. The 39th display flashed real time video feed of heads of state from members of the United Nations Security Council, including an unforgettable image of the Chinese president having his armpits waxed. The 40th display, at 10 o'clock, played live feed of Lestrade, who recorded a case note on his phone, 'Where's Tuesday Hudson?' and flashed it at the blank 41st display located at 11'o'clock.

"Cool your jets, lover boy," the voice stated.

"Madam, I don't have time for this. Moriarty—"

"You favor your mother when you're upset, Archie," the voice said.

The very mention of Lestrade's mother caused his stomach to jump or perhaps, he thought, it was the goat curry he consumed on the plane.

"You knew my mother?" Lestrade asked wistfully.

"Yes, Archie."

"Enough of this charade! Who's in charge here?"

"Depends?"

"On what?" Lestrade queried.

"Whether or not you accept the position?" the voice replied.

37

"I can't fit it in from this position," Tuesday said.

"Open wider," Eren replied.

"Get that nasty thing out of my mouth," Tuesday said.

"Just the tip," Eren replied, coaxing it in front of her.

"Fine, but I'm not swallowing," said Tuesday, nibbling the banana. "How long was I out?"

"Hours. You were telling me about Vivian's proposal, which was, I imagine for Sherlock, through his governmental connections, to delay Rock Hudson's official date of death until Sherlock and Vivian could produce a child who would carry the Hudson name. This would allow Sherlock to experience an intimate human relationship with someone other than Dr. John Watson and have a child who could secretly, without fear of retribution from his enemies, carry on his work."

"Quite right, Feelometer Boy. It was widely known, other than honey, my grandfather avoided sticky things, like sex and relationships, thus he was certain no one would suspect his secret role as my father's father or Vivian's lover. Sherlock died at the ripe old age of 103 and no one was the wiser that Dylan Hudson D.D.S., was in fact, Dylan Holmes, Consulting Detective.

"When my father came of age, he approached his longtime friend Inspector Leslie Lestrade, spilled the beans, and presented a different proposal. If Leslie were to share certain classified information, Father, while continuing his dentistry cover, would covertly consult on high-profile cases, and in so doing, teach Lestrade Sherlock's methods. But Leslie was a loyal copper and wasn't about to give away secrets of the realm, even to his best mate, even to learn Holmesian methods, until he was called to 10 Downing Street where the prime minister gave him the rah, rah speech about how working in this manner would prove to be of highest service to his country. He shared besides the reigning monarch and himself, nobody would be aware of this arrangement and should Lestrade be caught, the realm would disavow any knowledge, blah, blah, blah. From that point forward, Leslie and Dylan worked every official and, at times, unofficial case presented. When I came of age, I established the same relationship with Leslie's son Archie while maintaining my cover in the coroner's office."

"So, your boyfriend's name is Archie?" Eren teased.

"HE'S NOT MY...Ha! Whatever."

"It's a relief to know your father wasn't cloned. That never turns out well in the movies."

"My father was the most brilliant detective who ever lived! He uncovered seventeen international crime rings, foiled three attempts on Her Majesty's life, was responsible for putting thousands of criminals in jail, but did he ever get any credit? The poor man had to play dentist, when all he wanted to do was solve crimes. He was addicted to it ... like Grandfather ... like me. Long line of addicts."

"Self-realization is an important part of the recovery proc—"

"Hush, Feelometer Boy! I've been to rehab. I've examined my past, ad nauseum. I suffer from intergenerational trauma, learned behavior, genetic predisposition, escapism, blah, blah, blah. Truth is, I love getting high and I can stop anytime. I just did."

"Because you're trapped underwater. Truth is, you take those drugs to get an edge, and for a detective, you're failing to observe it having the opposite effect," Eren said.

"I don't need an edge."

"When's the last time you solved a crime straight?"

Tuesday fell silent for several moments, offering a meek. "I was twelve."

"And how did that make you feel?"

"Shut up, wanker!"

"As soon as you answer the question," Eren said.

"Like I was bloody Sherlock Holmes!"

"Why'd you use?"

"Come now! Have you ever been in a cannabis dispensary? It's like a bloody grown-up ice cream shop. Everyone is blissed out of their brains. You must have done some good stuff in your day, Feelometer Boy?"

"Sure, but not to excess, and you're no casual marijuana user, Tuesday. You're an addict."

"Yes, yes. An addict from a family of addicts. Sherlock used cocaine and opium to think on a higher level. Father wrote his own painkiller scripts to deal with having his face buried in people's disgusting mouths all day long, and—"

"And you're deflecting. Addicts are great at that. Now tell me, Tuesday Hudson, M.D. why do you use? To be the next Sherl—"

"I didn't want to be Sherlock Holmes!!! I wanted to be better! Better than him, better than Father. Better than everyone. I knew I could. Drugs make it easy. I can stay up for days. Solve three crimes at once. Beat Lestrade at every turn. Up to the day he found me with a mouthful of feathers."

"Snacking on your pillow?" Eren laughed.

"A raven ... from the Tower of London. The Queen ordered me to rehab. I'm supposed to be there now. You're a therapist. Does this count?"

"Not even close, but I think I can keep you straight long enough to help your cousin solve this case."

"HELP THE REALTOR. I'm the detective!" Tuesday exclaimed.

38

All these years, I could have been a detective. I would have been happy, or at least not such a bitch. Eren wouldn't have left. Hell, we might have had a kid by now. It's Father's fault. He didn't want me snooping around. He knew I'd discover the truth about him and Mother. My dear mother! Never said a word about my life choices. She was always kind, in her tight-ass British way … like Mary Poppins. I can't believe Mother was a secret agent. I can see it now. Poppins. Mary Poppins. Licensed to bake! God! Did she kill anyone? Worse thing I ever saw her do was sink a soufflé.

"Snap to, Watson," said Shadow as we exited her vehicle at house number five, a two-story Mission style fourplex in North Miami, painted a loathsome gray. A lone car occupied one of the eight parking spots. She opened the lock box, removed a key and unlocked the door which opened into a foyer with an apartment to our east bearing the letter A on the slightly askew door, an apartment to our west bearing a B on its door, and dividing the two, a stairwell leading upwards. The smell of Caribbean delicacies lingered.

"Anyone home?" Shadow asked, knocking on unit A's door, which creaked opened.

We entered the dainty one-bedroom, one-bath unit, smelling of cleaning vinegar, and in serious need of a coat of paint. The living room was starkly furnished, with a loveseat positioned in front of a large TV which overlapped the small table it rested upon. A crucifix adorned the far wall. The outdated kitchen contained a small dining table with two chairs and a fridge which held condiments, a carton containing three eggs, and a near empty milk jug. A quarter loaf of moldy bread lay upon the counter next to the toaster oven. Shadow walked through, thinking, *this place, is awful. It's owned by some shady LLC. Father would never list this dump. Stop being nasty, you little witch. This is probably another murder scene.*

We examined the bedroom containing a perfectly made double bed, nightstand with a Bible, lamp, and an empty denture case. The closet held vintage clothing suggestive of a woman of a certain age. *These clothes are fabulous*, thought Shadow as she examined the pocket of one of the colorful sweaters, removed a transit schedule, a business card for a medical clinic, and studied them. A set of nesting suitcases rested on a shelf above the clothing. She took them down, *Hmm. Missing overnight bag. Nobody here for at least a week.*

The remainder of the sparsely furnished abode was unremarkable. As such, we ventured into unit B. This unit was similarly meager, and although the bed was made it was not as neatly kept and smelled of fermenting fruit, which rested in a bowl atop the lacquered dining table.

The vibrant paintings decorating every available piece of wall space suggested a woman of strong spirit and artistic nature. Clothes were strewn about the bedroom floor in a most disgraceful manner, as if someone in search of a winning article of apparel had tried on each and discarded the losers. A series of hooks on the closet walls held hats, purses, backpacks. *Same jitney schedule and business card*, Shadow thought, examining leaflets poking out of a purse on a lower hook.

We explored the bathroom. Shadow opened the medicine cabinet. *Hmm. No toothbrush. No trash. No signs of foul play. Listen to me, foul play! Really getting into this spy shit. Another person murdered. For what?*

We exited the unit and onto the infernal stairwell. I battled nerve pain as Shadow outpaced me taking two steps at a time. Mercifully, either her powers of observation or my mind-reading worked in reverse, as she stopped halfway up, turned to me, and offered, "Sorry, Watson."

After proceeding up the stairs at a more reasonable speed, we entered the open door of apartment C. A small rolltop desk and one chair in need of reupholster were the only pieces of furniture in the living room. Shadow opened the desk and found yet another jitney schedule, and shook it in my direction, "Consider how many crimes are linked to trains and buses alone, Watson."

So as not to be rude, I gave a wee bark in acknowledgement.

Great. Now I've gone over the edge talking to this dog, Shadow fretted. *Nonetheless, public transportation is the vascular system of every metropolis, pumping the working class to and fro, as a heart moves oxygen-rich blood through a body. Since Miami's transit system sucks, private jitneys pick up the slack, particularly in impoverished areas. Committing these routes to memory is a trivial, yet crucial obligation in the life of a consulting detective. I memorized every one of these before my seventh birthday. Before Father ruined my dreams. The Hialeah route on these pamphlets terminates at a row of low-end medical practices. Hmm.*

The bedroom was tidy, although the bed was hastily made. An ancient radio sat on a wooden dresser. Shadow turned a knob and the device's tubes lit and crackled as the room came alive with the sounds of a Creole station. She listened as she examined the room, studying a shelf in the closet. *Hmm. Dust outline of a rolling backpack. Three empty units, three dead?* Shadow paused, attuned to the radio, playing an advertisement for Trevelyan Klinik Medical. We examined the bathroom, and finding nothing of import, she turned off the radio and we exited the unit.

As we approached the closed door of unit D, a delightful scent aroused me. Shadow knocked on the door.

"I already found Jesus," a striking young woman wearing a Casa De Nueva Vida tee shirt said, slamming the door in our faces.

Shadow knocked harshly on the door, "Hello! Hello!"

"Well, hello to you," the stouter of two police officers coming up the landing asked in a most inappropriate manner.

Shadow considered the constable, thinking, *asshole. Don't be mean, Shadow. More flies with honey.*

"We're here about the missing person," the slender constable offered.

Another one, Shadow mused, handing the officer her business card, as the striking young woman opened the door to unit D. "Shadow Holmes of Homes by Holmes and Holmes. This is one of our listings."

The slender officer addressed the young woman, "Ma'am. We're here about the missing person."

"About time," the woman said.

"Name?" the stout constable asked.

"Mine or the missing person?" the woman questioned, rolling her eyes.

"Let's start with yours, honey" the stout constable smirked.

"Josephine Fox, HONEY."

"Fox with one x, as in Foxy?" The stout constable smirked.

"Charlie! Didn't they teach you anything at the academy?" the slender constable scolded.

"Sorry, miss. Victim's name," the stout constable questioned.

"Victim!?" the woman asked.

"Sorry, ma'am. He's a rookie. He meant missing person. Just fill out the report, Charlie," the slender constable scolded.

"Victim's, er, missing person's name?" the stout officer continued, as he shook his ballpoint and mashed his pen against the form, his face reddening, "Cheap-ass pens!"

"Here!" the slender officer said, offering his partner another writing implement.

"Marie Benoit," Josephine said.

"Age?" the stout constable asked.

"73," Josephine responded.

"How are you related to the vic, er, missing person?" the stouter constable asked.

Shadow peaked in the open door and grinned, thinking, *daily double with this cop, rude and dumb. Stop it, Shadow. On second thought, perhaps it's okay when they deserve it?* "Obviously, she's Benoit's social worker," Shadow blurted.

"You're one of those Holmeses! Ms. Benoit told me the owner listed this place with your company. Love how you rock that outfit," the woman said, high fiving Shadow.

"How'd you know she was her social worker?" the slender copper asked.

"Her tee shirt and the clipboard with the assessment form on the foyer table," said Shadow.

"When's the last time you saw your grandmother?" the stout constable questioned.

"Not my grandmother."

"Sorry. He's new. Pay attention, Charlie," the slender constable scolded.

"Last Friday for my home visit," Josephine said.

"Does she disappear like this often? How was her mental state?" the stouter constable asked.

"A lot better than yours! Ms. Benoit didn't wander off. Is this all you people do? Ask stupid questions?" Josephine said.

I like her, Shadow thought, a sentiment to which I wholeheartedly concurred.

"We're just taking a report, Ma'am," the slender constable offered.

"To issue an Amber Alert,' the stouter constable added.

"Silver Alert, Charlie. Geez! Amber is for kids," the slender constable said.

"Mind if we look around?" the stouter constable asked.

"Mind? Why do you think I called you? How about you, Shadow Holmes? You like solving mysteries?" Josephine asked.

Hmm. I love solving mysteries! Is this a setup? Is she working for Moriarty? Why would she call the cops? No, she's legit and worried. I can sense it. God, I sound like Eren.

As the constables aimlessly poked about, Shadow explored the residence. It was similarly sparse and tidy. The bed was made. Shadow examined the Bible on the nightstand. A jitney schedule served as a bookmark. Shadow opened it and studied the verse. The refrigerator with the exception of a half-full Tupperware was barren. She reached for the container, opened it, and sniffed. The aroma was heavenly.

"Shame someone would let this delicious oxtail go to waste," said Shadow, winking at Josephine.

"Oh, you're good!" Josephine whispered.

"What's that?" the slender constable asked.

"I'm sure Ms. Benoit will show up," Shadow said, once again winking at Josephine, who although puzzled, was amenable to Shadow's deception.

Shadow smiled, thinking, *what a bright young lady. She could be helpful. I need to get rid of the cops.*

"That's right. Ms. Benoit must have gone on that church retreat she was telling me about. I'll check with the deacon. Sorry I bothered you," Josephine said.

"No worries, ma'am. That's why we're here. Call us if she doesn't turn up and we'll issue the alert," the slender cop said as they departed.

"You knew! Mrs. Benoit's sister always brings her oxtail after church. She eats half Sunday, calls me every Monday morning to complain it needs salt, then the eats the other half. There's no way she wouldn't call to complain. No way Ms. Benoit would let oxtail spoil either. That woman never wasted a speck of food in her life," Josephine said.

"You're very astute," Shadow said.

"I heard you banging around in here since you pulled up. Are the other residents missing too? One of my coworkers had a client go AWOL last week. Still hasn't turned up. Why didn't you want the cops to know?"

Shadow cogitated, *if I don't tell her something she might keep snooping and get hurt, or worse. But I can't afford to trust anyone. I'll tell her—*

"I get it. I read all the Sherlock Holmes stories as a kid. You're onto something big and the cops would just get in your way, right?" Josephine, who was studying Shadow's face interrupted. "Cute dog. Is he like your bloodhound or something?"

God, she's delicious, Shadow thought, replying, "Something like that."

"She's not coming back, is she?" Josephine asked.

Crap! She's clever. Play dumb, "Why'd you ask?"

"Ms. Benoit was a private person. She had cancer a couple years back. Never told me until she was done with chemo, but she read the same Bible verse every night."

"Exodus 15:26 'For I am the Lord who heals you,'" said Shadow.

"You don't miss much. Please, don't lie to me, Shadow. What do you think happened to her?"

Shadow remained silent, pondering, *what do I think? God, you don't want to know what I think. It's unimaginable.*

39

"I can't imagine you're asking me to be director? Of The Bee?" Lestrade questioned, the thought of it hitting him hard in the abdomen, or perhaps he considered it might have been the sketchy bag of Skittles he discovered in the cupboard.

"That's right, Archie," the increasingly familiar, synthesized voice replied.

"I'd only heard tales of this organization. Clever name. A well-deserved tribute to the great man himself. Who are you?" Lestrade asked.

"I can't share that information with you, unless ..." the voice replied.

"Unless I accept the post. Why me?" asked Lestrade.

"You have the perfect skill set and personality for this position. Arthur hand-picked you as his replacement."

"The antidote worked?" Lestrade inquired.

"It was too late," the voice responded.

"But you said he chose me?"

"He did, Archie."

"Who are you, madam? I'm growing weary of this game."

Speaking of game, mate, you don't get to be the head of the world's most secret spy outfit without having game. Arthur Conan Holmes had more game than Nintendo. An imposing figure of a man, with a twinkle in his grey eyes, a perpetual smile, and British accent, Arthur was bloody enchanting! Kids loved the bloke and Arthur appreciated youngsters. He relished watching them grow, learn, become good citizens, and mature—and mind you, not in a creepy way. Arthur was a man with strong conviction and open pockets. Homes by Holmes & Holmes sponsored the majority of the community's youth programs. Everything from karate to karaoke. Arthur and Guinevere attended all the events. Shadow, not so much. Over the decades, Arthur mentored dozens of kids and, you guessed it, recruited the best of the lot to become spies. A few other fortunate ones became the spy-adjacent Biscayne Park Irregulars who were modeled after Sherlock's network of street lads employed as intelligence officers throughout London. Arthur, however utilized his crew differently. None of the Irregulars knew Arthur was a spy, and none knew of the others' involvement. Arthur convinced the youngsters he would mentor them in improving their cognitive abilities via the presentation of tests of discernment and if they passed, he would pay their college tuition and upon graduation, buy them a house. It was a simple test requiring watching and reporting, so, basically spying, mate.

Arthur Conan Holmes was a man of rigid routine. He never left his residence for more than three days. When he was home, every evening ended in the same manner. At precisely 10:01 p.m. Arthur turned on the string lights hanging from the colossal oak in his yard, took out the trash, sat in the comfy rocker on his deck, exchanged pleasantries with patrolling police officers or the occasional late night dog walker, and consumed a humongous bowl of coffee ice cream, topped with hot fudge, marshmallow fluff, peanuts, and whipped cream. (Not a bad way to close out the day, eh?) Arthur maintained a crew of seven Biscayne Park Irregulars at all times. Their test was simple. They were to discreetly monitor the Holmes's household. If Arthur's routine remained unchanged, they were to do nothing. If, however, the routine deviated in the slightest fashion, or ceased for four days, the Irregulars were to don masks, appear in the Village's recreation field at 11:01 p.m., present in line formation in their designated spots, and using American

Sign Language, sign the letter each was assigned, which spelled out the name of Arthur's replacement. None of the Irregulars knew the others, nor the others' assigned letters. Arthur tested the Irregulars twice a year by coming out at 10:02 p.m. or something trivial, such as going light on the marshmallow fluff, which he naturally remedied after the fact. Arthur was on his seventh generation of Irregulars when Moriarty did him in. He knew he would never live to thank the ones who donned masks and signed the name of his replacement.

"Go ahead, Archie, trust those detective instincts of yours," the voice said.

"I am flattered, madam. However, I made a commitment to the prime minister."

"Don't worry about that dolt, Archie," said the Queen who suddenly appeared on display number two.

"Your Majesty!" Lestrade said, snapping to attention, bowing his head.

"Enjoying your 'holiday', Archie?"

"I apologize for the decep—"

"I don't have all day, Archie. Do you accept the post or not?" asked the Queen.

"And Tuesday Hudson?" Lestrade probed.

"Tuesday is certainly brighter than you, and a better detective, however unlike you, she's not cut out for the job. She's undisciplined, impulsive, and shows no respect for authority. A real throwback to Sherlock if you ask me. At least he kept his drug use under control. And while Shadow Holmes is likely the smartest human alive, I promised her parents I would keep her out of the spy trade."

"I simply meant to ask Tuesday's whereabouts."

"Get your mind in the game, lover boy. I'm certain you've deduced the future of this entire planet is at stake. Once we get that sorted, we'll come up with a suitable arrangement for you and Dr. Tuesday Hudson to continue solving crimes, only on a grander scale. Do you accept the post or not?"

Lestrade set a thirty second timer on his phone and recorded a case note, 'to Bee, or not to Bee' and stared at it pensively.

"Don't you ever do anything spontaneously, Archie?"

"Hadn't planned on it," Lestrade replied dryly. The timer buzzed. "I accept, under one condition, Your Majesty."

"A condition—for your Queen?"

"With all due respect, Your Majesty, no more wall calendars, please."

"No worries, Archie, The Bee has been kind enough to provide me with a wide array of your pics. Congratulations, Director Lestrade. Your new post begins immediately. By the way, Archie, there is a probationary period of 48 hours. If we're all still alive, we'll make you permanent."

Lestrade tapped his phone, setting a calendar event with an alarm for precisely 48 hours, the thought of which caused his leg to shake, causing his right foot to hit a button on the floor, raising a walk-in vault, which opened to reveal a vast array of advanced weaponry.

"I see you've found the armaments. You'll be needing those. And before you inquire again as to the whereabouts of Tuesday Hudson. I'm afraid The Bee temporarily lost—"

"Am I to understand, Your Majesty, you've lost track of the granddaughter of Sherlock Holmes?" Lestrade interrupted.

"Most impertinent, especially considering you're the director of The Bee now Archie, so technically you've lost track of her! Clock's ticking, Arch … pardon, I mean, Director Lestrade."

"Apologies, Your Majesty. Are we to apprehend Moriarty?"

"Oh no, Director Lestrade. You're a Bee agent now."

"Your Majesty, you don't mean?"

"Kill the cunt," the Queen ordered.

It was at that very moment Lestrade finally understood the freedom Tuesday, Dylan, (who knew his way around a dental drill, if you know what I'm inferring, mate), and Sherlock experienced when they administered justice as they deemed fit.

40

"You'll fit through here. When you get inside, open the door," said Shadow, thinking, *I must be out of my mind! Breaking and entering a medical practice with a dog accomplice. Like he can understand me.*

Hoping it would instill confidence, I fixed my gaze upon her and barked my acknowledgement.

"Clever dog!" Shadow said, lifting me through the space created by removing the glass slats of the jalousie windows.

Finally given the opportunity to prove my worth, I pushed aside my smoldering pain and slipped into the room with the grace of a prima ballerina, pirouetted to the doorknob, grasped it in my paws, turned it counterclockwise, (not an easy feat I remind you, sans opposable thumbs), and pushed open the door.

"Good job, Watson!" she said, tussling my fur.

Let's see what Dr. Percy Trevelyan IV is up to, Shadow thought, considering the documents strewn atop the not-so-good doctor's desk, raising her eyebrow, which brought about a fleeting recollection. Percy's great-grandfather, a client of Sherlock Holmes featured in the 'Adventures of the Resident Patient', inadvertently helped him solve a bank robbery. Turns out, Percy IV was more likely to commit one, as I learned when Shadow read a newspaper article found amongst the papers. *'Asinine Jury Verdict for Butt-Lift Butcher ... in addition to illegally supplying ketamine, oxycodone, and a variety of prescription drugs for off-off-label use, Trevelyan specialized in the practice of what is known to locals as a Miami butt-lift, which utilized his artisanal, occasionally lethal formula, of window caulk, cement, and soggy pork rinds.'* How the hell was this monster found not guilty? Moriarty got to the jury!

Whilst I too contemplated the competency of such a justice system, a horrific aroma sickened me. GREAT SCOTT. I smelled dead people! I tugged at Shadow's skirt.

"What is it, Watson?"

I relinquished my grasp of her skirt and led her to the source. Opening the door to the back room, she gasped at the ghastly sight, as there before us, on a crammed array of operating tables, lay six bodies. *I never wanted to be so wrong about anything, Shadow reflected. Ms. Benoit and the others. That heartless whore. The Baskerville paper! Moriarty's murdering people for their bones. They're making phosphorus bombs. Enough to ignite the entire planet.*

Whilst Shadow contemplated her horrendous hypotheses, the scent of garlic, formaldehyde, and stress sweat approached. I fell into stealth mode straightaway.

"Hand's up!" a man with a revolver said.

Thankfully, he failed to see me. I crept, leapt, and clamped onto the man's wrist with my teeth, causing him to relinquish his weapon, which Shadow swiftly retrieved from the floor.

"Good job, Watson!" she exclaimed, as we turned the tables on the bloke.

"How'd you find me?" the man said, nursing his hand.

"Tell me where to find Moriarty and I won't call the cops," said Shadow.

"Who are you?" Trevelyan asked.

"Tell me where she is, or I'll shoot you dead!"

"Go ahead," Trevelyan scoffed.

Hmm. I thought I really sold that line. Plan B. "Will $100,000 loosen your tongue?" Shadow said, pulling a wad of cash from her purse.

"What would a dead man need with money?" Trevelyan stated, waving his hand about.

Shadow grabbed Trevelyan's sweaty hand, regarding his fingers as one might the tentacles of a rotting squid, thinking, *if Sherlock were here … I couldn't. Go ahead, you're a freaking Holmes*, "Hullo! You've been to Bone Valley," she said with prideful amusement.

"How could you possibly know?" Trevelyan asked.

"The tiny stone fragment lodged under your thumbnail. Based on the ratio of phosphorous, sand, limestone, and clay, its common to that area. You're luring elderly people with no next of kin to your clinic, willfully misdiagnosing them with cancer, offering free operations, administering lethal doses of anesthesia, and sending their corpses to the mines in Bone Valley, where phosphorous is extracted from their bones. And you're transporting these innocents here using the jitney routes in the poorest neighborhoods in Miami. Based on the number of stops, extrapolating for other major metropolitan cities in Florida with a large indigent population, I calculate … you're murdering 24 people every day. You bastard!"

"Only a goddamn Holmes could know that! The Professor is going to kill me for leading you here, but not if I kill you first."

It occurred in the blink of an eye. Trevelyan grabbing a scalpel off an operating table, lunging at Shadow. My teeth sinking into his ankle. Trevelyan, screaming, falling, landing most unfortunately on the surgical blade, which lodged in his chest. He writhed on the floor, until alas blood sputtered from his mouth, along with his last words, "Fucking dog!"

In the event you're speculating regarding my feelings related to such an insult, or my taking of a human life, to my astonishment, I felt no remorse whatsoever. However, I could observe in Shadow's expression, killing, even in the act of self-defense, was foreign to her. With great uncertainty I walked to Shadow's side and investigated her eyes. Would she welcome my aid or consider me nothing more than a murderous twat like Trevelyan?

"My hero! You deserve an entire wheel of cheese!" she exclaimed, scooping me into her arms, kissing my nose. Finding myself much relieved, I kissed her back with great vigor.

Shadow drew sheets over the heads of the elderly, supposing, *I see why Father didn't want me to be a spy. How awful! Bone Valley.*

Now, I enjoy a good bone as much as the next chap, however Bone Valley sounds ominous, eh? And, due to the fact that this adventure takes place in Florida, it is indeed a real place. Fortunately for you, I know all about it.

If you believe in science, (and I am hopeful, dear reader, you do), millions of years ago, Central Florida was covered with seawater. Imagine huge swathes of Florida underwater, (and believe me, mate, with climate change, they will be again). During said period, inland Florida was an underwater playground for giant sharks, whales, and assorted fishy things. As sea creatures died off, their bones sunk. Fast forward a few million years to receding water and the resultant land rising from the ocean, and just like that—Bone Valley, high and dry, an hour inland, as the pterodactyl flew from Florida's west coast. High ground attracted humongous beasts like giant sloths and three toed horses. As land creatures died off, what was left? A colossal number of bones, and I'd imagine, giant piles of sloth dung. Rivers and streams crossed the land carrying a gravedigger's smorgasbord of giant terrestrial animal bones into the shallows, where they combined with the aforementioned sunken sea creature skeletons along with naturally occurring phosphorous, forming an ore. Cover it all in a 50-foot layer of sand, clay, time, and voilà! The richest deposit of phosphorous in the Colonies.

About now, I'd wager you're thinking, Watson is more than just a pretty face, and more importantly, you're wondering why in bloody hell I'm blathering on about bones and phosphorous. Because, mate, phosphorus is an indispensable fertilizer. Because elemental phosphorous can't be manufactured or destroyed. Because due to its nasty habit of igniting upon exposure to air, it's used to make incendiary weapons, thus, earning its nickname as the devil's element. And the really, really, ginormous because—because at the rate humans are going, Earth will run out of phosphorous in this century. Sounds like something you'd read in a science fiction novel, eh?

Turns out, Bone Valley, produces 75% of the phosphorous used in the United States and 25% of the phosphorous in the world. There are dozens of phosphate mines dispersed over the half million acres which comprise Bone Valley. Mining operations are near medieval, leaving behind a radioactive byproduct known as phosphogypsum, and lots of it. Indeed, for every ton of phosphoric acid fertilizer produced, Florida gets five tons of glow-in-the-dark radioactive waste. It's no wonder residents of the Sunshine State are a bit off-kilter, especially our governor. Seems Shadow was thinking the same thing, *Fester Fahrenheit. Those are his phosphate mines. Moriarty is working with him. Murdering old people for their bones. I sure as hell hope someone at The Bee knows what's up.*

41

"I imagine someone is going to pop in and brief me, Your Majesty? Your Majesty?" Lestrade questioned.

"Good evening, Director Lestrade. Agent Hopkins. Congratulations on your new post. I'll be bringing you up to speed," the agent, who had beamed into the room, remarked.

"Hopkins. Any relation to Stanley Hopkins?" Lestrade questioned.

"Yes, sir. My grandfather was just a lad when he started at Scotland Yard. He worked many a case with Sherlock Holmes. It was the greatest honor of my life to work with Arthur. Rest his soul. Hooooonk," Hopkins emitted, blowing his nose into his hanky. "Of course, I look forward to working with you, Director."

"Thank you, Hopkins. Moriarty survived," Lestrade stated.

"His brother, sir. We're dealing with Jane Moriarty, his ruthless great-granddaughter. First female of the Moriarty bloodline. While the males had enhanced levels of influencing pheromones, hers are ... intoxicating, sir. She's been working with The Bee for years, and quite brilliantly if I do say, sir, until recently. Killed her own father, Arthur, Guinevere, and countless others. Afraid we lost her after Reichenbach."

"Locate all known intelligence on Jane Moriarty and all her ancestors. I want everything: holdings, known associates, recent travel, medical records, dating history, purchases, debts, allies, enemies, and cross reference everything to Reichenbach, and James Moriarty's book. Nobody could ever make sense of the thing," Lestrade stated.

"Already done, Director. Just needs an update."

"Fine work, Hopkins. Please download the data onto my phone."

"No need for that, Director Lestrade."

"Of course there is. I developed a crime solving app. I call it, 'Deduce This!' It started as a video game, however—"

"We are aware, Director. Guinevere Holmes discovered you were working on that app years ago. After she worked her magic, we found it to be 98.24% accurate—almost as good as Arthur Holmes," Hopkins chuckled.

"98.24%? The most I ever achieved was 92.09%," Lestrade muttered, taking out his phone, recording a case note, 'The Bee—Patent Infringement?'

"Would you like me to proceed with the download to your phone, Director?"

"98%! Go on then," Lestrade muttered.

"Yes, Director. Might I brief you on our current gadgetry in the interim?"

"Proceed," Lestrade replied.

"These nasal swabs provide your best chance against Moriarty's pheromones. Thirty minutes until you're fully inoculated, remains effective 24 hours post insertion," advised Hopkins.

"Side effects?" Lestrade questioned.

"Permanent loss of sex drive, foul smelling penile discharge."

"Pardon?" Lestrade questioned.

"Hahaha. Apologies, sir. Just a bit of hazing to put our new director at ease. Welcome aboard. No known side-effects, Director."

Lestrade sneered, took a swab in each hand, plunged one into each nostril, winced, swirled, and set a 30-minute timer and 24-hour alarm on his phone. "What else do you have for me?"

"This gun transmits a fatal pathogen dart. A shot anywhere on the body results in immediate death."

"I am an excellent marksman," Lestrade replied.

"How fortunate, Director, as with this weapon, you only have one shot. And I believe you're going to be happy with this tie. It doubles as a garrote. If I do say so myself, the color compliments your wardrobe. And given you're the first director we've had who didn't carry a briefcase, I developed this bulletproof rucksack containing a parachute. The chute offers cloaking protection, thus neither you, nor the chute will be detectible. I only created it moments ago; it hasn't been field tested."

"I'll keep that in mind should I find myself aloft, Hopkins."

"Very good, Director. And if you find yourself in an underwater pickle, your new cell phone functions as a mini-scuba tank."

"New cell phone? But I just arranged this one to my liking."

"Not to worry, Director. I took the liberty of synching it to your current phone's set-up."

"Would have liked the opportunity to delete some of those pics," muttered Lestrade.

"Those pics are old news, Director. We've been tracking you since you were a wee thing."

"Bad form, Hopkins. When this undertaking concludes, we'll be having a word regarding The Bee's snooping protocols," Lestrade said, recording a case note on his phone, 'The Bee-review invasion of privacy practices'.

"Of course, Director, although you might want to avoid using words such as undertaking in your new line of work. Shall I continue?"

"Proceed," said Lestrade.

"Very good, sir. I call this little baby The Narcissist," Hopkins said, tossing Lestrade a smartwatch. "It transmits a holographic mirror, causing egomaniacs like Moriarty to freeze in place and stare at their own image for a period of three seconds."

Lestrade fixed the watch to his wrist and pushed a button. An image appeared. "My word! I need a bath," said Lestrade, observing his hologram. "What do we have in the way of transportation?"

"Wait until you see this chariot in action!" said Hopkins, as images of a car appeared on a large monitor which dropped from the ceiling.

"How pedestrian."

"White Teslas don't draw attention in Miami, Director, however I assure you this vehicle is far from uninspired. Please observe the monitor."

A video of a white Tesla clocking 300 kilometers per hour on the Seven Mile Bridge in the Florida Keys played. The Tesla rapidly overtook the cars in front of it. It appeared a crash was eminent, the Tesla however, had loftier plans. It extended a set of wings, glided over the cars and launched into the clouds, where it destroyed two incoming fighter jets with a sonic blast.

"I didn't see a cup holder?" Lestrade japed.

"I was saving this, Director. Tess, demonstrate refreshment station," Hopkins beamed, whereby the back hatch of the vehicle sprung open revealing a mini bar, including Guinness and Boddington draft taps, a high-end espresso machine, a fast-boil tea kettle, and a tiny fridge, stocked with Caesar salads.

The thought of Caesar salad reminded Lestrade, as it always did, of his first kiss, which reminded him he was wasting valuable time better spent locating Tuesday Hudson, causing him to become unnerved, causing his leg to twitch, causing his right foot to strike a button on the floor, causing the lift to appear.

"Ahh. Perfect timing, sir. The analysis is complete," Hopkins remarked.

"Fine work, Hopkins."

"Thank you, sir."

"Well?" asked Lestrade.

"There is a 98.24% probability that … Fuuuccck!"

"Bad form, Hopkins!"

"I beg your pardon, sir. After scorching the planet's surface with phosphorous, Moriarty will cause meltdowns in several key nuclear plants … and create a New World in a hollow Earth," said Hopkins.

"My f-ing word! Which nuclear plants?"

"According to our White House sources, a lease was recently executed at the Crystal River nuclear plant."

"Who initiated the lease?" Lestrade asked.

"Governor Fester Fahrenheit."

"That bloke always seemed dodgy. Do we have eyes on him?"

"Yes, Director. He's in the governor's mansion."

"Tuesday Hudson?" Lestrade asked.

"No word, yet Director."

"And Shadow Holmes?" Lestrade questioned.

"Selling real estate."

"Selling real estate? Right after her parents were murdered?"

"We are monitoring her, sir. So is Moriarty."

"Run a list of the addresses she's visited through 'Deduce This!' and send me the results. In the meantime, how soon can you get me to Tallahassee?"

"The Bee has transportation stations at every major airport. We can beam you there in 3.2 seconds. From there, it's a ten-minute drive, eight if you run the lights."

"Very good, Hopkins. Dispatch Bee agents to every nuclear power plant in the southeastern United States."

"Yes, Director."

Lestrade placed the pathogen gun in his vest pocket, removed his mud-stained tie, and disposed of it in the trash. He transferred the contents of his old rucksack into the new one, retrieved his new phone, fastened the smartwatch to his wrist, aimed the mirror hologram at himself, and tied a perfect Windsor knot in his new tie.

"Other orders, Director?"

"Yes, Hopkins. Run every piece of information you have on the likely whereabouts of Tuesday Hudson through 'Deduce This!' and send them to me immediately."

"Indubitably, sir. The Queen herself made finding your girlfriend our second highest priority."

"Thank you, Hopkins, but she's not my girlfriend," Lestrade replied, wishing it were in fact true.

42

"I'm not your bloody girlfriend, Fester!" Moriarty said, tossing the box of two dozen long stems, along with the governor's amorous aspirations into the rubbish.

"Sorry, Professor," Fahrenheit said, digging the box from the trash.

"Don't grovel, Fester. Men! Needy little bastards, the lot of you. Where's my lease?"

"Tada!" Fahrenheit announced, plucking a damp envelope from the bottom of the roses.

"Ttssssss!" Moriarty emitted, snatching the document from Fahrenheit's hands. "Good job, Fester. Now run along and play. Mummy has work to do."

"Before I go, Professor, I was thinking."

"Thinking, you, Fester? How uncalled for."

"Why was Fission's foot glowing?"

"Glowing! Nosey cow couldn't resist my stacks," Moriarty said under her breath.

"Can't really blame her, Professor," said Fahrenheit, ogling Jane's breasts through her untied robe.

"Not these stacks, tosser! Men like you are the reason I so relish killing your gender. Fission visited the phosphogypsum stacks near the phosphate mines, hence the glowing. Why did you specify her foot? FESTER. What have you done?"

"Fission wasn't cooperating. I got your lease," Fahrenheit sheepishly replied.

"I suppose you did. I didn't tell you to kill anyone, however it shows initiative."

"Thank you, Professor," Fahrenheit puffed.

"I despise initiative! Thanks to your foolishness, people will be looking for Fission. They'll retrace her steps, leading them to you, and eventually drawing attention to my plans. No matter. You're dispensable. Thankfully, I've accounted for such variables as your incompetence. I'll have to accelerate my timetable."

"Sorry, Professor," a dejected Fahrenheit said, walking toward the door.

"FESTER." Moriarty called with open arms, her head oscillating side to side.

"Oh, Jane!" Fahrenheit exclaimed, careening toward her like a labradoodle at a dog park.

"Ttssssss," Moriarty emitted, whilst connecting a perfect left hook to Fahrenheit's incoming nose.

"WHAT THE? We had a deal!" Fahrenheit said, nursing his pounding probiscis.

"That was for offing Fission. As for our deal, did you actually believe we were going to shag? Don't look at me like that, Fester. I'd never stoop so low as to do a politician. You're even slimier than me, and I'm a murderous cunt. And your name is Fester! However, since you've procured the lease, be a good lad and make sure my body is flawless before anyone of import sees it. And, FESTER."

"Yes, Professor?"

"Moving forward, be honest with me, or there will be consequences. Nod if you understand," Moriarty commanded, seizing Fahrenheit's face, squeezing his cheeks together with great force.

He nodded.

She shed her silk robe to the floor.

He crept closer, trembling with every step. His nose throbbed.

Her eyes glowed. Her head oscillated. Her scent puffed through the air as she patted her reddened fist. She closed her eyes, pictured killing him, wobbled and righted herself.

Finding himself dizzied, and forgetting his injury, Fahrenheit instinctively grabbed his nose to quell the scent. The agony was reminiscent of being on the losing side of a badger fight, however he found her aroma less maddening than was typically the case. Indeed, for the first time since he whiffed Professor Jane Moriarty, Governor Fester Fahrenheit could think clearly. He had to focus. What did she mean by dispensable? Did she forget he was going to be president? No! She was going to kill him. He had been too intoxicated to realize it before. PAIN. Pain was key. His freed him. Hers amped his bondage. Pain! He needed to achieve a delicate balance.

Fahrenheit filled with dread. His insides stung. His hands leaked cold sweat. He needed to buy some time, plus, she was never going to fuck him. He needed a plan. He was never good at plans. He always paid someone to do his thinking. He deduced he needed to stay alive. Keep breathing until someone catches her or gives him a chance to kill her. Be useful. Do as he's told. Tell her she's flawless. Or not? How could he tell her if she wasn't flawless?

He dropped to his knees and viewed her toes. Toes! Toes were safe. He was never a toes bloke. He would start with her toes and work his way up. Toes looked fine. No! Fine wasn't good enough. She wanted flawless. Moriarty's toes were a far cry from the bruised and blistered mess they were days ago, but flawless? Okay, they were flawless, although he wasn't a fan of crimson polish. Ankles, check. Calves, smooth, curvy, and tanned. Knees. Never been a fan, with knee wrinkles and such, but he considered them flawless front and back.

Thighs. Although short, her previously frostbitten thighs were completely healed. They were in fact, tanned, toned, and appeared to be supple as the belly of a newborn pup. Flawless.

Arousal fell upon him. Fahrenheit squeezed his nose, generating enough misery to allow him to return to task. His eyes drifted up. He slammed them tight as her aroma filled him. He felt a stirring below.

Plan B. Skip right over the main event and head for the stomach. The stomach seemed safe. That was the new plan. Head for the gut.

Moriarty's musk and Fahrenheit's plan skirmished toward the inevitable. What could he do? His plan was slipping away faster than a strapless prom dress. Pain! He needed pain. He made two fists, jabbing his fingernails into his palms until they bled. Pain revived his focus.

He held his breath, thrust his neck upward and attempted to time the opening of his eyes with their arrival on his target—her stomach. As per usual, Governor Fester Fahrenheit undershot his goal. His eyes opened in the general vicinity of Moriarty's minge. He caught a whiff of her. His manhood rammed against his tropical wool pants and let loose a torrent.

"Ttssssss!! Did you just? How marvelous, Fester. Hahahaha!"

"That never happened before!"

"Whatever you say... Fester."

"Honest, Professor, it never—"

"Come now, Fester. Never happened; with the exception of two days ago in that corner of this very room. I never miss a thing, Fester, and how would you have shagged me when you can't even make it out of the gate!? HAHAHAHA. Now, be a good lad, and complete your inspection."

Humiliated, nonetheless temporarily relieved from his desires, Fahrenheit conducted a brief assessment of the remainder of Moriarty's body commencing this time with her head. Upon his eye's arrival at her breathtaking breasts, he once again found his excitement building.

"Fester!"

"Yes, Professor?"

"Am I flawless?"

"Flawless," Fahrenheit responded, squeezing his bloody, sweaty palms.

"LIAR. Thanks to those blasted Holmeses, my right nipple is far from perfect. I told you Fester, they're consequences for lying," Moriarty said, reaching for her phone and snapping a picture of Fahrenheit—evidence of his embarrassment front and center.

"What are you doing?"

"This ought to keep you in line in case you consider crossing me. And, I have one more assignment for you, Fester."

"Yes, Professor?" Fahrenheit said, squeezing his nose long enough for his focus to return.

"Issue an executive order expanding the use of phosphogypsum."

"But Professor. It's radioactive and causes red tides. What do you need it for?"

To dump into oceans, lakes, rivers, and streams, causing algae blooms which produce red tides killing all marine life, along with anyone on the sea, generating foul air on the coastlines and driving all terrestrial beings inland, you idiot. It'll be fabulous! Moriarty thought, stating, "Are you questioning me, Fester?"

"No, Professor. It's just that it took years to get these stupid Florida legislators to allow its use just to build roads. All that fuss about a little radon and dead fish. It won't be easy."

"You'll figure it out, or consequences," said Moriarty, reaching for her phone and sending Fahrenheit a text.

Fahrenheit opened the compromising text photo of himself, and swallowed, hard, "What do you want the order to do?"

"I'll send you a list."

Fahrenheit deleted the text photo and shrank from the room, squeezing his fingernails deeper into his palms, wincing in pain.

43

What a pain. I can't meet with the owner of the next house until tomorrow morning. All the way in Homestead, Shadow mulled, as we pulled into the drive and entered her cottage, where she flopped on the couch. Momentarily forgetting my condition, I hopped up to join her, causing me to yelp in pain. Shadow patted my head to comfort me, "My dear Watson," said she, a greeting as familiar as mother's milk, hence stirring a flurry of memories. My dear Watson, spoken through the lips of a tall slender man next to a beehive. My dear Watson, from the lips of a robust man in an armchair with eyes that twinkled as Shadow's. My dear Watson, called a grey-eyed lad with a fishing rod. Whilst these perplexing images invaded my brain, I lay my head on Shadow's lap, sighed, rested my eyes, and tuned to her churnings.

Five houses down, one to go. What do we have so far? Enough phosphorous from people's bones to ignite the planet. A human cloning machine. A Hollow Earth. A man immune to snake venom. Could that villainous viper really be trying to scorch the planet with phosphorous and create a Hollow Earth below? The great-niece of the Napoleon of Crime ruling a Hollow Earth. Who would be left to rule? The people she clones with Ms. Wilson's uterus. She must have found a way to accelerate the maturation process. Otherwise, she'd wind up with a planet of babies. Hmm. I read a paper hinting at the development of a new cellular division algorithm ... and Moriarty's math skills may even be superior to mine. Who would she clone? Hmm. And the snake venom? Is that alone responsible for her crazy level of pheromones? Sure, I was attracted to Moriarty at the seminar, but it wasn't until we were in her boat that I felt super horny. Does seawater bring out her aromatic powers? No, human blood is basically 85% seawater. Think it out! Could sunlight power her pheromones? Come on, Shadow. Powers from the sun. She's not Supergirl. Head in the stars! But what if a star ... our star amplifies her powers? She has that whole cold-blooded reptilian thing going, and snakes warm up in the sun. Wouldn't be the craziest thing in this investigation, and as Great-Granduncle Sherlock used to say, 'When you have eliminated all which is impossible, then whatever remains, however improbable, must be the truth'. So why would she want to shut her superpower off inside a dark planet? Does she have some perverse sense of fair play to rule without them ... does she have daddy issues too ... or does the darkness allow her to think clearly? Hullo! That's why Dolly said Father was worried for her. Her scent is driving her mad. She really is a sick serpent! She'd have to be to come up with a plan like this. Hollow out the planet! That's insane. How would she even access it? It's not like she can cut a giant hole in the Earth.

44

The straight edge cut a shallow groove into Fahrenheit's stomach. He winced, applied bandage, tucked his shirt, wiped blood from the blade, and thrust the razor into his pocket.

"Good morning, Professor."

"You're much too chipper, Fahrenheit. And you're not drooling? I saw your bloody palms last evening. Idiot! You think a bit of pain is going to stave off my charms? Ttssssss!"

Fahrenheit squeezed his self-inflicted wound and yelped.

"Why Fester, is that a razor in your pocket, or are you just happy to see me?" Moriarty snarked, snatching the straight edge from Fahrenheit's pants.

"Please don't hurt me, Professor. I have the executive order. You can do whatever you want with your phosphogypsum. You … you need me."

Moriarty wielded the razor slowly round her face, gazing upon it in an intimate fashion. Her eyes burned a devilish red, which shimmered onto her nakedness in the semi-darkness. Her head slowly oscillated. A battle waged in Moriarty's warped mind, *last chance to boost your powers before they're gone forever. No! It will put you over the edge. You can beat them on your own. But what fun is that? Wait for that stupid girl to find it. No! I should get a leg up on those blasted Holmeses. No! Both legs, around their necks. Squeeze them. Slice them up! No! You're better than this. Then again, are you? Go ahead, Jane. Embrace your inner serpent!*

Moriarty's cranium ceased its gyrations. She held the straight edge vertically before her lips. "TTSSSSSS." She struck, plunging her tongue deep into the blade, followed quite understandably, by the sound of her screaming her bloody head off.

Blood spewed from Moriarty's tongue, which divided into equal parts, thrashed wildly from both sides of her mouth. Moriarty's pain skyrocketed her pheromone levels. The air smelled like the basement of a brothel.

Fahrenheit was overcome, nauseated—and erect. He ripped off his bandage and dug his fingernails into his open gut wound; alas it was of no use. His mind clouded with desire.

"TTSSSSHHHHHHHHHHHHHHHH." Moriarty screamed. Her scent was everywhere.

Fahrenheit collapsed to the floor, shaking in terror as if dropped into a horror film on Halloween—at midnight. He found himself unprecedentedly spellbound. He felt his brain melting into a lump of Silly Putty. He held his breath as he knew one more whiff would finish him. He attempted to rise. The struggle for air overtook him. His chest pounded. His head spun. He tried valiantly to hang onto whatever was left of him, yet all he could think of was her. He gasped for breath and the last independent thought Presidential Candidate Governor Fester Fahrenheit would ever have, along with half a liter of ejaculate escaped him. He lay vacuous.

Moriarty had never experienced such agony, and it drove her to a state of incommunicable thoughts of treachery, "ARCTICCCC," Moriarty screamed before blacking out.

Arctic ran into the room, giddy. Moriarty's scent overtook her. Arctic's face and neck reddened. She crossed her legs, erupted in pleasure and groaned gleefully, thus rousing Moriarty.

"TTSSSSHHERVITTCCCCHH ME," Moriarty demanded, sputtering blood all about Arctic's face.

Dr. Arctic jerked toward Moriarty's naked form like a rabid kangaroo, fighting her way through one spontaneous orgasm after another. Dazed and confused as to her objective, Arctic pulled her laser from the case, and thrust it between Moriarty's lips.

"ARRGGGGHHH. Not down there," Moriarty screamed, as the device short circuited in her wetness.

45

At least the roads aren't flooded, Shadow thought as lightning crackled through ominous clouds. "Last stop, Watson."

We exited the car in front of house number six, a three-bedroom, two-bath, canal-front rancher with native landscaping. *God, it's humid*, Shadow thought, ringing the video doorbell.

"Door's open. Out back," came a reply.

We entered the house. The smell of death hung fresh in the air. The body of a small, long-haired man lay upon the floor. The victim's neck bore the marks of a struggle. Shadow drew Trevelyan's revolver and examined the scene, fretting, *poor man. Strangled. By one enormous hand.*

Shadow took in the room with furious speed. Pictures of springs and cave divers adorned the walls. A bookcase containing innumerable volumes on aquifers of the southeastern United States stood against the far wall. *Hullo! That's how she's going to do it. The Floridan Aquifer. One huge underground water fountain tapped for residents of the southeastern United States. It's buried under tons of limestone. Covers 100,000 miles under Florida, Alabama, Georgia, Mississippi, and South Carolina. Sure, the aquifer is being drained and contaminated by growing populations, agricultural run-off, pollution, algae blooms, saltwater intrusion, but that's more of a slow death. To dry it up you'd need ... Head in the stars again. Don't even think it,* Shadow shuddered.

I was at a loss to comprehend her train of thought, however the smell of fear which emanated from her person kept me close. Gusts of wind contested our exit through the sliding glass doors to the backyard. Lightning lit the sky. An enormous man, with a mammoth mustache sporting a guayabera and Panama hat sat atop a cooler on the dock. A cat circled his feet.

"You're late," the man said, whilst doting on a float of eleven crocodiles in the canal below.

"I'm only fashionably late. You killed the owner," Shadow said, training her revolver on the man.

"Who says he didn't choke himself? I heard he was into that," the man snarked, taking a cigarette from a pack.

Shadow studied the man and began her assessment. "Your cigarette, a Russian Java and the insignia on your ring, Moscow State University, famous for their nuclear physics programs. The phosphorous scar on your right thumb, the careless result of a recent burn rate experiment. Obviously, you're Moriarty's top henchman in this fiery fiasco."

"What can I say, lady? I like burning shit," said the man, striking a match, watching the flame dance in the wind, deftly lighting his cigarette with the last flicker.

"Strong facial features, although you should get that nasty mole on your cheek examined, dark eyes, black hair, and the sheer size of you ... you're a descendant of Colonel Sebastian Moran!" exclaimed Shadow, raising an eyebrow, releasing another remembrance.

I stood in Camden House, opposite 221b Baker Street. A gargantuan bloke fired an air rifle through a window in yet another failed attempt on his part to kill Sherlock Holmes. Colonel Sebastian Moran was apprehended and sentenced to hang. Only he didn't. He escaped prison, fled to Cuba and changed his surname to Havana. I growled at his progeny.

"Ricardo Havana, at your disservice. You Holmeses could get top booking as a cruise line act. It's the Moran square ears and strong jawline, right?" he said, taking a crinkly drag of his cigarette.

"That and the set of your eyes."

"I got a pretty face, no?" Ricardo commented, batting his eyes in an exhaled cloud of smoke.

"Your grandfather was once considered the second most dangerous man in London."

"My grandfather was a bad ass British soldier! He was so tough he followed a man-eating tiger down a drain!"

"Your grandfather was a ruthless assassin!"

"MY ABUELO WAS A GOOD MAN. Until James Moriarty got to him. My grandfather went to Oxford and Eton. He authored two books. His father was the British minister to Persia, but does anyone talk about that? But Abuelo falls under Moriarty's spell, gets ordered to kill Sherlock Holmes and he's the villain! Moriartys and their damn pheromones!!"

"Hullo!" Shadow stated this time with authority. "So, they all had the power, but Jane's gender amplifies hers. And now she controls your nephew."

"I warned Fester not to trust that witch. My sister's dying wish was for me to watch over him. I told Harmony that Fester was a bad seed when the little maniac was five years old. She tried everything, medication, behavior modification, crystals, new-age mumbo-jumbo. Fester beat up three therapists—set one on fire," Ricardo chuckled, taking another drag, puffing out a cloud of smoke. "Our family paid them all off. Florida is the only state where that idiot could get elected governor. Fester was a disgrace to begin with, now he's completely shot out from her stink. La Serpiente is running things."

"The stains on your shirt. You've been to Conchy Joe's and had a bowl of their conch chowder."

"How'd you know it wasn't a cup?"

"I mean, just look at you. I'd wager you haven't had a cup of anything since you were a toddler." *Be kind*, Shadow thought. *Screw that. He's a Moran and he just strangled a man.*

"HEY," exclaimed Ricardo, rising.

"Come any closer and I'll blow your ginormous head off," Shadow said taking aim.

"You couldn't tear up my baby picture."

Maybe he's right, but I better look convincing, Shadow deliberated, cocking the trigger. "SIT," she commanded, to which Ricardo returned to his seat. "The residue on your trousers is from polishing off the seafood sampler of fried shrimp, crab cakes, conch fritters, fried fish and a variety of sides from my favorite motorcycle bar, Alabama Jack's in Key Largo."

"You forgot the chocolate peanut butter cheesecake. Talk about melt in your mouth," Ricardo added in a cloud of exhaled smoke.

"Those restaurants are close to the Port St. Lucie and Turkey Point nuclear plants. That's how Moriarty is going to hollow out the planet. Naturally, you've synched those reactor melts with Crystal River?"

"Naturally."

"With your knowledge of physics, you realize the consequences. Phosphorous and nuclear holocausts roasting all life on earth."

"Not all life," Ricardo crossed himself.

"Of course! There's only one reason you're helping her. The medallion around your neck. St. Joseph, patron saint of families. When you spoke about your promise to your sister you rubbed it. Moriarty promised to clone your sister for her New World."

It was at that point Ricardo, whose frame dwarfed that of a silverback gorilla, rose from his cooler, "LEAVE HER OUT OF THIS," erupted from his mouth as he charged Shadow like a mad bull, only to be stopped in his tracks by an exacting shot from her revolver, thereby separating the Panama hat from Ricardo's humungous head.

"I said SIT. How's she going to eliminate the radiation?"

"You're a Holmes, figure it out," Ricardo replied, reclaiming his seat.

"Hullo! A Miami Outboard Club sticker on your cooler!! Watson Island. The seaport! That sick serpent isn't going to bore into the Floridan Aquifer using nuclear matter. It's too deep. It'll take too long. And even Moriarty can't decontaminate an environment full of nuclear radiation. The reactors are a ruse to keep The Bee busy while she uses the nearly completed Port of Miami tunnel to dig into the more easily accessible Biscayne Aquifer where she'll build her vile New World. But she needs something from me to do it. Something to dry it out. Something, you were supposed to follow me to fetch for her. *Hmm. So why isn't this gargantuan goon following Moriarty's orders? Think it out. Of course,* "Moriarty's hormones have driven her insane, so now you can finally get revenge on her, and on my family!"

"You Holmeses. Always so proud of yourselves when you've solved the case. Too bad you won't live long enough to tell anyone. For Abuelo!" Ricardo said, crossing himself, retrieving his laser, shining it on the lever on the dock.

Shadow turned her attention to the feline, who, raised a paw and took aim. The dock beneath us dropped away. (As I said, mate, never trust a cat.)

46

Lestrade dropped through a window of Governor Fahrenheit's mansion like a cat burglar, disabled four Florida Department of Law Enforcement officers and made his way into the dimly lit basement, where he was greeted by a horrific scene. A razor wielding, red eyed Moriarty, her forked tongue lashing blood to and fro, her oscillating head straining against the slamming acrylic door of a departing transportation pod. A tall blonde woman lay on the floor, her neck pulsating blood.

"Tuesday!" Lestrade anguished, charging forth, reaching for Moriarty's throat, his hands recoiling off the vessel as it sailed down a tunnel. Moriarty hissed her farewell. Her stench filled the chamber. Lestrade took several shaky breaths and turned over the body. "Thank God!"

Ghastly smell! This paint prevented our sensors from locating Moriarty, Lestrade supposed, running his hand along the wall, until he reached Fahrenheit and attempted to nudge him from the pathetic fetal position he had assumed, "Governor! Wake up! Hello!" *Seems he's cooked, but then again, he was already half-baked. I'm going to tag him, in case he revives*, Lestrade thought, tapping a transparent GPS tracker patch onto Fahrenheit's neck.

Her pod went down a well and exited sideways? How did she tunnel horizontally through solid limestone? The walls are covered in algae, moss, mud, stained mineral deposits, indicative of a cavern which was further hollowed out. A test perhaps?

"Who is this poor unfortunate?" Lestrade asked, pointing his cell phone camera at the body of the deceased woman.

"Angelina Arctic, sir. The world's former leading authority on frostbite. Given your demeanor, Director, I assume none of that blood is yours and you failed to kill Moriarty?" Hopkins asked upon examining Lestrade's blood splattered clothes on videochat.

"Missed her by that much," said Lestrade, pinching his fingers together, contemplating, *or did I?* "Hopkins, I imagine our tracking technology is superior to Scotland Yard's?"

"Indubitably, sir!"

"Can we track my DNA?"

"Well done, Director. Well done, indeed. She's heading to the airport."

47

Moriarty's pod bounded through the winding tunnel faster than a speeding bullet, culminating in its arrival at her private airstrip in four minutes and thirty-one seconds. Arctic's laser, after being rewired and redirected into the proper set of lips, had effectively quelled the ache of her tongue, which flopped in her mouth like a pair of inebriated eels. *How'd that Scotland Yard copper turned TV star find me? I pay off their director just like the rest. Did Arthur put him onto me? Or is he working with the other Holmes? Tuesday Hudson. Looks like a bloody basketball player. No matter, I'll kill them all soon enough. Knives. Sharp ones,* Moriarty mused, shoved open the blood-splattered hatch, stepped naked onto the platform, and hissed at the approaching pilot.

The pilot, wearing an astronaut suit, slogged their way toward her from the stolen military jet, "Fueled and ready, Professor."

"The ttsssshhuit'ttsssshh a nittcccchhe touch," Moriarty hissed.

"No offense, Professor. After I heard what happened to Maverick, I thought my own air supply would come in handy," the pilot replied.

"Come now. He died with a ttssssshhmile on his fattcccchhe," Moriarty said, her tongue flashing here and there. "Marvelouttsssshh! I've developed a littsssshhip. Don't you juttsssshht love it?"

"Geez, Professor. What happened to your tongue? You want me to get a medic?"

Moriarty's eyes glared. She brandished her razor near the spacesuit, "I TTSSSSHHAID don't you juttsssshht love it?"

"Sure, Professor. What's our destination?"

"Opa Locka Airport."

"Geez, Professor. Won't we draw attention landing a military jet at that tiny airport?" the pilot asked as they traversed the runway.

"The governor attsssshhured our privattcccchhy. Now ttssssshhut up and fly," Moriarty ordered, as she climbed the jet ladder, the pilot a step behind.

"Uh, Professor. I've got a spare jumpsuit if you need something to wear?"

"Am I turning you on?" Moriarty asked, attempting to flick her tongue, which spilled from her mouth like two over-cooked strands of spaghetti.

"No offense, Professor. I'm non-binary and asexual. Just trying to keep the seats clean."

"Ttsssshh," Moriarty hissed softly, remaining otherwise silent for the duration of the 18-minute trip, landing, and deboarding.

"Hope you had a smooth flight, Professor. Anything else?"

The Miami sun glistened off the hot tarmac. Moriarty's eyes glared. Her head motioned side to side. She hissed and walked briskly to face the pilot, causing them, encumbered by the clumsiness of their suit, to fall backwards onto the runway.

Moriarty was upon them before they could rise. Her tongue thrashed wildly as she went Sweeny Todd on the pilot's suit, eventually resulting in a small slit in the fabric. Moriarty smiled as the pilot's wee, but erect penis pushed against their suit, "Attsssshhettxxxxhhual my attsssshhsssshh!"

The pilot lay helpless on the ground. Moriarty was overcome with murderous thoughts. She dizzied. *Noooooo. It's happening without the pain. You're running out of time, Jane. Blasted snake venom!*

She raced to the jet ski tied to a stake in the adjacent canal, jumped on, started the engine, revved the throttle, opened the glove box, retrieved a gun, fired an entire clip into the pilot, hissed, reloaded, untied the vessel, set a southernly course on the Biscayne Canal and was off in a flash.

48

It all occurred in a flash. The lumber below us vanished. We plunged downward. In an unrivaled feat of midair marksmanship, Shadow fired a fatal head shot directly through Havana's mustache. His massive form collapsed to the dock, quaking the pilings. I attempted valiantly to get to her, my paws dancing in the air like a mime who's consumed a pot of over-brewed tea. We plummeted into the snapping jaws of death below. The gun slipped from her hand. She looked my way. I heard her parting thoughts, *if Mother were alive, she'd say a prayer. For all the good it did her.*

I'm not one who believes in prayer, or nay a deity, however, the arrival of Dolly Jolly's submarine, which had mercifully separated us from the snapping crocs, was indeed a godsend.

"Fancy a lift?" said Dolly, through the submarine's hatch.

Looking up at us through the glasslike vessel with a mix of amusement and relief, a sober Tuesday and love-sick Eren, who came rushing forth to greet us as we slipped inside.

"Nearly got yourself killed without me, Realtor," Tuesday said, tossing Shadow a towel.

"You should see the other guy," Shadow replied.

"Shadow, my love—" Eren's voice trailed off in tears.

Shadow was overcome with emotion. She gazed upon him … Ahem. She viewed him … Ahem. She … Apologies. English is not my native tongue, thus, if you'll pardon my language, dear reader, I shall express Shadow's physical reaction in a loose translation of canine. She looked at him like a bitch in heat.

Whilst I understood the love Eren and Shadow shared, I still didn't trust the bloke, thus much to the amusement of my comrades, I shook myself off in a most vigorous manner, dowsing him thoroughly.

"Good job, Watson," Shadow laughed.

"What have you discovered, Realtor?" Tuesday questioned.

"Moriarty is—"

"Don't you dare! I've been locked up with Feelometer Boy and his magic banana for—"

"The fuck you say!" Shadow exclaimed, staring them down.

"I laced the fruit with a Naltrexone derivative," Eren replied.

"Mr. Adler always knew how to make good use of his produce," said Shadow.

"Eww! As I was saying, I've been locked away underwater for days. That's the longest I've gone without a mystery since I could say the word, and I'm an addict! Clues! I need clues. For the love of all things Holmesian, give me BLOODY CLUES," Tuesday screamed, then composing herself, "Please, Cousin."

"Miami Serpentarium, Supergirl, Alice in Wonderland, the devil's element, Octomom, Koreshan, nuclear ploy, Watson Island, Monty Python. Now that you're straight, think you can solve it in say … 60 seconds?" Shadow posed.

"60. I can do it in 49," said Tuesday, throwing her arms back and attempting to pace in the sub, which given her stature, proved challenging.

"Shadow, my love—"

"Does he ever shut up?" Tuesday questioned, whilst still pacing.

"Not really," replied Shadow.

"Got it! Moriarty's powers come from snake venom, the sun fuels them and she wants to rid herself of them because they're driving her mad as a hatter, thus she's planning to scorch the Earth with phosphorous, create a Hollow Earth, and populate her New World via a human cloning machine. The nuclear burns are a ploy to distract The Bee while she accesses the Biscayne Aquifer via the soon to be completed Miami Tunnel on Watson Island. And finally, you've yet to discover the Holy Grail Moriarty needs. How'd I do?"

"Looks like a few days with Mr. Adler's banana straightened you out," Shadow smiled, moving closer to Eren, to which I growled my objection.

"Looks like Shadow has someone new to protect her," Tuesday said winking at me.

The word protect accompanied by Tuesday's wink, caused my brain to buzz violently. I shook my head in response. Protect, protect, protect, hammered away. I once again experienced an ephemeral lapse, and upon regaining my composure, I found Shadow gingerly removing my shredded collar from my teeth.

"Watson! It's okay, old fellow," said Shadow, raising an eyebrow.

My head buzzed louder. An image flashed. A stout, youthful, man with watery grey eyes—Shadow's eyes. 'Watson! It's okay old fellow,' said he, attaching my dog tag.

I snatched the remnants of my collar from Shadow's hand, dropped it on the floor, and pawed feverishly at the tag.

"A few days in your company has driven the poor creature mad, Cousin," Tuesday scoffed.

"Far from it," Shadow said, feeling the edges of my dog tag.

Shadow moved to Eren, thrust a hand into his trouser pocket, (to which I snarled, and he smiled) removed a Swiss army knife, opened the screwdriver, inserted said tool into my tag, and popped it open. GREAT SCOTT. Had the answer to my past been locked away on my very being all along? The irony. I couldn't bear the suspense. My tail thumped furiously against Shadow's calf. I am not proud to admit I found myself panting, drooling, even whining with anticipation. (I trust, dear reader, you will find it in your hearts to forgive such a display. It shan't happen again.)

I knew I was meant to find you ... or you me, Shadow thought examining the inside of my tag. "You've had the clue all along, Watson!"

"Let me see," Tuesday said, snatching the tag. "Blow me back to Baker Street!"

"Care to clue us in, dearie?" Dolly said.

"It was my 21st birthday. Father and I were polishing off a bottle of port, joking about how many years I had left until the color of my hair matched my eyes, when he announced a surprise. Father knew I wanted to get inked and knew even better my lazy ass would never put the energy into getting one. He told me he once dreamt of becoming a famous tattoo artist. He apprenticed in a tattoo shop in Japan one summer in his youth, so naturally, I believed him. How could I have been so naive? I sat for seven hours while he toiled away. When I saw it finished, I asked Father why it took so long to ink a simple, yet elegant tattoo. The lying, spying prick told me it was all in the shading, which other than being the lightest shade of violet imaginable, appears to be, as Father would say, 'unremarkable,'" Shadow said, turning about, lifting her hair off her neck.

"Blimey. It's the spitting image of the violin and bow inside Watson's tag. Clever girl, Arthur would be so proud," Dolly beamed.

"Care to do the honors, Cousin," said Shadow, smiling at Tuesday, offering her my tag.

"Don't get sappy on us now. Go on, Realtor. You've earned it."

Shadow rubbed the inside of my tag over her tattoo in a circular motion. It glowed violet. A series of numbers appeared.

"GPS coordinates. No Name Key. One of Father's favorite fishing spots. Is The Bee monitoring this sub, Dolly?"

"Heavens no. This was a gift from a baked goods heiress whose cookies I—sorry, dearie. The sub is untraceable. Where to?"

"Head here," Shadow said, handing Dolly my tag.

"On it, dearie. But I should notify The Bee. They must have found a replacement for Arthur by now," Dolly said, thinking, *Moriarty wants to destroy the world and she wants to take a fishing trip. And they call me looney. But what do I know, I've only been spying for half a century.*

"Moriarty will be monitoring communications," Shadow said.

"I could send a message over a secure channel," Dolly replied.

"Knowing Moriarty, she has agents planted at The Bee. We can't risk it," Tuesday said.

"I have to agree with Dolly. All due respect, but what chance do the four of us have against Moriarty's crime empire?" Eren asked.

GREAT SCOTT! Four of us! Four of us! Either Eren's math skills were inferior to mine, (doubtful), or he had neglected to include me. Believing the latter to be true, I barked vociferously.

"Sorry, Watson. Five of us," Eren said, bowing.

Lightning broke across the sky. Heavy rain fell. The wind blew angrily. The submarine bounced violently in the surf. The crocodiles, frustrated by their inability to reach us, snapped away at our tasty forms through the hull of the transparent vessel. I positioned myself between Shadow and the crocs and growled.

"Anything unusual about this dog you wish to share, Cousin?"

"Assuming the top speed of this thing is 45 knots, we should have the answer to that in ... approximately 62 minutes, right Dolly?' Shadow smiled.

A new side of Shadow emerged. She was light of spirit. Dare I say, cheerful. I was glad for her, yet uneasy this newfound mood might hinder our assassination, er, investigation.

"Spot on, dearie. Unless one of those toothy beasts makes its way through the hull or this storm gets worse," Dolly said, her mind once again failing her, *who are these people? Where did I leave my car? Blimey! I parked underwater again. Shake it off, old girl. For Arthur!* "Buckle in everyone. Down we go."

49

Moriarty's jet ski bounced up the floating ramp, flew high in the sky, plummeted nose-down and submerged in a most ungraceful manner. She turned her wrist hard on the throttle, raising the bow, and sputtered to the dock behind her new home on Lake Mitchell.

"Ttsssshh!" Moriarty hissed at the humming in the sky which descended upon her. Waves lapped the shoreline as a small silver seaplane popped out of nowhere, set down on the lake, and ferried to the dock.

You see, mate, Moriarty might be mad enough to slice her tongue in two, however she wasn't daft. Having deduced The Bee would be monitoring Reichenbach Falls, she dispatched a metamorphosizing drone coated with a material which rendered it undetectable, to retrieve James Moriarty's treasure from the falls.

The seaplane withdrew its wings, tilted its frame upright, shrank, transformed into a robot, extended a set of track rollers, glided toward Moriarty, and deposited a small black box at her feet. Moriarty's eyes glared red. She anxiously broke the seal, opened the box and upon finding it to be quite empty, screamed, "ARGHHHHHHHH."

"Guten Tag, Frau Professor," a woman exiting the sliding patio doors said.

"About time you convinttcccchhed the owner to ttssssshhell thittssssshh dump," Moriarty hissed.

"He recently had a change of heart, Frau Professor," the woman grinned, wiping blood from her hands.

"Have preparationttsssshh been made?"

"Ja, Frau Professor. Love the tongue. It's spicy," the woman responded, anxiously removing her blouse.

"Are you the only one left?"

"Only you and only me, Frau Professor," the woman responded, tearing off her bra.

"Marvelouttssssshh. Ttssssshhtep closer."

"Ja, Frau Professor. You smell wunderbar," the woman sighed as she pranced over to face Moriarty like a kid at an ice cream counter.

"Do you know why crimelordttsssshh don't like Jehovah'ttssssshh Witnettssssshhttssssshhettssssshh?" Moriarty asked, eyes aglow, head oscillating.

"Why, Frau Professor?" the woman replied, ripping off her shorts, moaning in ecstasy.

"We don't like any witnettssssshhttssssshhettssssshh," Moriarty responded, raising the black box in the air, bringing it down so forcefully on the woman's forehead as to render her dead. "Dittssssshhpottssssshhe of that, R3," Moriarty said, to which the robot extended a vise-like appendage, clamped it onto the woman's ankle, and rolled deep into the lake.

Moriarty felt a mess, inside and out. She surveyed her blood-covered body thinking, *shame none of this blood belonged to that copper. He'll die soon enough. Along with the rest of them.*

Moriarty walked to the deck of the infinity pool, tossed the box on a lounge chair, and dove into the lukewarm water, which was soon tinged red with blood. Swimming calmed her. She attempted to overcome her sense of failure with positive thoughts. One for each stroke.

I killed Arthur and Guinevere Holmes.

Their stupid daughter will lead me right to it.

I discovered Sherlock Holmes' offspring.

I'm going to kill the bitch.

I recovered ... an EMPTY FUCKING BOX.

Moriarty exited the pool, shook off, and entered the house. She had only seen pictures of the place. It was dreadful. She only coveted it due to its location. Remember, mate, the number one rule when purchasing real estate: location, location, location. In this case the neighborhood was sketchy, however this 1950s ranch style waterfront fixer-upper was situated on Lake Mitchell, right off the Biscayne Canal. Why, may you ask is this a good location? Fair enough. It's 0 nautical miles to its own lakeside seaplane dock. It's 11 miles to the Port of Miami. And the final selling point, it's 2.1 nautical miles via canal to the Opa Locka Airport, which is remarkably unguarded by way of water, making Moriarty's international comings and goings a piece of cake—and as I'm certain astute readers have observed by now, I do relish cake.

Moriarty walked to the bedroom and studied herself in the mirror. She hoisted her curvaceous right breast in her left hand, rotating her index finger and thumb slowly round the rose-colored nipple, causing it to harden, highlighting the infinitesimal imperfection to her eyes, which glowed red in angst.

Now, hang on. Humans don't typically pay any mind to having dogs around when showering, dressing, even dare I say, mating, thus, I've seen my share of bosoms and what I'm trying to get across, mate, is you'd have to be outright loopy to give a shite about a flea-sized nipple nick on those glorious girls. Indeed, she could nourish an entire litter with just one of those beauties. Moriarty however, felt otherwise.

"BLATTSSSSHHTED HOLMETTSSSSHHETTSSSSHH," Moriarty screamed at her disfigurement, and in so doing, caused her tongue to spill from her mouth.

She hadn't seen the results of her tongue barbering until that very moment. Her heart hurried at the sight of it. It twitched. Her head oscillated. The back of her throat ached as she attempted to further extend her tongue.

The musculature of the tongue is a fascinating thing, mate. Turns out each side has its own set of muscles, own nerve supply, and own mind.

Moriarty clenched her throat and forced her tongue from her mouth. "Marvelouttssssshh!" The aching was brilliant. She struggled to master something she had long taken for granted, and in so doing, pain fell upon her. She wished for a moment she hadn't killed the German so soon. Her head oscillated side to side. Her eyes shone scarlet. She thrust her tongue to the mirror and reveled in her cobralike image. The pain was exquisite. Although her mind filled with images of knifing the Holmeses, watching them bleed out, and despite innumerable fainting spells, Moriarty managed a full hour of exercises at which point her embattled tongue had been tamed sufficiently as to obey simple commands: in, out, up, down. Controlling each side independently, or the ultimate act of flicking, still works in progress.

Moriarty felt a mess. She looked in the mirror. Her hair was out of control. She jumped in the shower, rinsed off, picked up the shampoo bottle, and fumed, *EMPTY. Arghhhh! Empty! Just like that stupid box. Bravo, Great-Granduncle. Another disappointing man in my life. What the hell am I supposed to do with an empty ...* And then it hit her.

50

It didn't really hit me until now ... how much I love him ... how much I hurt him ... how much he hurt me. Time to let him know how you feel. Make things right, in case we ... "You shattered me, Eren!" Shadow blurted.

"Oh Shadow. If there had been any other way. Staying away from you has been the hardest thing I—"

"Shh! Not a peep, Eren! If I wasn't such a bitch, you wouldn't have left me. You saw past my meanness, but you couldn't handle my lack of compassion when you needed it most."

"Shadow. I—"

Shadow raised a finger to her lip. "It's not about you, Eren Adler! And don't give me some bullshit about how you were protecting me. I don't blame you for leaving. God! For a person with so much emotion, I must have been a nightmare for you. It took this tragedy to unlock my feelings. My passion was as buried away as my cousin's phone number. I was shut down. I couldn't even get myself excited enough to finish one of my doctorate degrees. Instead, I hermitted my days away reading, eating, and drinking wine. Not that there's anything wrong with that, but I was hollow. Then you came along and loved me. Just being around you makes me ..." Shadow's words drifted off, replaced by her innermost emotions, *makes me simultaneously sharper and keeps me on the edge of dampness. I want you inside me. I want to have a baby with you. But you left me! Asshole! But I still love you. Tell him, Shadow ... while there's still time.* "You were my only source of joy. I realize now how that burdened you. I was empty and I let you fill me. I should have been filling myself. Fulfilling myself ... Still, you told me you would always love me and then you went poof, so now that my emotions are in full play buddy, SCREW YOU AND YOUR FEELOMETER, EREN ADLER."

I must confess, I was rather enjoying this, mate.

"I do love y—"

Shadow held her finger to her lip, "It's not your fault, Mr. Adler. On the contrary, I owe you. You saw me before I did. You loved me before I loved myself. My parents' murder and my near death woke my slothful ass up! I've been robbed of so much ... by that sick serpent, by Father, Mother, but mostly by myself. I'm done being my own villain, especially when there's a real one to catch. I've taken a deep look at myself, and I'm going to change. Finish what I start. Be kind. More importantly, I found my purpose. I'm a detective! And a fucking extraordinary one. Well, at least better than Tuesday."

"Are not!" Tuesday replied childishly, sticking her tongue out.

"And one more thing, Mr. Adler," said Shadow, walking to face him.

"Yes, my lo—"

Shadow held a finger to her lips, embraced Eren, and snogged him in a manner so revolting as to cause me to cover my eyes with my paws, until after an indeterminably painful period of time, Eren's wee moans broke the silence.

"Just when I thought you found a way to shut him up," Tuesday japed.

"Aww!" Dolly said.

"If you lovebirds are through inhaling each other's innards, I have details on the coordinates we're bound for," Tuesday offered.

"Watson Boulevard," Shadow muttered, her lips back upon Eren's.

On most occasions, the sound of my name rolling off Shadow Holmes' tongue is music to my ears; however, I found this public display of affection quite disturbing. Nonetheless, given this was the first occasion since I bore witness to Shadow's exceptional mind that I experienced in her the uncustomary emotion of bliss, I did not permit my bad feelings concerning this bloke to fester.

51

Governor Fester Fahrenheit's SUV came to a halt in the emergency lane of the Julia Tuttle Causeway. The driver opened the door of the black Hummer. County Manager Bill Brown entered and greeted Fahrenheit like bloody royalty.

"How was your flight, Governor, or is it too early to call you Mr. President?" Brown groveled.

"Here," Fahrenheit stated robotically, showing Brown a text.

"Hold on, Governor. Nobody hates these bastards more than me, but I didn't agree to wholesale murder."

"Comply," Fahrenheit stated coldly.

"Look, Governor, with Eren Adler on leave, this was the perfect time to ship these scumbags off. You didn't tell me you were going to kill them! What if we get caught?"

Brown's phone dinged with a text. 'When he's elected president, he'll pardon you. They might even hail you a hero, Brown. Stop squirming, get out of the car and introduce the idiot. M.'

Fahrenheit waited for Bill Brown to conclude his introductory remarks and made his way through the vast crowd to the sunbaked podium. His face was drenched with sweat, however, in his robotlike state, it went unnoticed, as he made no effort to hanky off before approaching the microphone. Ironically, prior to his zombification, Fahrenheit would have delighted in Moriarty's elegant solution. Now, he was but a puppet in her frightful play.

"Floridians! Are you ANTI a society that places the rights of these vile sexual predators above your own?" Fahrenheit read from his phone.

"ANTI, ANTI," the crowd cheered.

"Floridians! Are you ANTI a criminal justice system which places the safety of our children at risk?"

"ANTI, ANTI, ANTI," the crowd roared.

"Floridians! Are you ANTI your government spending millions of dollars a year housing and monitoring predators?"

"ANTI, ANTI, ANTI, ANTI," the crowd hailed.

"Miamians! Are you ANTI this horrible encampment of monsters, who use beautiful Biscayne Bay for a toilet, and lie in wait for your children?"

"ANTI, ANTI, ANTI, ANTI, ANTI," the frenzied crowd screamed.

"Thankfully, this is Florida, where I make the rules, and today I am proud to introduce a bold solution. A program I call, Up The ANTI".

"UP THE ANTI, UP THE ANTI, UP THE ANTI, UP THE ANTI, UP THE ANTI," the crowd yelled.

"Behind tourism, agriculture is the Sunshine State's largest employer, providing two million jobs and over 100 billion dollars in annual revenue. For those who don't know, phosphorous is critical to the production of fertilizer which our farmer's rely on. Florida's phosphate reserves are plentiful; however, we lack the manpower to mine it. These 'people' have no place to live, limited work opportunities, and no future. I do not condone their monstrosities, but keeping them here, unsupervised in close proximity to our children, is not the solution. My fellow Floridians, whatever shall we do?"

"UP THE ANTI, UP THE ANTI, UP THE ANTI, UP THE ANTI, UP THE ANTI, UP THE ANTI, UP THE ANTI," the crowd roared.

"Upon the conclusion of my remarks, law enforcement shall escort these bridge dwellers into those buses lining the emergency lane. Once they've exited, this area will be sanitized and secured. The predators will be driven to remote phosphate mines in central Florida where they will be provided supervised living quarters, food, training, jobs, and zero opportunity to offend again. Further, our criminal justice system has been directed to refer all predators being discharged from incarceration into our program so they can be afforded the same opportunity as we UP THE ANTI."

"UP THE ANTI, UP THE ANTI, UP THE ANTI, UP THE ANTI, UP THE ANTI, UP THE ANTI, UP THE ANTI, UP THE ANTI, UP THE ANTI, UP THE ANTI, UP THE ANTI," the crowd chanted.

"Before I wrap up, I know certain liberals will complain about violating the human rights of these 'people' who served their sentences, but honestly folks are these predatory beasts really people?"

"UP THE ANTI, UP THE ANTI, UP THE ANTI, UP THE ANTI, UP THE ANTI, UP THE ANTI, UP THE ANTI, UP THE ANTI, UP THE ANTI, UP THE ANTI, ANTI, ANTI," the crowd yelled.

"I want to thank County Manager Brown for his ANTI predator stance and willingness to be first to forever rid his community of the plague of sexual predators. Now, who's ready to UP THE ANTI?"

"UP THE ANTI, UP THE ANTI, UP THE ANTI, UP THE ANTI, UP THE ANTI, UP THE ANTI, UP THE ANTI, UP THE ANTI, UP THE ANTI, UP THE ANTI, ANTI, ANTI, ANTI, ANTI, ANTI, ANTI, ANTI, ANTI, ANTI, ANTI, ANTI, ANTI, ANTI, ANTI," the crowd cheered as Fahrenheit concluded his remarks.

"You know how to rile up a crowd, Governor," Brown said, escorting Fahrenheit to his vehicle. "For a minute, you had me believing it. I still don't feel right about slaughtering them like this."

52

Like lambs to the slaughter, Moriarty thought, watching the video feed of the departing buses. She called for R3 who glided into her bedroom.

"Instructions, Professor?"

"Ttsssshhsseaplane mode."

"Yes, Professor," R3 replied, gliding into the water, transforming into a single passenger seaplane.

Moriarty's heart raced. Her head oscillated, her tongue slithered from her mouth, "Ttssshhoon, Great-Granduncle Jamettssshh. Ttssshhoon." Moriarty fetched the four things she needed: the empty box previously hidden in Reichenbach Falls, her copy of The Dynamics of an Asteroid, a metal tube containing dry ice and Mrs. Wilson's uterus, and a shatterproof container of test tubes containing DNA samples of the most ruthless criminals and the most revered good chaps in human history: Mahatma Gandhi, Michelangelo, Marie Curie, Abraham Lincoln, Albert Einstein, Martin Luther King, Jr., Mr. Rogers, Mother Teresa, Nelson Mandela, Charles Darwin, Genghis Kahn, Lizzy Borden, Fidel Castro, Nero, Attila the Hun, Hitler, Stalin, Idi Amin, Saddam Hussein, and, naturally, Napoleon.

Moriarty walked to the dock, clothed solely in her red-flowered bikini bottom, the one she promised to wear when she killed the last of the Holmeses, opened the plane's door, slid the test tube container into the plane's side panel, and tossed the book, box and uterus onto the floor.

"Firttsssshht ttsssshhtop, Bittsssshhcayne Park. The Log Inn," Moriarty hissed.

R3 rocketed from the dock, and following a brief journey atop the lake's choppy surface was airborne.

"Marvelouttsssshh!" Moriarty hissed, opening the side window for a better view. She garnered strength from deep within her throat and attempted to flick her tongue into the oncoming air, however the force of the wind in the opposing direction slapped the right side of her tongue against the left corner of her mouth and the left against the right. The pain was indescribable. Her eyes glimmered red. Images of stabbing Shadow Holmes and Tuesday Hudson, their bodies oozing blood, consumed her. She blacked out, awoke, got her bearings, and began her countdown. If she didn't encounter any gawking kayakers, she would arrive in … ten, nine, eight …

It was upon the count of three Moriarty saw them: five blondes in peacock blue monokinis, four brunettes and a redhead in lavender bikinis, all riding inflatable flamingos. The women were of course in an Olympic-sized pool playing a bastardized version of water polo, and the setting, was of course, the infamous, Log Inn.

Built in 1923, the Log Inn, a 3,900 square foot log cabin constructed of termite resistant Dade County Pine featured five bedrooms, a rustic kitchen, a loft which ran half the length of the building, a fireplace, and an indoor loo—somewhat of a luxury at the time. In modern days, the Log Inn abounds in sumptuousness.

The original owner of the property was a crusty tart by the name of Amy St. Clair, who after a particularly bitter London winter, took holiday on the sunny shores of Miami Beach. St. Clair's father made a substantial living as a beggar on the streets of London until he was found out by Sherlock Holmes as documented in 'The Man With The Twisted Lip', however by the time his misdeeds were uncovered, St. Clair had stashed away a tidy sum and left it all to Amy, who upon seeing an advertisement for a log home in her hotel lobby promising a free strawberry shortcake just for touring the place, purchased the property on the spot. Further, I am told the shortcake, made with fresh local strawberries, was delectable.

Those were the days of the Miami land rush, where real estate changed hands ten times over before the property appraisers' office could even record the deed and selling homes was, dare I say, a piece of scrumptious cake.

The log home was designed for a household of ten. Amy, being a keen businesswoman, had other plans—a home for wayward girls. Okay, you got me, chum. It was a brothel. Thus, was born the Log Inn, a place a bloke could patronize when they desired, as the inscription over their mantlepiece read, 'a place to put your log in'.

As madame of the Log Inn, Amy St. Clair served as mentor to wayward girls, never failing to inspire her ladies, even personally servicing a few clients, (the ones with mommy issues if you ask me, mate). Upon her death, Amy's daughter Gretel, the surprise result of a geriatric pregnancy, took charge. In addition to holding the brothel's record for highest ever daily earnings whilst dressed in a yak costume, Gretel was a world-renowned broker of curios and oddities. And the more curious and odder it was, the higher the cost. For the right price St. Clair could obtain anything from shrunken heads to rare animal organs for her exclusive clientele, however her fascination lay with ancient knives.

R3 coasted to a stop at the dock behind the Log Inn. Moriarty exited the plane, instructed R3 to secure the doors, and walked topless across the pool deck.

"PROFESSOR. We missed you!!!" the girls skreiched.

"Back off, Bitchettsssshh. Buttssssshhhinettsssshhttsssshh," Moriarty hissed, sashaying through the covey of swooning lovelies to the main house.

"I have your knives, Professor. They're incomparable. I'm tempted to keep the flaying ones for myself. Carbon steel blades. Bejeweled rhodium plated platinum handles. You're going to just die when you see the design."

Someone is going to die, Moriarty thought to herself and hissed, "Ttssssshhow me!"

"Here you go, Professor," St. Clair said, opening a small silk lined suitcase.

Moriarty had never seen such perfection in craftsmanship. Each handle was fashioned into a different species of venomous snake. Her head oscillated. Her eyes glowed red. She removed a knife from the case. Its platinum handle was fashioned into a black mamba, with two large ruby eyes, "Marvelouttsssshh!"

"That'll be $16 million," St. Clair said, without batting an eye.

Money! What's wrong with this whore? Last time I was here she was all over me, and she never charged me, for anything? Moriarty's head oscillated. Her eyes were ablaze. Her tongue slithered from her lips. Moriarty hefted her left breast toward her mouth in a failed attempt to flick her nipple, lapping at it like a nursing kitten. "Ttsssshh! Can't we work ttsssshhomething out?" Moriarty hissed seductively.

"Nice trick, Professor. That's one helluva ouchy you got on your tongue. One of my girls used to be a surgeon, but I pay better. You want her to take a look?"

Why isn't she gawking at my tits? It's the blasted nipple wound! No! Something's different about her face. This should do it, Moriarty thought, stretching to place her armpit under St. Clair's nose, "SMELL ME."

"Sorry, Professor. Ever since my botched rhinoplasty, I can't smell a thing. It was worth it for this nose though, right?" St. Clair laughed, turning her head to the side, pointing at her profile. "Kiki out back digs sniffing stuff. Gets off on the smell of old bookstores. Want me to get her?"

"That won't be nettcccchhettsssshhttsssshhary," Moriarty hissed, slicing St. Clair's throat.

Blood spurted from her carotid. St. Clair slumped to the ground. *Marvelous! A madame with her skills will come in handy in my New World,* Moriarty mused. Utilizing a flaying knife with a coral snake handle, Moriarty peeled a gossamer-thin sheet of skin from St. Clair's thigh and tossed it in the open knife case. Her tongue danced violently from her mouth. She bit it hard. The pain, the killing, was exactly what she needed to ready herself for the end of it all, and a new beginning. Moriarty's brain pumped full of images of hacking the Holmeses to pieces. She passed out, awoke, replaced the knife, picked up the valise and walked to the pool deck, her ever increasing scent proceeding her.

Stepping onto the deck, a bee buzzed past her calf. "Blattsssshhted bee!" Moriarty yelled, squashing the creature with her bare foot.

"PROFESSOR. Let's play," the women, drawn in by her allurement, screeched, as they scurried in her direction.

Moriarty turned her back toward the women, bent over, paraded her bikinied rump high in the air, placed the valise on a lounge, opened it, and removed two knives, one with a water moccasin handle, the other that of an inland taipan.

Moriarty turned to them eyes aglow, her head shifting in a snakelike fashion, her split-tongue jetting here and there.

The first girl didn't see it coming.

The others never stood a chance.

53

What are the chances? Pizza! My favorite food group. No time to stop for a pie, Shadow. Not when you're so close to catching her. The coordinates should be right around those ... hives, Shadow thought, smiling brightly.

The scent of melty cheese summoned me, yet much to the dismay of my rumbling belly, my comrades passed the No Name Pub without sampling its delicacies. I, on the other hand, headed straight for the trash bin. (I am, after all, a dog.) GREAT SCOTT. Shadow was fifty paces ahead. I had forsaken my vow. I sprinted toward her. Several wee deer the size of golden retrievers looked on in amusement as my paws sunk into the muddy soil. As I quickened my pace, Shadow, Tuesday, Dolly, and Eren strode through a field abuzz with bees, stopping at a tall beehive, where they were greeted by a woman, beer in hand, wearing a long-sleeved tee-shirt bearing the image of a sailfish, a seashell print skirt, a large-billed fishing cap, wrap-around sunglasses, and muck-stained sandals. Whilst the sun had taken its toll on her skin, her warm smile projected a youthful image. A bewildering, yet familiar scent filled the air causing my tail to drop. Unable to discern whether this woman was friend or foe, I concealed myself behind a hive, standing ready.

"I'm —" Shadow said.

"Oh, poor Arthur!!!" the woman bellowed for some time.

"Excuse me. I'm—"

"Geez! You Holmeses! Always in a rush. Give me a minute to grieve, Shadow!" the woman yapped.

Shadow pensively observed, whilst Tuesday thrust her hands behind her back and began to pace round the woman.

"Who the hell are … those eyes! Arthur had another kid! That lying, spying, jerk of a boyfriend!" the woman huffed.

"The fuck you say!?" Shadow questioned.

Disregarding Shadow's comment, the woman stared Tuesday up and down, chuckling, "Geez, you're a big one. Two questions. How long does it take to shave those legs and more importantly, who's your daddy?"

"I have them waxed and Dylan Hudson, THE GREATEST DETECT—"

"Cool your jets, Stretch. Hudson, huh? So, Sherlock boinked his landlady," the woman said, backing off.

"Eww! And my grandfather certainly did not BOINK her. Dr. Tuesday Hudson, consulting detective. And you are?"

"I'm Honey. Sorry about your dad, Shadow. And your mom. May their souls sail free. And look who you brought to visit. Hello, Dolly! BIG FAN. I broadcast your mermaid shows during mating season. Drives the bees wild."

"Lovely to meet you, dearie," said Dolly, thinking, *drives the bees wild. This one's crazier than me. But she knew Arthur. And Guinevere. Blimey. Is she one of ours?*

"And this tasty bite?" the woman questioned, regarding Eren as if he were a fresh baked biscuit.

"Eren Adler. Sorry for your loss," he said, extending his hand.

"Eren!" Shadow admonished.

"She is genuinely grieving, my love."

"You have questions," the woman stated, rather than asked.

Shadow puzzled over the woman, *who does this tramp think she is? Damn straight I have questions, Honey! Who names their kid Honey? Hmm. Her mother was a beekeeper. These hives are ancient. European honeybees. I recognize the pattern. A variety found in … Hullo!*

Fun fact, mate. Bees are highly intelligent creatures who communicate in a variety of manners. Through a waggle dance, they show their hive-mates the nearest nectar source. They can sense magnetic fields. They emit and receive a variety of pheromones which play a role in every aspect of the life of a hive—defense, mating, locating food, thus allowing the hive to behave as a superorganism. In fact, Sherlock Holmes was so fascinated with the subject of bee society, he even wrote a book on it, 'Practical Handbook of Bee Culture with Some Observations Upon the Segregation of the Queen'. A real snoozefest if you ask me, unless you happen to be fond of bees, which these days most humans are, with our planet in danger of the loss of pollinators, global warming and such. Perhaps not everyone believes this to be so? (I mean, really, some Yanks even believe elections can be stolen.)

Shadow struggled to focus on the case, *hmm. Why would she have those hives? And that slut referred to Father as her boyfriend! Remember new leaf, Shadow. Be kind. More flies with …* "Honey, this is awkward. There's a lot I didn't know about Father until recently. You and he weren't still?"

"I wish! Once Arthur met your mother, there was no room for anyone else in his heart, except you. Not that I didn't try to tempt him, I mean just look at me," Honey smiled, smoothing her skirt. "But you don't really need me to tell you much. Go ahead. Do your Holmes thing. You know you want to."

Shadow examined Honey and her surroundings, blurting, "Father met you at fishing camp as a teenager. He fell for your hippie charms, keen mind, artistic nature, and mutual love of fishing."

"We met the summer I turned 17. Arthur was 16. Poor Arthur," Honey wailed.

"You left the Keys decades ago. Based on the callouses on your left hand, you spent a great deal of time wielding a geologist's rock hammer. Your father died ten years ago. Your mother took ill soon after. You gave up your career, returned home to tend to her and the bees. She died seven years ago, and you've been stuck here ever since, which explains why you drink so much—even for someone who lives in the Keys," Shadow said.

"Rude, but you nailed it. My family lived in a little apartment on top of Daddy's bait store, right there," Honey said, pointing. "Believe it or not, I still live there."

I believed it, mate.

"Arthur came in every day, listening to Daddy's fish stories. He told some whoppers. Most people wrote Daddy off as a blowhard, but he knew more about bait than anyone in the Florida Keys. Understand, there's fishing and there's catching. Daddy loved preaching his catching credo for doing things right—"

"Right bait, right guide, right place, right time, right conditions, right lucky," Shadow muttered, thinking, *so that's where he got that ridiculous saying.*

"I heard you hated fishing, but you're a good listener, like your father. Arthur would sit quietly, soaking in whatever anyone said, and never uttered a whisper, until he had something worthy to say or ask. Something so very important, yet the rest of us would never have even conceived to consider it. I never met anyone as warm and clever as Arthur Holmes. I tingled every time he spoke. I taught him how to kiss like a French girl and he taught me how to speak like one. I can't believe he's dead. Ohwahhhhhh!!"

"Fascinating account. The bees. They were Great-Granduncle Sherlock's," Shadow offered, peering at one of the surrounding hives.

"How'd you know?" Dolly asked.

"Obviously, she recognized the pattern of the subspecies," Tuesday offered.

"If they were your grandfather's bees how'd they wind up with Arthur, dearie?"

Bad enough the man was a dentist, I can't tell them about his phobia. I watched my father hunt down the most vicious criminals on earth. The man was fearless, except when it came to bees. He never explained it. Poor thing wouldn't even take honey in his Earl Grey, Tuesday thought, responding, "Never fancied them I imagine."

"After Father learned your mother was a beekeeper, he asked if he could bring over some bees from Sherlock's original hives. He told you something along the lines of 'poor creatures would welcome the holiday from the cold Sussex air'," Shadow said, in a deep British accent.

"Hey! That's a pretty good Arthur Holmes. Mine's better though," Honey said, bellowing forth a deep British voice, "These bees have been in my family for generations. You must promise me, dear girl, promise me you'll protect—"

The word protect droned in my head. I experienced yet another lapse, this one quite wee, after which the hives came alive. Bees consumed the entirety of the space around me. My ears rattled from the deafening buzz. I faltered toward Shadow, my courage, along with the word protect departed, replaced by a singular terror, PAIN.

54

I'm not proud to admit, mate, pain was the first thing that popped to mind as a swarm of bees enveloped me. Not a fan of things which can prick you. Don't get the wrong impression. I'm not one of those anti-vaxxers, however the idea of being covered in a multitude of stinging insects induced in me a state of terrified mummification rivaling that Han Solo bloke when they froze him in carbonite.

The bees whirled round my face like dervishes. Remarkably, the creatures did not sting. I found myself quite relieved, whilst regaining my steadfast resolve to one thing and one thing alone—protecting Shadow Holmes. That however presented a challenge, as with the swarm upon me, I was blind as an ungroomed sheepdog. In an effort to separate myself from the noisy creatures, I shook my head, releasing a recollection more vivid than any which had come before.

I found myself in a Sussex meadow. A wee lad with mischievous grey eyes held in his grasp ... GREAT SCOTT. A ball! I danced at his feet. Ball. Ball. Ball. What was he waiting for? "Toss it! Toss it," I barked. (Regrettably, the lad was past the age when interspecies communication still proved possible.) A gent tending a beehive looked on with merriment. Despite his advanced age, the beekeeper was remarkably spry, bore a

Roman nose and eyes identical to the child's … and Tuesday's. GREAT SCOTT. Sherlock Holmes!

A man approached. His forehead jutted beneath the railway cap which sat upon his oscillating head. His eyes shone red. He carried a stick with a cobra-head handle. He smelled like the lipstick, the water cooler, the Serpentarium postcard. Moriarty, the station master! The rogue rushed forward, raised his stick to the lad, and shouted, "Hand it over, Holmes, or the boy dies!"

Sherlock dove to intercept him, exclaiming, "Protect!" The hives buzzed to life. I darted to their aid, leapt for Moriarty's stick, which he brought down upon my skull, dropping me to the grass. I lifted my throbbing head and clenched Moriarty's ankle in my teeth with all the might I could muster. The wee lad punched the rogue, right where it counts. Sherlock pummeled him. Moriarty collapsed, landing unfortunately on my flank. The pain was excruciating. The bees were upon us, followed by … stinging. So much stinging.

"Back off, buzzers. Leave that baby Key Deer alone …" Honey's words and the bees drifted off, along with my memories, as well as the smoke emitted from the device she swung about in her hand. "Your dog?"

"Yes," Shadow responded, causing my tail to wag with great vigor.

"Better check him for snake bites," Honey said.

Eren dashed to my side and inspected my coat and underbelly, which I must admit came as a shock, especially considering my past behavior toward him. "All clear. Do you have a hose so we can check his paws?"

Honey pointed to a nearby spigot. GREAT SCOTT. Bees, followed by a hosing off. Things were certainly not going my way.

"The bees only did that twice before, when Key deer fawn had been bitten by a snake."

"The deer survived," Shadow stated.

"No shit, Shadow!" Honey chortled.

"Hullo!" Shadow and Tuesday exclaimed concurrently.

"Hey! No pilfering my grandfather's expression, Realtor," Tuesday winked.

Their lack of concern for my well-being, notwithstanding, I knew I had not been bitten by a viper, however I failed to understand what those two had deduced, thus I tuned into Shadow's thoughts, *the bees! Of course. Their stings counteract Moriarty's pheromones! But how? And if they do, why wouldn't Father just give them to her? Hmm. Maybe they don't work on Moriarty? Perhaps an antidote … or vaccine? And what does this have to do with Watson? He doesn't seem like he was bitten by a snake, but just in case,* "Let's clean you up, Watson," Shadow said, turning on the spigot. Despite my distaste for baths, I complied.

"Smart dog! What's his name?" Honey asked.

"Watson," said Shadow, whilst she cleaned and inspected my paws.

"Your dad name him?" Honey questioned, removing her sunglasses, studying me.

"Why?"

"When we were kids, Arthur was always going on about his dog. Red and white border collie named Watson. Green eyes, too. He never told you about him?"

Shadow's mind raced, *no, the lying, spying prick, and Watson's tag led us here. I swear this dog understands everything I say. And the bees … did they respond to the word protect in Honey's lame imitation of Father's voice or is it something about Watson that made them swarm? Maybe they're trained? Yeah, right, Shadow, trained bees. Head in the stars. But why would Father leave Sherlock's bees with this squinty eye tramp? Hmm. Hadn't noticed her right eye through her shades. She's probably been looking up someone's ass. New leaf, Shadow. Be kind. Hmm. Why would her eye … Of course!* "Honey, your last name wouldn't happen to be Penny?"

"Yes and keep the jokes to yourself."

"Honeypenny," Dolly snorted, thinking, *this one's either barmy, or she stumbled into the wrong storyline.*

"As in Dr. H. Penny, the astrogeologist who postulated the theory that water on Earth originated via ice contained in asteroids?"

"See, you're not the only one with your head in the stars, Shadow Holmes."

How the hell does this tramp know what Father used to say to me!? Be kind, Shadow. Focus on the case. Think it out! What are the odds of an astrogeologist taking care of Sherlock's bees? Seventeen million, two hundred thousand—Not the time for math, Shadow. Think it out! Shadow told herself, flopping into a soiled camping chair and assuming her 'I'm most certainly going to apprehend you' posture. At the same time, Tuesday paced about wildly.

"They okay?" Honey inquired.

"It's their way," Eren replied.

Their Holmesian minds bombarded me so rapidly, distinguishing between the two proved a challenging task, *astrogeology. Asteroids. Snake venom. Bee stings. Tramp. Key deer. Trained bees. Vaccinations. Aquifers. Energy sources. Watson. Slut. Bee stings. Protect. Murderous cunt! Meteorites. Properties of meteorites. Iron cells in bee abdomens. Magneto reception. Lying. Spying. Polarity. Desiccant. Two meteorites! Reichenbach. Sick serpent. James Moriarty. The Dynamics of an Asteroid. Blow me back to Baker Street! It's ele-freaking-mentary!*

"The central hive," the cousins chimed, racing toward the ancient tin roofed structure, Shadow grabbing Honey's smoke machine en route. Naturally, long legged Tuesday had the advantage, arriving first.

"Ha! I'm quicker … Apologies, force of habit. I believe you have the honors, Realtor," Tuesday said, backing away.

"They were your grandfather's bees," Shadow smiled, spraying smoke over the hive.

"Together then," they said, removing the top, peering in.

55

Hold it together for a few more hours, Jane, Moriarty thought, as she hopped in the seaplane, "Watttsssshhon Ittsssshhland ttsssshheaplane hangar, R3. Ttsssshhtep on it!"

R3 plotted a southeasterly course, revved its engine and sped from the dock.

Moriarty opened the knife case, slid her fingers along the elastic of the velvet side pouch, tossed in the container of test tubes, including the ones most recently filled with thin pieces of tissue skinned from Gretel St. Clair and her trollops, closed the case and placed it in the plane's side panel.

Still titillated by her recent wickedness, Moriarty hissed in delight and initiated her countdown. She reached 248 seconds when she heard a blast and felt a vibration below. Her body shook. Her tongue whipped furiously from her mouth. Looking out the window through glaring eyes, she saw him on the far side of the footbridge bordering the Miami Shores Golf Course. A dashing man comfortably reclined in a golf cart, smoke billowing from a rocket launcher—and his cigar. Moriarty fumed.

"TTSSSSHHOOT HIM," she ordered, causing R3 to lay down a round of machine-gun fire obliterating the cart. "Marvelouttsssshh!" Moriarty hissed and continued her countdown.

At 99 seconds, they reached the blue-green waters of Biscayne Bay. Below, a stingray, attempting to elude a bull shark, leapt from the water. The shark thrust its open maw through the surface, pulling the unfortunate creature below. *How glorious*, she thought.

At 48 seconds, Moriarty peered nostalgically upon the city she once loved, its rhythm, food, culture, people, and depravity that was Miami of the past, before the developers moved in for the sake of AirBNB McMansions, replacing many of the splendid drug and arms dealers of the past with oligarch landlords who had no need of her crime syndicate. She pondered the Drake equation, which in addition to foretelling intelligent life on other planets, predicts the number of years an intelligent civilization may sustain itself. *They already killed it. I'm just speeding things along. A new sinister world is coming, Great-Granduncle. Just wait until you see how we torture the righteous ones this time around. Just like you envisioned. Just like I planned.*

At 33 seconds, R3 veered. The sun glared through the plane's window. Moriarty's mind flooded with images of wrapping her legs around the tall one's neck, whilst stabbing the stupid one over and over again, until it all went black. R3 skipped along the surface of the waters surrounding Watson Island and ferried to the seaplane dock, thus awakening Moriarty, who threw open the plane door, retrieved her knife case, and stepped onto the dock. "R3! Engage ttsssshhecurity protocol Ttzzzzhheta," to which, R3 issued a series of flashing lights.

A man wearing a gas mask greeted her.

"How deep?" Moriarty questioned.

"10 meters below the tunnel, Professor. As instructed," the man responded, backing away, fast.

Moriarty turned her attention to the center of the hangar where a group of men shoveling the contents of six dump trucks into a sand pile which reached the ceiling, began sniffing the air like a pack of bloodhounds. The men made a mad dash for the wee, blood-splattered topless knock-out strutting their way, only to be yanked back by the chains which bound their shackled legs to the walls.

"MARVELOUTTSSSSHH," Moriarty hissed, thinking, *everyone who ever double-crossed me. Everyone who isn't dead—yet. Just wait until Fahrenheit brings the predators. They'll make a fine addition. And that stupid girl. She's found it by now. I can feel it.*

Moriarty set her valise on the floor, bent over, opened it, and removed two knives: the one with the black mamba handle, the other, a tiger snake. Her head began oscillating, her tongue darted across her face as she gazed down upon her red-flowered bikini bottom—because the time had finally come to kill those blasted Holmeses.

56

The cousins gazed at the inside of the hive as if they had indeed located the Holy Grail. Bees circled their heads. Shadow plucked a square rock from the hive, removed a compass from her purse, placed the rock atop, and observed the needle, which did not react, leading her to poke her finger into a cell and remove some goo. Royal Jelly. Yum! Fun fact, mate. Bees feed copious amounts of Royal Jelly to a female bee and magically she becomes the Queen with powers to reproduce. Shadow placed a wee dab of Royal Jelly upon the compass. It twitched. A large bee, twice the length of the others, buzzed past and came to rest on the compass. The needle spun off its base.

"Kiss my asteroid!" Shadow roared.

The cousins shared a smile.

"How's it feel to solve your first case, Realtor?"

Freaking heavenly, Shadow thought, blurting to Honey, "Reichenbach was a test site!"

"Your father called it the Moses stone," Honey said.

"And Moriarty has the other half," Tuesday added.

"You've been studying it," Shadow said.

"For half a century," Honey stated.

"I'm afraid I'm as lost as my car keys, dearies," said Dolly.

"Seems you have the honors, Realtor."

Shadow lifted the rock, started to speak, paused, and turned to her cousin, "He was your grandfather."

"Together, then, my dear cousin."

"Great-Granduncle Sherlock wasn't running from James Moriarty when they wound up at Reichenbach. He discovered that Moriarty found two meteorites, each from the opposite pole of the same massive asteroid."

"When the negatively charged and positively charged meteorites were placed together, they absorbed tremendous volumes of water. When separated, the water released," Tuesday said.

"James Moriarty planned on slurping up the water supplies of entire nations and blackmailing them for the return of their most precious commodity," Shadow added.

"Cornering the bottled water market without bottles!" Eren offered.

"Grandfather and James Moriarty battled for the stones at the Falls. Sherlock snatched one meteorite, while the other, along with James Moriarty fell deep into the chasm of the falls."

"Great-Granduncle Sherlock hid his meteorite in the hives for safe keeping, where unbeknownst to him, the bees, with their natural ability to absorb iron into cells in their abdomen for magneto reception, depleted the meteorite of its polarity."

"Which transferred to these bees and somehow gave them the ability to counteract Moriarty's pheromones via their stings," Tuesday said.

"Arthur visited every year for a booster sting. He was overdue," Honey sniffled.

Shadow peered deep into the hive, pondering, *every year? Bees don't live that long. And what about their stings effect Moriarty's pheromones? Did the meteorite cause that too? And what's this all have to do with Watson? What am I missing... Of course! It's freaking bee-lementary!* "No dead bees!"

"Took you long enough," Honey chuckled.

How did I miss that? I need drugs. No! Be strong. She is after all Mycroft's spawn, Tuesday considered, stating, "Not bad, Realtor! Are you certain you didn't know your parents were spies?"

"Dead bees?" Eren questioned.

"There's always several in a hive; sometimes as many as a hundred a day," Honey replied.

"And Watson?" Eren asked.

And Watson, indeed! I barked to indicate my impatience.

"I was getting there," Shadow said, extending her open palm toward her cousin, at which point Tuesday, tossed her a compass from her backpack. Shadow held the compass to my head. It spun round and round, causing her to shout, "Hullo!"

"Sounds better when I say it, but well done, Realtor."

I was endeavoring to grasp the significance of my magnetism, when the large bee which had been resting on the compass earlier, landed upon my nose. I stood petrified, whilst she moved her appendages about, her eyes fixed upon me—all five of them. Just as I smelled something familiar, she buzzed off.

"Vicky used to do the same thing to your father," Honey said.

"Vicky!" Dolly questioned.

"Short for Victoria," Tuesday chuckled.

"The Queen," Shadow said.

"Sherlock named her," Honey added.

"Sherlock Holmes named her? And you think I'm the one losing my wits, dearies?"

"I thought queen bees only live a few years?" Eren asked.

"A five-year-old queen is considered ancient, Feelometer Boy."

"Do you expect us to believe these very bees belonged to Sherlock Holmes," Dolly questioned.

"Arthur said you were a bit slow, but always came through in the clutch," Honey said.

"Why you—"

As the two boomers quarreled, the cousins turned their attention to a wayward hummingbird.

Shadow thinking *cinnamon colored tail feathers. That's not a ruby throated hummingbird. It's a broad-tailed hummingbird. Never been a recorded sighting in the Florida Keys.*

Tuesday pondering, *something off about the rhythm of its wings.*

"Fascinating visit, Honey, but we have to split. Whatever you do, guard this meteorite with your life," Shadow said, returning the rock to the hive, winking at Honey.

Honey returned the gesture as she slipped on her sunglasses.

"But you said—"

"Don't worry, Dolly. The meteorite will be safe with Honey," Shadow winked to the spy.

She's onto something. I can play along, Dolly thought, stating, "Where did I park my car? Who are you people? Oh my, I've gone off again, haven't I, dearies?"

"It's been most enlightening, Honey Penny. Send my best to Pussy Galore," Tuesday japed.

"Couldn't resist, could you, Stretch? Don't worry about the meteorite," Honey winked. "And one more thing, Shadow Holmes."

"Yes?"

"Arthur would be proud," Honey sniffled.

57

Jane is going to be so proud of me. She was right not to trust Uncle Ricardo. Jane's so bright. She smells like sex. And nobody ever made me come like that.

She promised to take me with her if I found it. I'll just wait until these jerks leave, and my little birdie friend will retrieve it. Jane is going to be blissed out, just like me when I see her. When I smell her. And the best part, the very best part, Jane is going to kick my idiot brother to the curb!

I wonder what she needs it for? Who cares, Tiffani. The sooner you give her the stupid rock, the sooner you get your rocks off. I hope it's not too heavy. Maybe I should have used the red breasted robin?

58

Well, that was a bust, thought Lestrade after his 1-hour 36-minute inspection of Moriarty's airstrip yielded no results. "Any word on Tuesday Hudson?" Lestrade questioned through his phone.

"Afraid not, Director," Hopkins replied.

"Moriarty?" Lestrade asked.

"Nothing, Director. However, the tracker you placed on Governor Fahrenheit proved useful. After a rousing speech at the Julia Tuttle Causeway—"

"The infamous predator encampment?" Lestrade interjected.

"Indubitably, sir. He's taking them to Watson Island."

Now why would Fahrenheit be headed to Watson Island? The irony. If only Tuesday could hear this. Tuesday ... Lestrade worried to himself, causing a knot in his gut, or perhaps he thought it was the bag of gummy worms he unearthed in the rental car. "Map of Watson Island, please, Hopkins."

"On your phone, Director."

"Thank you, Hopkins," Lestrade remarked, opening the text, thinking, *at Scotland Yard, I'd have to fill out a request form. I could get used to this. If I survive. Let's see. An animal park, children's museum, boat ramp, Japanese gardens, boating clubs, heavy duty construction equipment, and a hangar owned by Citrus Industries!* "Hopkins, what's the purpose of the construction equipment?"

"A tunnel to the Port of Miami, Director."

A tunnel, Lestrade considered, pronouncing, "it's not what's on Watson Island Moriarty is after, it's what's under it! I'll be beaming back momentarily, Hopkins. Have Tess waiting."

"Bravo, sir. If it's not too impertinent, might I say, I see why Arthur selected you. Shall I dispatch agents, Director?"

The question bobbed about Lestrade's brain, *more agents? Not until I rescue Tuesday. If she's even there. Oh, Tuesday… Clear your head, lover-boy. WWTD?* "If you don't hear from me within the hour, send in the troops," he replied, setting a one-hour timer on his phone.

59

"Based on my calculations, Moriarty will be reaching the requisite depth below the Port of Miami tunnel within the hour," Shadow said.

"Blimey! I've been watching them build the tunnel from my yacht," Dolly remarked.

"It's 120 feet down, nearly a mile long, and wider than two semi-trucks. It's due to open this year," Eren said.

"Moriarty's paid you quite the wicked compliment, starting her mad new world there, eh, Watson?" Tuesday said, patting my shoulder.

Imagining I should feel honored to have my name associated with Moriarty's murderous intentions upon Shadow, my comrades in arms, and every living creature on earth stirred me to my core. Shadow however, seemed cool, calm, and collected, "Can you manage a bit more speed, Dolly?"

"I'll have us there in 48 minutes, dearie, but I'll likely blow my engine."

"Thank you, Dolly," Shadow replied.

"No worries, dearie, besides, you know how I like blowing things," Dolly chuckled.

"Shall we discuss strategy?" Tuesday asked.

"Actually, I'd like your advice," Shadow said.

"It's about bloody time," said Tuesday.

"I was asking Dolly," Shadow said, to which Tuesday pouted.

"Why I'm no Arthur Conan Holmes, dearie, but I worked by his side for decades, and I'd like to think I learned a thing or two. Arthur advised, first and foremost, always, always, stay attuned to your adversary's deepest desire, dangle a means to obtain it within their grasp, take it away, then hit them while their mind's set on a way to get it back. Equally important, never underestimate your opponent. And finally, gather and analyze all available recognizance."

That's the same advice Father gave me about selling houses. Never realized espionage and real estate had so much in common, Shadow thought, responding, "Actually, Dolly, I was asking for your advice."

My advice. Blimey! Least somebody still thinks I'm good for something, Dolly considered, responding, "Find a way to piss off your enemy. Throws them off their game, you know. Then shoot them, dearie. Shoot them dead."

"Thank you, Dolly," Shadow replied.

"About that reconnaissance. Can you brief me on your deductions, dearies?"

"It's elementary, Dolly—"

"Now you're pilfering elementary. Bad form, Cousin," Tuesday huffed, thinking, *bad form, I sound like Lestrade. I shouldn't have left him that clue. He'll get himself killed.*

"As I was saying, Moriarty is utilizing phosphate mining equipment and Citrus Industries' fleet of trucks to dig under the Port of Miami tunnel during its final construction phase."

"Naturally, nobody is paying any mind to all the trucks coming and going, permitting Moriarty direct access into the Biscayne Aquifer where she will attempt to construct her villainous Hollow Earth. Enough chatting, my dear cousin! How about me and Dolly go down and blast them? I'll bet you want in on it, eh, old fellow? You look like you've got some fight left in you," Tuesday said addressing me.

The thought of ridding the universe of Jane Moriarty appealed to me. Her great-grandfather robbed me of my past, and I craved vengeance. I steeled myself for the challenge, picturing Moriarty's throat in my grasp, her screaming for mercy, me permitting none, when Shadow's voice intruded upon my fantasy, "No blasting, please, my courageous cousin, and stand down, Watson. I have a better idea. And, when the time comes, I promise you dibs on sending Moriarty to the hell she deserves."

60

The occupants of the buses following Governor Fester Fahrenheit's Hummer into the Watson Island hangar entered a hellish scene. A short, stacked, blood-soaked woman adorned in only a bikini bottom, wielding knives in each hand stood carving the image of a serpent into the chest of a large screaming man shackled to the wall. Surrounding them lay the bloody carcasses of a dozen men also in chains, a dozen more pleading for clemency, along with a half dozen drivers dead in the cabs of their dump trucks. The woman completed her macabre artistry, lifted her oscillating head, stared down all three of the buses, and having finally mastered her tongue, flicked it in and out. The bus drivers slammed on their brakes. The occupants, although terrified by the sights before them, were indescribably aroused by Moriarty's escalating scent and clamored to get out. One bold bloke opened the door handle and sprang forth.

Moriarty shrieked, "Defend me, Fettssssshhter!"

Fahrenheit peppered the man's body with an assault rifle. It was at that very moment, we arrived, and somebody, as anticipated, was expecting us.

"MARVERLOUTTSSSSHHHHHHH. Ttsssshhtupid girl. You even brought your couttsssshhin!!" Moriarty hissed, wielding her weapons before her as if performing a dance of veils.

"I've got the meteorite," Shadow said, presenting a square stone.

"No. I have it," said Tuesday, holding an identical stone.

"No, I have it," Eren said, holding yet another stone.

"No, I do," said Dolly, with yet another square stone in hand.

"Do you think me that ttsssshhupid, Holmettsssshh?"

Sure as hell hope so, Shadow thought.

"Tiffani!!!!" Moriarty screeched.

Tiffani Fahrenheit skipped toward Moriarty, placed the meteorite in her hand, and burst into pleasure, "You smell sooooo good, Jane."

"Ttsssshh!" Moriarty's eyes flickered brighter and brighter. She brought the meteorite to her lips and flicked it repeatedly, lost in thought, *the taste of ultimate power, of freedom. Finally, Great-Granduncle James. Didn't think I could do it, did you, Daddy?*

"Oh, Jane, I can't wait—"

"Annoying girl," Moriarty said, slashing Tiffani's throat.

"That's not the meteorite!" Shadow said.

Does that stupid girl honestly think I'm going to fall for that old trick? Still, she is Arthur's kid. I'll play along, and then I'll kill her, just like her parents, "R3! Robot mode. Polarity check," Moriarty commanded, to which the seaplane transformed and rolled past our party coming to rest before its master.

"This one," R3 stated, pointing its robotic arm toward Tuesday.

"Impottsssshhttsssshhible! Tettsssshht mine again!!! NOW."

"No magnetic properties," R3 stated.

"ARGHHHHH. How'ttsssshh it feel to have ttsssshhomething taken from you, Holmettsssshh," Moriarty screeched, throwing a knife straight into Eren's gut.

61

Lestrade's gut rumbled with anxiety, or perhaps he considered, it was the three Caeser salads he consumed en route. While twenty well-armed mercenaries guarded the hangar's street entrance, there was an absence of airborne devices patrolling the airspace, no boats policing the seawall, and one unoccupied seaplane at the dock.

"Tess, fire a sonic knock-out blast at the gentlemen below, please," Lestrade requested as they hovered above Watson Island.

"Yes, Director," Tess replied, as the soldiers collapsed to the ground.

"Fine work, Tess. Lovely day for skydiving. Take the wheel, please," bade Lestrade, slipping on his backpack.

"Target location, Director?"

"Hangar roof, Tess."

The Tesla reached 3,600 feet in altitude, stating, "Your stop, Director."

Lestrade had never worn a parachute, and the one in his rucksack was untested. His right leg twitched, causing his foot to jerk and strike the ejection button on the Tesla's floor. Lestrade found himself propelled through a hatch in the vehicle's roof. He held tight to the straps of his pack. His ascent ceased. Gravity took hold. Lestrade was freefalling, and not at all pleased. A voice came through his cellphone, "Deploy your chute, Director."

Lestrade pulled the cord on his rucksack. Much to his relief, he felt the chute release, accompanied by the sound of wind dancing in his ears. The force of the straps against his groin was jarring. Lestrade fumbled for the chute's toggles, took hold of them, and steered toward the hangar roof. Once in control, he rather enjoyed the ride. The wind blowing against his face, the cruise ships across the channel, the grey-blue water of the harbor below, the flock of pelicans heading his way!

Fun fact, mate. Pelicans have keen eyesight. They can launch an airborne assault on a school of fish from high above the beach on a cloudy day, however they most certainly cannot see an invisible parachute. Lestrade and his chute, bearing three flapping pelicans, careened to the water below.

Lestrade prided himself on his athletic abilities. Rugby, gymnastics, cycling, skiing, water polo. He was a strong swimmer, however having been forced to watch the movie 'Jaws' at a formative age, he was never comfortable outside a well-chlorinated pool.

Lestrade hit the water hard, submerged, popped up, and expectorated a mouthful of seawater tasting faintly of motor oil. He treaded in place whilst regaining his bearings. The hangar dock was approximately 20 meters away. He freed the pelicans, punched the chute retrieval button on his pack, and recorded a case note on his phone, 'parachute-for the birds'. Lestrade pushed the scuba setting on his phone, gripped it in his mouth, and swam underwater to the dock.

The water was murky, something bumped him, causing his right leg to twitch, causing his foot to hit the submerged ladder of a transparent submarine. Lestrade grabbed a barnacle covered rung, gashing his forearm, causing blood to drip around him. A blast of shark-fear adrenaline propelled him up the ladder like a trapeze artist, just in time to see Moriarty's knife pass straight through Eren Adler. And straight through it went.

Lestrade concealed himself, determined the bloke was unscathed, deduced it was a hologram, and assessed the scene, "Tuesday," he mouthed to himself, his eyes fixated upon her, whilst fumbling in his pack for his pathogen gun.

"BLATTSSSSHHTED HOLMETTSSSSHHETTSSSSHH," Moriarty yelled, running toward Tuesday, who after tossing her stone to Shadow, retrieved her gun from her skirt waistband and got off seven shots. Unfortunately, Moriarty having swooned from her slaughter-filled fury, a result of one of the slugs grazing her arm, fell out of reach of the remainder of the bullets. She popped up and was upon Tuesday before she knew it, slashing the gun from her hand with the mamba knife, and in a move befitting a professional wrestler, bounced off the side of the hangar, flew in the air, thrust her strapping thighs round Tuesday's neck, dropped her to the ground, held the knife to her heart, and hissed at Shadow, "TTSSSSHHH. The meteorite or your couttssshhin diettsssshh."

Lestrade aimed his gun at Moriarty, whose thighs were gripped firmly around Tuesday's neck. He couldn't risk the shot.

"Release her!" Shadow exclaimed, rushing forward, tossing the stones between Moriarty and the sand pile.

"But ttssshhhe'ttssshh nearly dead!" Moriarty hissed in delight, squeezing her legs tight round Tuesday's throat, pushing the knife through the fabric of Tuesday's tee-shirt, demanding, "ttssshhend out the otherttsssshh. The real onettssshh."

"Keep your britches on, though I doubt you're wearing any," Dolly yelled from her spot next to me and the real Eren, who were concealed on the other side of the sand pile.

"Tottssshhttsssshh out your gun, Mermaid," Moriarty demanded.

Dolly tossed out a weapon and stepped forth.

"And the boyfriend," Moriarty commanded.

"Coming," Eren replied as he and Dolly strode toward Moriarty. As Shadow predicted, Moriarty failed to call me forth, thus, as designed, I used this to my advantage and lay in wait.

A few paces in, Eren, also as devised, let loose a sneeze that would put a Great Dane to shame.

"Oi! Snakeface!" yelled Dolly, retrieving a wee gun from her hair, taking aim at Moriarty. Unfortunately, Governor Fester Fahrenheit, positioned in his nearby Hummer, was quicker, opening fire on Dolly, who fell to the ground.

Shadow predicted a 16% likelihood of an event such as this to occur. She presented every possible scenario, and in each and every one, I was to hold my ground until she beckoned. However, at the time, the only sound I heard was the pounding in my ears. They killed Dolly and I wanted bloody revenge. And I do mean bloody! I fell into stealth mode and crept round the mountain of dirt until Moriarty was in view—at the very moment she raised her knife to Tuesday's chest! This did not sit well with the bees. Remember the bees, mate?

Vicky and a dozen worker bees appeared out of nowhere, wielding their stingers over and over again upon Moriarty's hands. "BLATTSSSSHHTED BEETTSSSSHH." The serpent's mind filled with images of murder. She collapsed, dropping her knife and releasing her grip on Tuesday, recovered and charged toward the sand pile, swatting bees as she ran. The pain induced by the stings triggered the intensification of Moriarty's scent, causing the predators to clamor in their buses. One dashed through the door. Fahrenheit riddled the escaping man with bullets, which proved to be an effective deterrent as the others settled back into their seats.

Shadow ran to her gasping cousin's side, placed Tuesday's head in her lap, pushed her chin upward to open her crushed airway, and whispered, "You shattered your record, Cuz. Three minutes, forty-eight seconds."

Lestrade aimed his weapon at Moriarty as she dashed toward the dirt pile, Vicky and her entourage in hot pursuit. Lestrade had never killed anyone in cold blood before. *WWTD?* he thought to himself and squeezed the trigger.

62

Lestrade's lethal pathogen dart was headed straight toward Moriarty. Unfortunately, so was I. Moriarty who prided herself on never missing a thing, failed to see me coming until I was upon her. She turned to face me. The dart whizzed past. Moriarty's eyes glared red. She flicked her grotesque tongue and given it was the nearest thing to my grasp, I launched myself in the air and latched onto it with my teeth. That's right. My teeth! I did what I had to do, so don't go getting judgy again—MATE.

I clung to the villain's tongue with all the strength I could muster. We fell to the ground, me atop her. Bees buzzed round, getting in stings here and there. In her effort to free herself Moriarty punched me repeatedly about my face and ribs. For a human of such short stature, she pummeled me like a prize fighter. Mercifully, I could take a punch. Incensed by her blows, I dug my claws into Moriarty's bounteous bosom and tightened my hold. *FOR DOLLY*, I thought, chomping down harder, and nearly bit Moriarty's bloody tongue off! Her torso convulsed. She shrieked in pain, which without use of her tongue was broadcast not unlike the call of a forlorn moose, as were her rapidly building pheromone levels. Her mind filled with murderous thoughts of slashing my throat. The bees got in a few more licks of their own, causing Moriarty to writhe on the ground like the sick serpent she was. She blacked out, only for a second, came to, reached for my ear, yanking it with great force, causing me to do the one thing I somehow knew I was never to do—expose my neck.

Moriarty saw her advantage, retrieved a folding razor from her red-flowered bikini bottom, flung it open, and slashed my throat.

Whilst a surgically sharp blade certainly induced less pain than a bullet, the net effect was remarkably similar. I wilted to the hangar floor. Blood leaked all about, the scent of which irritated my bladder—and I really needed a piss.

"Watson!" Shadow cried out, running to my aid, thinking, *please be okay, please.*

In the mayhem Moriarty dashed toward the sand pile, retrieved both of the stones and called out, "R3, THE BOTTXXXXHH."

"Yes, Professor," R3 responded, as its robotic arm presented James Moriarty's invention.

"MARVELOUTTSSSSHH," said she, thinking, *our time has come, Great-Granduncle.* She plunged one of the stones into the box; nothing occurred. *"ARGGHHH!"* she shrieked. Tossing it aside, she snatched the other rock, thrust it into the box, yielding the same result, screaming, "HOLMETTSSSSHH."

I felt my life force seeping out. At least the world was safe for now. However, our mission was incomplete. Shadow had yet to secure the box. Protect! I had to get to Shadow, however I couldn't so much as raise a whisker, and she was several meters away. My eyes closed in defeat! Shots rang out. I opened my peepers to witness a most remarkable scenario.

Shadow was holding Tuesday's gun, having shot Governor Fester Fahrenheit, who lay slumped over his Hummer. Whilst Vicky's stings, given to us en route, were doing an admirable job protecting our party from the effects of Moriarty's rapidly escalating scent, her musk filled the hangar, overtaking the occupants of the buses, who upon finding themselves unguarded, bolted forth in a stampede of more than a hundred sexual predators headed her way.

Oblivious to the events around her, Moriarty was otherwise occupied, screaming, "NOOOOOOOO," at her great-granduncle's box, which despite her thrusting every square rock within a 10-meter radius deep within—did absolutely nothing.

Moriarty ran, snatched two knives from her case, one with a rattlesnake handle, the other a cottonmouth, and sprinted toward the Holmeses. She was nine meters away, well within the range of the gun in Shadow's hand. I couldn't fathom why she had not taken the shot, until I realized the weapon only held eight bullets, Tuesday fired seven, and Shadow put either one or two bullets to good use on Fahrenheit. Or had Tuesday only fired six shots and the gun held nine? Or had Shadow fired but one shot, Fahrenheit five from his gun? Told you, mate, I was never good at maths. I was attempting to reconcile the number of rounds an Israeli .22 LRS held and how many shots had been fired by each party when the rumble of feet on the hangar floor deafened my ears.

Moriarty saw the mob of predators out of the corner of her eye. She turned to face them, her head oscillating, eyes glaring, tongue flicking in and out. She calculated the arrival time of the deviants to her position as well as her distance to her sworn enemies, began her internal countdown and bolted toward the cousins. Four, three, two, one. Moriarty stopped in her path and launched her knives. I cringed.

They were goners, mate, however the Universe, or in this case, a couple of mad bastards, had other plans. One of the predators, Eren's predator, Peter Kent to be exact, who due to his castration found himself immune to Moriarty's scent, leapt into the path of the knife headed for Shadow, felling him dead. The other knife lodged into the heel of Lestrade's right shoe, as he dove and stumbled into a cartwheel in his attempt to intercept its path toward Tuesday.

"BLATTSSSSHHTED HOLMETTSSSSHHETTSSSSHH," Moriarty screamed, turned, and fled from the predators.

She was but a few steps from the dock when Lestrade pushed a button on his watch directing a mirror at Moriarty who found herself so overtaken by her own reflection, froze in place for three seconds, then resumed her hasty retreat, Lestrade, Tuesday, and Eren in hot pursuit.

Protect! Protect! Protect! The call to action rang in my ears. It was at that point nothing short of a miracle occurred. I came to my paws, sprinted, soared, and grabbed the only thing within my reach:

Moriarty's red-flowered bikini bottom, (the one she promised to wear—well, you know, mate). The bikini slipped below her ample arse, over her brawny thighs, down round her tanned ankles, tripping her, causing Moriarty's slightly prominent forehead to smash into a cement dock piling, which soon dripped crimson and yellow with bits of brain which spilled from the viper's skull. It was over.

Disappointed? Come now, I'd wager you were expecting a different outcome, with a different sort of piling, you sick bastards? Perhaps something along the lines of … Moriarty tripped, righted herself, flicked her tongue, and hissed, "I HATE BLOKETTSSSSHH." The highly aroused predators piling atop her naked form, pawing her body like jackals. Within moments, Moriarty's scent dissipated. Layers of dazed predators peeled off. Moriarty's tongue dangled from her blue lips, her once fabulous form flattened against the hangar floor like roadkill.

Might I say, dear reader, if the latter scenario is what you had in mind, you really should seek counseling, or perhaps a career as a novelist? As to the events which indeed transpired that day …

It was over. I lay down and closed my eyes for my final rest. Even with my second wind, I sensed I was soon to leave this world; however, my heart was light. We had prevailed! I felt someone stroking my face. Shadow! *Brave, brave, Watson. I'm sorry, old fellow. I was so sure …* she thought, tears streaming down her face.

It was good not to be alone at the end. I gazed lovingly at my mistress and drew my final, final breath, causing that godawful scent of Moriarty to fill my olfactories. However, there was another scent in the air. One I nearly recalled in No Name Key. Vicky!

It was then my memory of the Sussex meadow resumed. I lay bleeding on the ground, Moriarty, the station master drooped over my flank, thrashing in pain from Vicky and her swarm, their stingers entering the rogue's skin, with a few misaimed stingers slipping into mine. The stinging! So much stinging. The scent of serpent and Royal Jelly thick in the air. I attempted to rise. The pain was unbearable. Amidst the bees and my own blood in my eyes, I could barely make out Sherlock pushing the boy into a shelter beneath the hive, reaching for something. Dr. Watson's old service revolver. BANG. A single shot through the station master's head. GREAT SCOTT. That's what happened to me! Moriarty! The bee stings!

Not so fun fact, mate. When a honeybee stings, it dies a macabre death. The bee's barbed stinger is structured in a manner that once it stings, the bee cannot retrieve it without it rupturing its belly, leaving the stinger embedded, pulling out instead its own guts, dying, soon after. All but the queen bee have barbed stingers, however Vicky's colony altered by the meteorite, evolved to have un-barbed stingers, thus they can sting with impunity—at least to themselves.

To my astonishment, I took another breath and opened my eyes to the sight of a tearful Shadow Holmes cradling me in her arms, applying pressure to my neck, saying, "Hang in there, Watson."

Eren observing us fondly, uttering, "I sense he'll be fine, my love, and what a story to tell our children!"

63

Turns out, mate, I'm not your run of the mill raconteur. It's the bee stings combined with Moriarty's venom that allows me to read minds. That's how I experienced all those Sherlock Holmes adventures as if I were there. I even read the mind of the great Sherlock Holmes. I realize it sounds mad. I believed so myself when I first read Shadow's thoughts, however if you 'think it out', like Shadow, it makes perfect sense. Fun fact, mate. Bees, wasps, moths, and a variety of insects communicate with pheromones. Mammals, (even you, dear reader), use pheromones to attract mates, even wee babies use them to locate their mother's nipples.

As to how despite losing the majority of my blood, I avoided death, turns out whilst I can't cure my nerve pain, dodge walking sticks or cutting utensils, thanks to those dreadful bee stings long ago, I can replenish my own blood supply. I can even grow a new organ or two if required, and I can live for ... well, that has yet to be determined.

"I said no heroics, Watson," whispered Shadow, whilst she gently stroked my head.

The bees buzzed over, circled, and covered my muzzle. Just when I thought I was safe, the day went straight down the loo! I was too terrified to move a muscle, until I smelled it, until I tasted it. Royal Jelly! It was delectable. And as I would later learn, accelerated my healing.

Lestrade wrapped his tie around Tuesday's bleeding hand. She retrieved her pack and knelt at my side, the tug of her needle indicative of her suturing my neck wound in a most competent manner.

"You'll be okay, buddy. Won't he?" Shadow murmured to Tuesday.

"Fit as a fiddle," said Tuesday, tapping Shadow's tattoo, tugging the last stitch tight against my skin.

64

Speaking of sewing things up, I'd wager you've heard enough about me and are curious as to the ultimate outcome of the fascinating yarn I am masterfully weaving? Thought so, mate.

"You're late, Father's Android," Shadow stated, to which an attractive man smoking a robust cigar approached from the seawall, holding a box identical to the one at Moriarty's feet.

"I'm afraid it's me, Child," the android replied.

"Mother!?"

"Hello, Shadow. This was supposed to be your father's android, but he decided to play hero and programmed me in here with his dying breath. Silly old fool. Smartest man in the world, but he got flustered every time he had to merge calls on his cell phone. I couldn't get this device to work until a few hours ago and I built the bloody thing. Apologies for my tardiness, and the deception. Your father and I wanted to shield you from all of this; however, I must say, even with the abundance of death surrounding us, I've never seen you look so alive."

"Seems we underestimated each other, Mother."

"Indeed! When did you deduce I was an android?"

"A moment after I saw a young Sean Connery peeking around the hangar door."

"He always was my crush," the android giggled. "Your father would have looked dashing in here. He would have been so proud of you, Shadow. I am. Please forgive me. And him."

"Hard to be mad at a corpse, Mother."

"Thank you, Child. And Watson! It's good to see you, old fellow. I told Arthur you'd find your way home," the android stated.

I sniffed the air. I did not recognize the scent, voice, nor shape of this being, nor did it appear to be mammalian.

"Sorry, old fellow. How's this?" the android questioned, adjusting its voice, reaching into a compartment on its thigh, retrieving a piece of cake, kneeling to feed me.

I knew that voice, and that cake. (I never forget a cake.) Guinevere Holmes' famous coconut cake. Cake, cake, cake. I polished off every bit and licked the plate clean.

"I knew it! He was Father's dog. And Grandfather's. And Sherlock's before that," Shadow stated smiling.

"More like they were his humans. Seems you're his latest," the android replied.

"I knew I recognized that dog from Grandmother's painting! Arthur must have wound up with him because my father was allergic to dogs. I might have turned out differently with Watson around, but I suppose you make a good team, Cousin."

"Tuesday Hudson playing well with others! Extraordinary! Your parents would have been tickled pink," the android said.

"Thank you, Guinevere. Sorry you're dead. I feel awful for not warning you."

"It's not your fault, Tuesday. Obviously, your impulsivity was inherited from Sherlock. As long as you learn from your mistakes, and check into a proper rehab. As for you, Director Lestrade."

"Glad to see you're not entirely dead," Lestrade snarked.

"Sorry, Archie. We couldn't risk anyone knowing."

"Of course, I'll tender my resignation immediately," Lestrade said, removing the cottonmouth knife from the heel of his shoe.

"Of course, you won't! You've done fine work, Archie, and we can't have a machine running a spy agency. We're nothing without our humanity, especially in our line of work. Consider your probationary period over, Director Lestrade."

"Fine work—for a wanker!" Tuesday said, lifting Lestrade by his collar and kissing him hard.

"My word …" Tuesday muttered as they broke from their kiss.

"What about that bloke?" Lestrade questioned, nodding toward Eren.

"He's with me," Shadow offered.

"Some spy you are, Lestrade. Fortunately, you kiss like a girl," said Tuesday.

"Like a girl!?" Lestrade questioned indignantly.

"It's a good thing, Lestrade," Tuesday said, kissing him again, ever so softly.

"When did you switch out Moriarty's box, Mother?"

"A missile in the air on the way here. Mercifully, my android form is adept with a rocket launcher, even if it can't dodge bullets. Moriarty's seaplane landed several shots, hence my tardiness," the android said, pointing to holes in its shoes which leaked a brown-green fluid.

"Guinevere! Is that you or have I totally lost it?" Dolly shouted, much to my shock and relief, as she walked toward us, smiling, plucking lead from her bullet-proof mermaid sarong, blood dripping from her scalp.

"Dolly, your head!" Eren exclaimed.

"It's only a flesh wound, dearie. Seems we won. Whew! Good to see you, Guinevere, although I'm cross with you, even if you are dead. And Arthur?"

"Afraid he didn't upload in time," the android replied.

"And what of Moriarty's box?" Shadow asked.

"To think your father worked his entire life to find it. The good and evil which lie within," the android stated, contemplating the box in its hand. It was at that point, Vicky buzzed by and landed on the device. The box glowed a dark shade of indigo against the android's palm. The harbor waters banged against the seawall.

The good? What good could possibly come from … Shadow thought, exclaiming, "Hurricanes!"

"Blow me back to Baker Street!" Tuesday exclaimed.

"Measured doses of Vicky employed in James Moriarty's device, and so directed in a precise manner, could evaporate any hurricane nearing landfall. Think of the lives and property to be saved," the android said.

"And if another mad genius like Moriarty gets their hands on it, Mother?"

"The Bee can provide adequate safeguards."

"Says the murdered widow," Shadow snarked.

"Ouch! You're right, Child, but don't come crawling to me when the insurance companies raise your windstorm rates," the android said, tossing the box to the floor next to the other, lasering them both into oblivion.

"That must come in handy for s'mores," Eren joked.

"If you're going to tell dad jokes, Mr. Adler, you and Shadow might attempt providing me a grandchild or two. You know, you and your eggs aren't getting any younger, Child."

"MOTHER."

"Can't blame a dead mum for trying."

Lestrade strode to Eren, Shadow, and I, who were comfortably situated on the floor and offered his hand, "Inspector Lest ... Pardon, force of habit. Director Lest—"

"No need for introductions, Archie. Tuesday told us so much about you," Eren said, shaking Lestrade's hand.

"Doubtful. However, she's beat me to it yet again, even with all The Bee technology I had at hand," Lestrade said, then stood on tip toes and whispered into Tuesday's ear, "Do you know I beamed to Tallahassee? And I have a flying car. I'll take you for a ride. It's bloody brilliant."

"It wasn't me who solved it, Lestrade."

My word! Tuesday bested by the Realtor! And she kissed me. Best day ever, Lestrade considered, offering his hand to Shadow, "Well done! Well done, indeed. Pleasure to meet you, Ms. Shadow Holmes. I am at a loss as to how even the great-granddaughter of Mycroft Holmes deduced the unlikely chain of events which just transpired. As a student of Holmesian methods, would you mind terribly?" Lestrade asked, retrieving his phone, recording a case note, 'how Shadow worked it out', thinking, *and she better not say it's elementary.*

65

"It's elementary, my dear Lestrade," Shadow laughed, whilst stroking my head.

Bad form, thought Lestrade, as he busied himself taking notes.

"When I saw Tuesday's gun, the barrel had gun oil residue which looked and smelled to be a month old, predating the death of her mother, meaning my cousin hadn't shot it, leading me to predict her success at grazing a charging Moriarty to be 72%, but even if she missed entirely, being shot at would be enough to piss that psycho off."

"Piss her off?" questioned Lestrade.

"Sage advice from one of your finest agents," Shadow replied, winking to Dolly.

"You didn't want to kill her until you had the box, so you provoked her. Clever," Lestrade replied, whilst taking notes.

"And the wrestling hold?" the android asked.

"On our brief date, Moriarty told me about her favorite wrestlers, two of them loved that particular move."

"Date? With Moriarty!?" the android exclaimed.

"I didn't know who she was, and she poisoned me, Mother."

"You two didn't—"

"Mother!!!"

"Sorry, Child. Must be this male android programming."

"If I may, my dear cousin. While I estimated a 41% chance Moriarty would use those Herculean thighs for a chokehold after I grazed her with a bullet, Shadow estimated it double that. Thankfully, my free-dive training allows me to hold my breath for three minutes, which permitted sufficient time for Dolly to mount her attack."

"Although I predicted a 58% chance of Dolly pissing Moriarty off with a few rounds before Fahrenheit could shoot her, I was confident his chances of a head shot to only be 16%, and since Dolly's mermaid coverup is bulletproof, we deemed those acceptable odds," Shadow added.

"I would have taken 100:1 odds to rid the Earth of that twat, dearie."

"And your dog's heroics?" Lestrade questioned.

"Afraid I screwed the pooch with that one," Shadow sighed, tussling my fur.

"And that bloke?" Lestrade asked, pointing to Kent, who lay dead on the floor.

"A repentant soul," Eren offered.

"Cousin, you didn't predict anything about Kent's penance or Lestrade's clumsiness?"

"Clumsiness? I meant to do that," muttered Lestrade.

"I expected The Bee to come to the rescue, but I failed to account for something very important," Shadow said, pointing to Lestrade and Kent. "Human emotions. Including mine. Shortcomings I'll remedy before our next investigation. Right, Watson?"

I licked Shadow's face in agreement. It tasted of victory.

"I assume your agents have secured the nuclear plants and intercepted Moriarty's phosphorous and phosphogypsum?" Tuesday questioned.

"The nuclear plants are safe. The phosphorous will be converted to fertilizer for use in undeveloped countries. Bee technology will allow the extraction of the radioactive materials from the phosphogypsum rendering it safe for use in construction materials. The radioactive byproducts will be utilized to produce medical devices for the diagnosis and treatment of cancer in third world countries," Lestrade responded.

"Not bad—for a wanker!" said Tuesday, kissing him again.

Shadow rose, walked to the knife case, removed the test tubes containing the DNA, "To the Napoleon of crime, and all the rest!" she exclaimed, tossing the tubes to the hangar floor where the shattered glass and contents were incinerated by the android.

"That's the end of it, except for the robot. Imagine what we could learn if its computer system is linked to Moriarty's criminal enterprises?" Lestrade probed, nodding toward R3.

"Not bad—for a wanker! You've trained him well, Tuesday," Shadow laughed.

"His training has yet to commence," said Tuesday, squeezing Lestrade's arse cheek.

"THE ROBOT," Everyone in the room, with the exception of myself shouted.

In fairness, after chasing a murderous split-tongue villain in a transparent submarine with Sherlock Holmes' relations, Shadow's ex, and a mermaid-camgirl-spy, and defeating said villain with the help of a colony of magical bees, an android inhabited by Shadow's dead mum, along with the newly appointed director of the most secret spy agency in the world, and learning I was essentially an immortal mind-reader, I didn't immediately comprehend all the hullabaloo regarding a transforming robot. Until I saw the flashing light.

Moriarty was a lot of things, but stupid wasn't one of them, mate. The Zeta security protocol she instructed R3 to initiate included a self-destruct command to commence within moments of the cessation of Moriarty's life signs, which were linked to the robot's sensors.

Shadow's thoughts filled my head, *a bomb this size could wipe out Miami. Only seconds remain. I've got to get to it. I just need to recall those images of bomb wiring from the papers I read when I was nine.*

Tuesday was first to sprint toward the device. Whilst her long legs gave her advantage over Lestrade and Shadow, neither stood a chance against the android, who dashed to the robot, gathered it up, and took flight above the billowy clouds, where the AI devices of two eternally opposed family lines, one determined to save the world, the other to end it, exploded.

"You can come out, again, Mother."

"You know what they say, kill me once, shame on you. Kill me twice, most unlikely. I knew this shielding function would come in handy," the android said as it flew into the room and dusted itself off.

"And what of them?" asked Lestrade, pointing to the predators.

"Some will always be animals who can't control their disgusting urges. Others, like Kent, demonstrate rehabilitation is possible. The trick is predicting which is which," Eren said.

"So, scorch the whole lot of them?" Tuesday questioned.

"Why the hell not?!" Eren replied.

"EREN," Shadow admonished.

"Joking, my love. Joking. Although … Here's a thought. How accurate are those laser eyes of yours, Guinevere?" Eren questioned.

We departed the hangar along with three busloads of recently castrated predators who were dropped rather unceremoniously at the causeway and returned to Shadow's domicile for a wee celebration. Cake was involved. It was scrumptious.

As to my memory, it pains me, to report, dear reader, much of my past remains a mystery, however the details of Shadow and my adventures remain fixed firmly in my mind, and I am privileged to share them with you, as well as that which transpired since the conclusion of our first case a decade ago.

Tuesday threw a grand coming out party to announce her presence to the world who welcomed the granddaughter of Sherlock Holmes with reverence. She has not since wanted for new mysteries to solve. Further, on occasion, although it wounds her ego, she has been known to consult with Shadow on problematic cases. As to Tuesday's drug use, whilst she struggled with her demons, it pleases me to report, she recently picked up her five-year chip.

Lestrade oversaw the construction of the new Bee Headquarters in London, directly under 221b Baker Street, where he has successfully led the agency since our fateful encounter. As to their on again off again relationship, as of this writing, Tuesday and Lestrade are vacationing together in our home, and whilst I am always pleased for their company, I am reminded of the words of Benjamin Franklin, 'Guests, like fish, begin to smell after three days.'

Dolly donated her estate to her mermaids and threw herself a going away soirée on her yacht with her most intimate friends. You got me, chum; it was an orgy, after which she took a bottle of Quaaludes and signed off. The media ran a story which compared Dolly to a woman of great altruism. The headline read, 'Bon Voyage to Dolly Jolly, Miami's Mother Teresa of the Night.'

The bees reside with us and are happily buzzing about, pollinating the abundance of flowering plants and trees which share our quaint Village of Biscayne Park, thus permitting Dr. Honey Penny to lead NASA's deep space mission to sample the asteroid, Bennu.

The android containing Guinevere's consciousness most unfortunately ceased operating years ago, and despite the efforts of every computer expert in the known world, remains in storage to this day.

As to Shadow Holmes and me, we have solved many a gruesome mystery and sold oodles of murder scene homes since our first case, and, as I lie upon this bed, Eren's arm draped across my chest, his fingers tickling my ear, Shadow sleeping like a brick, my face pressed to her belly, the lot of us intertwined like a litter of pups, I am, dear reader, most appreciative of your dogged attention to our riveting adventure. (You were dogged and riveted, were you not?)

I'll be signing off for now ... What's this? My head is abuzz with a beating sound from deep within Shadow's womb, and something else; a thought so wee I can barely make it out, *the game is afoot!* GREAT SCOTT.

About the Author

David Raymond is a Miami native and bestselling author of books set in Florida, a state presenting infinite possibilities for fiction writers to 'not have to make stuff up'. David spent his public service career directing large governmental social service systems, including the Florida Department of Children & Families and the Miami-Dade County Homeless Trust. In the vein of truth is stranger than fiction, David, the victim of a sexual predator as a child, was responsible for the housing placement of over one hundred homeless sexual predators, who due to residency restrictions, were living under the Julia Tuttle Causeway, a situation which drew international media attention.

David holds a Master of Science degree in Mental Health Counseling and completed the Harvard University, John F. Kennedy School of Government Executive Education Program. Prior to working in the social service field, David sold real estate, taught middle school marine biology, managed a pathology laboratory, and was an environmental lab technician testing Miami's ocean waters.

Following a distinguished career, David successfully wrote over $1 billion in grant applications and four novels to date. His hobbies include playing guitar, learning the banjo, fishing, reading, hiking, and experiencing the wonders of nature.

David lives in Biscayne Park, Florida with his mystical wife Amy and their forever goofy Aussiedoodle, Starry. David and Amy are blessed by their extraordinary children, Mia, a gifted psychotherapist, Abraham, a legendary native fishing guide and best son ever, their wondrous daughter-in-law, Yudith, a teacher and mother, and their magical grandson, Ryder.

Acknowledgements

To Sir Arthur Conan-Doyle and his immortal creation, Sherlock Holmes, I offer my eternal gratitude for inspiring my love of fiction. This humorous homage would not be possible without your brilliance.

I also pay tribute to my late father, Jerry, whose correspondence with me as Dr. Watson, regarding such mundane things as nasal congestion, kept me wildly amused during some very dark times. You are always in my heart.

Writing without an editor is akin to hiking the Everglades without bug spray. I am fortunate to have had two such repellants of bad writing, awful grammar, and wandering musings. Thanks to Susan Barnes, developmental editor extraordinaire, whose input is like taking a writing master class and to Eileen Bryson, who not only knows her way around plot and punctuation, but also gets me. My book would be a mess without you!

I am forever thankful for my ongoing collaboration with Ana Chabrand and Leila Charur, who continue to dazzle with covers which are—most remarkable.

To Amy, my remarkable wife and partner, who has supported me in all my lunacy, forgiven my occasional moods, loved me, and guided my spirit. I cherish you eternally.

To Abie, Yudith, and Ryder who fill our lives with love and magic.

And finally, many dog lovers profess to having that one dog. You know the one. You gaze into each other's eyes and all is right with the world. To Sherlock, our first border collie, who, I would swear under oath, could read our minds.

Books by David Raymond

It's Like Having Sex With God

The Mermaid of Arch Creek

Time Noir

The Game Is Afoot: A Shadow Holmes & Watson Mystery